Praise for Wendy Francis

The Summer of Good Intentions

InStyle Magazine's 7 New Page-Turners to Read in July
Woman's World Book Club Pick
PopSugar's 23 Perfect Poolside Reads

"*The Summer of Good Intentions* is a tender and vivid portrait of a family by the sea, of three unforgettable sisters and the tidal pull of their love and secrets. Wendy Francis is a wonderful writer. She made me feel the salt air."
—Luanne Rice, author of *The Lemon Orchard*

"There is much to like in Wendy Francis's *The Summer of Good Intentions.* Love in all of its messiness is written with convincing thoughtfulness and insight, each flawed character beautifully and realistically portrayed. Feel the sand between your toes as you explore the special bonds of sisterhood and family in what promises to be one of the best books of summer."
—Karen White, author of *Flight Patterns*

"I was immediately engrossed by this story of three adult sisters who share their own bonds, heartbreak, and challenges. So much more than a beach read, this very real, poignant, and funny novel will make you look at your own family in fresh, new ways."
—Lee Woodruff, author of *Those We Love Most*

"A lovely summer read. Wendy Francis deftly explores the bonds of sisterhood and the complexity of family relationships."

—Wendy Wax, *USA Today* bestselling author

"Wendy Francis has created both a family and a story I did not want to leave. These three sisters on a summer vacation display the strong ties that can both hurt and heal a family. Filled with the sweet briny air of Cape Cod, this extraordinary tale shows that, together, we can weather all the seasons of life."

—Patti Callahan Henry, author of
The Bookshop at Water's End

"Wendy Francis's book thrilled me like a ride in a race car along the coast with the top down. It is everything a summer read should be."

—Elin Hilderbrand, author of *The Identicals*

"A compassionate and warm family drama filled to the brim with characters who feel like old friends."

—*Kirkus Reviews*

"An effective and smoothly written summer novel. . . . Skillful writing and realistic dialogue. Maybe this is what's meant by an 'addictive' summer read. We read on to find out whether, or if, these folks will re-order their lives and begin to pay closer attention to each other. Yep. Life *is* short. Summer only comes once a year. And some of the best parts are to be found in the little *Book of*

Summer in that quaint Cape Cod house, lovingly added to each year."

—*Barnstable Patriot*

"Touching. . . . An especially memorable, enjoyable read about family ties and the highs and lows of relationships between couples."

—Edge Media Network

"You are headed to Cape Cod even if you don't leave your front porch. . . . Watch as the family drama unfolds with lots of laughter, heartache and healing."

—*Sun Chronicle* (Attleboro, MA)

"A tale of love, loss, and repair, offering comforting themes and lessons about avoiding the mistakes of our parents."

—*Improper Bostonian*

"What do you get when you mix family, secrets and a mysterious accident? A messy and engrossing scorcher of a story that we couldn't walk away from even after the sun went down."

—Booktrib.com

"A *must* on any summer reading list."

—A Southern Girl's Bookshelf

"This book will be deservedly popular in the beach bags of Edgartown and Truro this summer."

—*Open Letters Monthly*

"A poignant and heartwarming novel. . . . Wendy Francis brings the seaside retreat vibrantly to life and the idyllic setting perfectly balances the characters' weightier issues. . . . A warm and inviting story with a close-knit family whose bonds are strengthened by crisis."

—Book Reviews & More by Kathy

"A wonderful summer read full of changing family dynamics, *The Summer of Good Intentions* is one you'll want to tuck into your tote bag . . . everything you could want for a perfect beach read."

—Sunshine State Tourist

"The perfect escape!"

—Liz & Lisa, "Best Books of July"

"A riveting novel of life and the unknown we all must eventually face."

—The Romance Reader's Connection

Three Good Things

"A toothsome tale . . . a debut as light, sweet, and fluffy as Danish pastry dough. Culinary romance lovers—fans of Sharon Boorstein, Susan Mallery, and Deirdre Martin—will devour it."

—*Library Journal*

"Like gossip over morning coffee in the kitchen . . . warm and comforting."

—*Kirkus Reviews*

"*Three Good Things* is a flavorful tale of sisters and second chances, fresh starts and sweet surprises. Wendy Francis has written a rich debut, sure to delight the lucky readers who discover her here."

—Barbara O'Neal, author of *The All You Can Dream Buffet*

"There are so many good things to say about *Three Good Things*. It's a warm, witty, and wise story of sisters on their journey through love and life. Wendy Francis's new novel is as delicious as the kringles made in Ellen's bakeshop."

—Susan Wiggs, author of *Family Tree*

"Wendy Francis's *Three Good Things* is as sweet, rich, and comforting as a Danish kringle, spiced with lots of good surprises."

—Nancy Thayer, author of *Secrets in Summer*

"A lovely story about people you wish were your next-door neighbors. I wish, too, the kringle shop were next door, because I loved the mouthwatering descriptions of its treats. Curl up with this book, along with a cup of tea and a kringle (what else?), and lose yourself in a world you won't want to leave after you turn the last page."

—Eileen Goudge, author of *The Replacement Wife*

The
SUMMER
SAIL

WENDY FRANCIS

TOUCHSTONE

New York   London   Toronto   Sydney   New Delhi

Touchstone
An Imprint of Simon & Schuster, Inc.
1230 Avenue of the Americas
New York, NY 10020

Copyright © 2018 by Wendy Francis

First Touchstone trade paperback edition May 2018

TOUCHSTONE and colophon are registered trademarks of Simon & Schuster, Inc.

For information about special discounts for bulk purchases, please contact Simon & Schuster Special Sales at 1-866-506-1949 or business@simonandschuster.com.

The Simon & Schuster Speakers Bureau can bring authors to your live event. For more information or to book an event, contact the Simon & Schuster Speakers Bureau at 1-866-248-3049 or visit our website at www.simonspeakers.com.

Manufactured in the United States of America

1   3   5   7   9   10   8   6   4   2

Library of Congress Cataloging-in-Publication Data

Names: Francis, Wendy, author.
Title: The Summer sail / Wendy Francis.
Description: First Touchstone trade paperback edition. | New York : Touchstone, [2018]
Identifiers: LCCN 2017050097 (print) | LCCN 2017060246 (ebook) | ISBN 9781501188923 (eBook) | ISBN 9781501188916 (paperback)
Subjects: LCSH: Female friendship—Fiction. | Female friendship—Bermuda Islands—Fiction. | Jealousy—Fiction. | Domestic fiction. | BISAC: FICTION / Contemporary Women. | FICTION / Family Life. | FICTION / General.
Classification: LCC PS3606.R36535 (ebook) | LCC PS3606.R36535 S88 2018 9(print) | DDC 813/.6—dc23
LC record available at https://lccn.loc.gov/2017050097

ISBN 978-1-5011-8891-6
ISBN 978-1-5011-8892-3 (ebook)

For my forever sisters, near and far

And for Mike, my rock

Prologue

⌒

Abby slid the invitation into the envelope. It was a lovely invitation, on sturdy cream card stock with blue script and a jaunty little boat sailing across the top. She knew it was silly to have ordered special cards in this day and age when everything got sent electronically, but a twentieth wedding anniversary seemed to demand a certain amount of decorum. And it was the perfect reason to celebrate. Every year, she and her two college roommates tried to meet up for a reunion somewhere in the States, but this year, she wanted to propose something different: a cruise, an island getaway to Bermuda. What could be more idyllic?

She sealed the envelopes, affixed the stamps, and addressed them in her loopy handwriting, one to Ms. Lee Minor in Charleston, South Carolina, and the other to Ms. Caroline Canton in New York. Abby smiled at the thought of her roommates' spotting the invitation in a sea of advertisements and magazines in their mailboxes. It was good to try something different every so often, and as she'd said to her husband, Sam, when first pitch-ing the idea, *If not now, then when?*

Frankly, she was desperate for a proper getaway, one where she would be among friends, plied with good food and drink, and tasked with nothing more than a decision on where to dine that night (the ship had five elegant restaurants on board). Abby had barely survived the homestretch of her boys' sophomore year—both twins seemed intent on growing up too quickly—and she was counting on the cruise to entertain them with its endless loop of activities. Meanwhile, she could lounge by the pool in peace.

It was, as Sam liked to say, a win-win.

Now if she could just twist Caroline's arm to take a full week off from work and Lee to treat herself and her daughter to a vacation, all would be well. Abby would call them later, once they'd had time to consider the idea. The sales pitch was easy—Caroline needed a break from her stressful editor's job at *Glossy* magazine, and Lee and Lacey could use some uninterrupted time together to smooth things out between them (Lee, a teacher, would be on summer vacation in June). Abby needn't mention any other reason—beyond her anniversary, of course— why it was so pressing that they come. They would find that out soon enough.

She licked the final envelope and addressed it to Sam's office on campus. He'd get a kick out of that, being invited to his own anniversary party. Somehow the formal invitation made the whole idea of a cruise—up to this point a dreamy mirage—crystallize into reality. Abby could almost smell the sea breeze, taste the margaritas, feel the sand between her toes.

She decided she would walk the letters over to the post office herself, only a few blocks from home. No point in worrying whether the invitations had actually made it into the mail. She headed out the door, envelopes in hand, and was flooded with a newfound sense of anticipation. A sail away to a tropical island. Yes, it was just the thing she needed.

She hoped her roommates would say yes.

The honor of your presence is requested at

A Renewal of Vows

On the 20th Wedding Anniversary of

Abigail and Samuel Bingham

The **Bermuda Breeze,** *Aequor Cruise Lines*

Departs from Boston Harbor

June 15–23

1

~

When the invitation arrived in her mailbox, Caroline didn't know what to think. She recognized Abby's handwriting immediately. Had she forgotten a birthday? Why was Abby sending her a formal note? She tore open the envelope and read. *The honor of your presence is requested at a Renewal of Vows. Oh,* she thought, *Abby and Sam's anniversary, of course.* The invitation was so old-fashioned, so pretty. *So Abby.* Caroline ran her finger over the swirling blue font. A twentieth anniversary celebration. It took her a moment to register the cruise part. *Oh,* she thought again. Weren't cruises for old people? Surely, their gang wasn't part of the senior set yet, ready to ring the bell on their last sunset. Why not a trip to Vegas—or someplace remote, like Iceland, to mark the occasion?

The last time Caroline, Lee, and Abby had all gotten together, it had been for their annual girls' weekend in Aspen. Each year, the three of them left their messy lives behind for a few days and pretended it was like old times. Which it kind of was, because every time they gathered, the years fell away and they might as well have been sitting on the frayed chenille couch in their dorm room and watching *Jeopardy!* Except the hotel rooms they stayed in these days had four-hundred-thread-count sheets, Wi-Fi, and room service.

On the bottom of the invitation, Abby had written: "Please come! It will be fun! You, me, Sam and Javier, Lee and Lacey. All expenses paid. Pretty please?" Caroline wondered if Lee's daughter, Lacey, would actually agree to join them or, now that she was a freshman in college, if she was too cool to spend a week with her "aunts." Still, a vacation was a vacation, and Abby and Sam were offering to pay. Caroline gazed out her apartment window at the Manhattan skyline.

A cruise?

As much as Caroline loved to travel, she had a thing about boats. She'd much rather be suspended forty thousand feet above land in an airplane than floating on a bottomless sea. The one time she'd gone sailing— years ago, on a yacht with the dashing editor of Milan's fashion magazine—she'd vomited over the side and ruined what might have been a promising evening. She supposed, though, that there were things like Drama-mine and those little acupressure bracelets she could wear now. Did people even get seasick on big cruisers?

Her mind darted to Javier. She checked the invitation again. *You, me, Sam and Javier.* Of course, Abby had thought to include Javier, even if Caroline's three-year-old relationship with him was nothing like her friend's sturdy, stalwart marriage of twenty years. And if she were being completely honest, Caroline occasionally had her own smidgen of doubt about her boyfriend, like an old back injury that resurfaced from time to time. But maybe a cruise, an *anniversary* cruise, would spark something in him. The idea that it was time to take whatever it was they were doing to the next level.

Whenever the roommates got together, Abby and Lee would press her for news. *Any ring yet?* And Caroline would wave it off, pretending not to care. The first year she and Javier had dated, she really hadn't cared. She was content to find someone so kind, so smart, someone who tolerated her insane work schedule now that she was a senior editor at *Glossy* magazine. Javier traveled almost as much as she did, jetting from vineyard to vineyard and sampling wines for his boutique stores back in New York. Her boyfriend was a sommelier. It had an appealing ring to it—plus, he was the most amazing lover she'd ever had. She didn't need someone to settle down with, had never felt the maternal tug.

But lately she'd been thinking more about having a permanent place they could call home, a dwelling beyond their loft apartment on the Lower West Side. A little house, maybe, in Connecticut, or across the way in New Jersey. Caroline wasn't getting any younger, and though Javier rightly pointed out that she'd always be younger than he (seven years to be exact), she was beginning to register that desire her girlfriends had described: a longing for a commitment with heft, a solemn oath that he'd spend the rest of his life with her, in sickness and in health. Javier had promised her all of these things, but Caroline was feeling the need to make it official. Was that so crazy of her? Abby, at least, told her no.

Caroline was happy for Abby, truly, genuinely glad that her friend had had the good fortune to be married to a solid guy like Sam for twenty years. She loved Abby like a sister. But, if she was being completely honest, she was also a tiny bit jealous. Because if Sam and Abby were celebrating their twentieth, what was Caroline celebrating? Fifteen years in the publishing industry? As if that deserved a candle! She, Lee, and Abby had all started out of the same proverbial running blocks at their small New England college, yet Caroline felt outpaced by both her best friends.

She wandered over to her desk and flipped ahead in her calendar to June. Ever since she'd jettisoned the world of wedding planning and neurotic brides fifteen years ago, *Glossy* had become her home away from home. Most nights found her in the office till eight or nine, but, aside from a few meetings she could pass along to her assistant, the week of the cruise looked wide open. Could she afford to take an entire week off from work? She was about to pencil it in with a question mark when her phone rang. *Abby*. Caroline picked up.

10

"Did you get the invitation? Are you coming?"

"Hello to you, too," Caroline said with a laugh. "Perfect timing—I just opened it. Wow, twenty years. Can that be right? We must be getting old." She settled onto her sofa and watched as the sidewalks below began to fill with purposeful New Yorkers striding out in the brightening Saturday afternoon.

"Twenty years is right. But since we were all in our *early* twenties when Sam and I tied the knot, I consider us still young."

"I'm happy to go along with that reasoning," said Caroline.

"So, you're coming, right?" Abby pressed again. "I realize it's short notice, but the cruise line has a great deal going, and Sam and I have been wanting to do something special to celebrate our anniversary. And, well, I haven't seen you in a year, and did I mention we can drink cocktails on the lido deck?"

Caroline smiled despite herself. Abby had always been a gifted saleswoman. A cocktail poolside sounded pretty appealing at the moment.

"Please tell me I don't have to wear that awful seafoam dress again." Abby had put Lee and Caroline in ridiculous ruffled bridesmaids' dresses for her big day—an unfortunate fact that they would never let her forget. The wedding itself, however, had been gorgeous, set in a quaint seaside town on the Cape.

"Ha! As if any of us could fit into our old dresses. I

gave away my wedding gown as soon as the twins were born."

Caroline laughed. Abby's twin boys, Chris and Ryan, were now sixteen. "I think I donated my dress to Goodwill the day after your wedding," she kidded. "Let me check with work and Javier and get back to you? You know I'd love to go."

"Fine, but even if Javier can't come, your presence is mandatory. You were my wedding coordinator after all." And with that, her friend buzzed off.

Caroline thought back to Abby's wedding day. One of her first jobs as a wedding coordinator, it had been all she could do to keep things running smoothly, what with the flowers nearly forgotten and then Sam fainting from the heat. But the day had been a success because Sam and Abby had gotten married. Finally! After three years of dating in college and four after that.

Of course, Abby would be the first of the roommates to get married. People were always drawn to her, the way she exuded an air of calmness and a certainty that everything would turn out all right. She'd easily assumed the role of den mother of their little college pack. Caroline was the driven one, the studious roommate who made sure everyone turned their papers in on time. And Lee, with her long golden hair and southern accent, was the kind of girl for whom college seemed tailor-made (Caroline remembered one boy actually dropping his tray in the dining hall when Lee walked in). If Lee weren't so nice and funny, if the three of them hadn't been assigned as roommates, Caroline would probably have hated her.

The summer before freshman year, they'd all filled out a questionnaire meant to pair them with compatible roommates. But when they'd shown up that first day— Lee from Charleston, funny, to the point, and with a predilection for saying "y'all"; sweet, down-to-earth Abby from the Cape; and Caroline from Long Island with a toughness that neither of her roommates seemed to possess—none of them could understand why they'd been thrown together. Aside from the fact that they'd all checked off Impressionist painting as their favorite art, they didn't appear to have much in common. They'd spent that first afternoon taking the measure of one another.

But then, after a day of unpacking followed by pizza, Abby had blasted "I Melt with You," and, like fools, they'd danced around their new room under the watchful eyes of Renoir's *Luncheon of the Boating Party*. Later that night, Abby had exclaimed, "I know why they put us together!" Lee and Caroline had gazed at her expectantly, as if she could read their tea leaves for the next four years. "We're together because we're all the 'only child.' No brothers or sisters. They wanted us to finally have sisters. Don't you see?" Abby's eyes had flashed as if it made perfect sense. "Henceforth, I hereby declare you, Caroline Canton, and you, Lee Minor, as my new and forever sisters!" After that, there had been no more judging. They were the forever sisters and that was that. Through thick and thin.

Caroline set down her phone. *A week sailing the seas to sunny Bermuda.* Assuming she could keep seasickness at bay, how could it be a bad thing? It might, in fact, be just what she and Javier needed. Her mind started to spin with the ways she could turn it into a story for the magazine, something that would justify *Glossy*'s footing the bill, even if Abby and Sam were offering to pay. Pink sand, martinis on the deck, white-hot parties—the images began to twirl in Caroline's mind like filaments of cotton candy wrapping around a stick.

She started to tap out an e-mail to her boss with the heading *Story idea: CRUISING TO BERMUDA.*

Lee sorted through the pile of bills with her morning coffee. That was all that ever seemed to come in the mail these days—bills and junk mail. She tossed a handful of supermarket flyers into the recycling bin, then noticed the corner of an ivory envelope protruding from the pile and pulled it out. A small wave of excitement rippled over her when she recognized Abby's handwriting on the front, and she ripped it open. *The honor of your presence,* she read, *is requested at a Renewal of Vows.* On a cruise! *Wait, a cruise?* she thought. Well, that was different. Expensive different.

So Abby and Sam had made it to twenty years. She hadn't been counting—who had?—but it didn't seem possible that twenty years had passed since that long-ago day in June. Lee still considered Sam to be one of the luckiest guys around—anyone married to Abby automatically lived under a charmed star. Of course, the fact that Lee's daughter, Lacey, had been conceived on Abby's wedding night probably made Lee disproportionately fond of them both.

They used to joke that if Sam hadn't fainted at his own wedding (a minor detail but still fun to mention) and pushed the ceremony time back by half an hour, Lee would never have met Lacey's father. She and Caroline had been sitting at a local tavern, long after the wedding reception wound down, replaying the highlights of the night, when Scott showed up. Lee was immediately intrigued by the handsome man in uniform whose arms looked as if he threw out a hundred push-ups each morning. When he offered to buy her a glass of wine, she said *yes, please*, the tips of her ears tingling. He told her he was home for a week before shipping out again. A few more glasses of wine, and, before long, they were back in her hotel room, Scott asking if she had anything to be safe. She brushed him off, told him not to worry, the odds of anything happening so very slim.

And then, a few weeks later: a blue line. *Lacey.*

For nearly twenty years, Lee had been a single mom. Even when Scott offered to get married (she'd tracked

15

him down overseas with the news), they both knew it wasn't right. Now he was only tangentially involved in their lives, retired from the Navy and living in a leafy Philadelphia suburb with his wife and three kids. Every so often a card and a check would appear in the mail for Lacey, but Lacey wasn't stupid. She knew dads showed up for recitals and soccer games, tucked you into bed. All things Lee had done single-handedly for Lacey's entire childhood and adolescence.

And now Lacey, the girl who could squeeze the strongest emotions from Lee—both a fuming, inconceivable rage and a love so uncontainable that sometimes Lee just had to pull her daughter's sweet, grown-up face into her hands and kiss it—was a freshman in college. Well, technically a sophomore. Exams had wrapped up last week, and Lacey was home to keep Lee company and also, quite possibly, to torture her for the remaining months of summer.

The honor of your presence is requested, Lee read again. Below Abby had written: "Hope you and Lacey can join us! All expenses paid. Please come!" Lee grunted at the mention of expenses. Sam and Abby had more money than they knew what to do with, thanks to Sam's family's good fortune—his dad, an investment banker, had come into a windfall during the dot-com era. An island cruise would be a mere blip on their bank account.

The sound of Lacey's feet hitting the bedroom floor banged overhead. Lee listened as her daughter made her way to the bathroom. Lee had been on Lacey's case to get a job for the summer, but so far nothing had materialized. Which struck Lee as sheer laziness. If nothing else, Charleston was a tourist destination—there were always jobs for the taking in the summertime. The toilet flushed. The bathroom door squeaked open.

"Mom?" Lacey called from the top of the stairs. "Have you seen my phone?"

Lee glanced around the kitchen island where she sat with the invitation, her coffee, and her laptop. It was her favorite place in the morning before she headed off to work, where she would attempt to coax unruly four-year-olds to behave. It was the last month of preschool, and the little miscreants only wanted to be let loose for the summer. Lee didn't blame them. She felt exactly the same way.

"Sorry," she yelled up now. "Maybe it's on your bedside table?"

"Yeah, maybe."

Lee cupped her hands around her coffee mug, feeling the warmth spread to her fingers, and sighed. She felt as if she'd sent one daughter out the door last fall only to have someone else's child return in her place. Lacey spent most of her days holed up in her bedroom with her iPad, doing who knew what. The long-ago days of lounging on the couch and watching *American Idol* together were a distant memory. It was as if the transformation Lee had been bracing herself for during Lacey's adolescence had waited to occur until her freshman year in college. Lacey wasn't sullen exactly, but whatever view Lee took, her daughter could be counted on to take the exact opposite.

Lee had been expecting changes in Lacey after freshman year, but more of the stretching-her-wings variety. Would she have dyed her hair? Pierced her nose, maybe? Lee remembered the intoxicating experience that college could be. But Lacey seemed to be floundering more than anything else. Instead of talking about what she wanted to do with the rest of her life, she gushed about Tyler, a boy from New York who'd wooed her during the first months of freshman year. Lee's daughter had fallen in love. And her grades had quickly tumbled downward, the causal link so obvious to Lee. This from the girl who'd been valedictorian of her high school class.

"I'm not paying for college just so you can meet some boy," she'd warned Lacey over winter break during one of their tête-à-têtes.

"Why not?" Lacey countered. "I thought you'd be happy that I can actually manage to hold on to a boyfriend."

The words cut, but Lee chose to ignore the bait. "And I thought I'd taught you better." After a few more harsh, regrettable words were exchanged, Lee stormed off in her car, like a defiant teenager rather than a middle-aged mother. *Where had feminism gone?* Lee wondered while she sat alone at a bar that night and twirled the olives in her gin martini. Where had she gone wrong? All those years spent nurturing, helping with homework, advising and consoling her daughter over the occasional mean girl. Hadn't she been a good role model for Lacey when some days she would have much rather stayed in bed?

As she'd helped Lacey pack her bags for college up North, Lee had secretly hoped her daughter would want to go into medicine. Lacey was strong in math and science, all the classes that had eluded Lee. *Was Lacey going to marry this guy?* The thought scampered across Lee's mind now, and she shoved it away. Lee had met the boyfriend once, at parents' weekend in October, and had been underwhelmed—Tyler someone (Lee always forgot his last name), who was tall with a mop of dark hair but who seemed incapable of forming an articulate sentence. Lacey said it was because Lee made him nervous. Which had prompted another round of arguments. How did Lee make him nervous? *Because you make everyone feel like they're not good enough!* Lacey had screamed.

Lee sighed at the memory. She typed *Aequor Cruise Lines* into the computer. What could it hurt to look? When the website popped up, tanned, relaxed, fit-looking people lounged by the pool. Lee scrolled through the pictures for the *Bermuda Breeze*, an enormous ship. There was a peanut-shaped pool, gourmet restaurants, a casino, and spa. And then the photos of Bermuda, all that pink sand and water so turquoise it seemed unnatural.

The more Lee considered it, the more the idea of a

cruise intrigued her. She hadn't seen her roommates in what felt like a dog's year. She and Lacey could relax in the sun, no pressure, maybe even share stories like old times. A change of scenery might be palliative for them both. She clicked on costs: it looked like roughly a thousand bucks per person.

Yes, a cruise might be just the thing to set them back on their old path, the mother-and-daughter team of two, making their way through the world, cresting one wave at a time.

∿

Abby double-checked her suitcase for the multiple bathing suits and tubes of sunscreen she'd laid out the night before. It was all there, tucked neatly beneath her outfits for each night, eight in total, Friday through next Saturday morning. She'd packed the black one-piece with the built-in Lycra tummy, the magenta two-piece with a ruffled skirt to hide her thighs, and, in the event she was feeling adventurous, the red-and-white striped bikini. The bikini would likely stay hidden away for the duration of the trip, but if she couldn't at least hold on to the *possibility* of wearing it, what was the point of going on a cruise for her twentieth wedding anniversary? She wasn't getting any younger. And her notebook, the one with the creamy leather cover, she double-checked for that, too.

"Honey, have you seen my charger?" Sam's head poked through the bedroom doorway. His cheeks were ruddy from the last-minute exertion of packing and loading up the car.

"Sorry. Maybe check the basket in the kitchen? There's a bunch in there." Abby tugged on her suitcase's zipper before realizing that she'd get better leverage if she climbed on top.

Sam shook his head. "Already looked. About eight different chargers but not the one I need." His footsteps thumped back downstairs.

There was something about packing that turned them all into maniacs. Or maybe it was the sultry June heat pushing through the window. She'd already changed her shirt once after sweating through the first. In one bad decision (of many) of late, they had decided not to buy a new window air conditioner until a true heat wave hit. Last year's AC had gone on the fritz, and it had seemed as if they had months to replace it until now, here they were, sweating like pigs without even a single fan.

At last, Abby managed to get the suitcase closed. After twenty years together, she and Sam had learned it was best if they packed separate bags. It avoided the inevitable packing confrontation, rendering obsolete questions such as *Why did she need all these shoes for one little trip?* and *Where did all the shoes come from anyway?* No, there was no point in arguing before they were even out the door. Traveling with separate suitcases was one of the secrets to a happy marriage.

"Cut it out, you idiot!"

Abby groaned. Chris and Ryan were at it again. She stuck her head in the hallway.

"Honestly, Chris. Do you have to talk that way? Please be kind to your brother." For some unknown reason, he'd taken to addressing his twin like a criminal lately, as if it were perfectly acceptable behavior.

"He's being an idiot," Chris said again, as if to further his point.

Abby shot him a look over Ryan, who stood a full four inches shorter than his brother. "If I need to speak to you again about your language, you might as well stay home. Going on this cruise is a *privilege.*" It was part threat, part reminder, one that she and Sam had been holding over the twins' heads at various times during the last week. *Please,* she offered up a silent prayer. Could they please just make it to the boat so she could plunk herself into a chair and leave her family to fend for themselves? What was the worst they could do? Throw each other overboard? She was pretty sure Sam would jump in after them or, at the very least, alert the captain. Meanwhile, Abby could enjoy her book in the sun.

"I didn't *do* anything. He's got my headphones and I want them back," Ryan pleaded. The second-born, only five and a half scrawny pounds to Chris's six, Ryan might have been a straggler, but he was a fighter. Though she wasn't supposed to have favorites, Abby's maternal, protective instincts had kicked in instantly when she sat beside Ryan in the NICU those first ten days, willing him to fatten up and his lungs to pump. It had been this way ever since, Chris being the handsome go-getter for whom everything seemed to come so easily, so naturally, and Ryan having to struggle to make good grades and find friends.

"Chris, give Ryan's headphones back right now. I mean it," she said in her firmest, I'm-not-messing-around mom voice. "You boys are going to kill me before we even get on the boat."

Chris tore the Bose headphones from around his neck and whipped them at his brother.

"Hey!" she cried. "That was totally unnecessary, and you know it." Abby tossed Ryan a beseeching look, one that she hoped conveyed that she was sorry his brother was being such a jerk but if he'd agree to ignore it, she would make it up to him somehow once they reached the boat. Ryan shrugged and stuck the headphones in his backpack.

The car horn beeped outside, Sam's five-minute warning that everyone—that is, the boys, who inevitably managed to lose their shoes in their own house—had better find their way to the car soon. Abby, however, took it as a good sign. If Sam was in the car, it meant he'd located his charger. She did one last check of the upstairs to make sure all the lights were off, then headed down just as Sam was stepping back inside. "Last call for bags. Honey, is yours all set?"

Abby nodded. "On the bed."

WENDY FRANCIS

"Great. I'll grab it."

She circled the living room and headed into the kitchen, where she double-checked the fridge door. Tightly shut. All the burners were turned off on the stove. She ran through the remainder of her mental checklist. The mail had been put on hold, the trash emptied. She'd already dropped off Wrigley, their golden retriever, and a ten-pound bag of dog food at the neighbors' house this morning. The family had never been away from Wrigley for more than a few days, but he'd padded right into their neighbors' house and settled on the kitchen rug, as if he'd lived there his whole life.

Yes, everything that needed doing before the cruise had been accomplished.

Abby went back into the living room and watched through the window as the boys lugged their bags out to the car. She could hardly believe that on another sweltering June day, almost twenty years ago, she had gazed across the church at Sam, so in love. Could she have anticipated all that had happened since? Not even close. Like how they'd tried for kids for so long, one frustrating month after another, until finally, miraculously, she was pregnant with the twins? Or, how the topsy-turvy world of tenure would lead them first to New York City, then to Philadelphia, and finally to Boston while Sam scaled the academic ladder as a history professor? Or that Abby, always one to be chasing her career, had more or less quit her job at the art gallery to raise the boys?

24

No, looking at Sam that day, she couldn't have imagined all that lay ahead: the loss of both her parents, the various trips to the ER for the boys, the endless battles over homework, the baseball and hockey tournaments. It was all there—the richest memories, the most challenging times—and she wouldn't change any of it. Well, maybe one thing. But what was the saying? *Whatever doesn't kill you, makes you stronger.* If that were true, then Abby was destined to be a Teflon woman. She just needed to stare down the one thing that threatened to steal away everything dear to her.

After the cruise, she'd promised herself, she would tend to it.

She pulled shut the front-window drapes. When she turned, Sam was back inside, waiting, pretending not to check his watch.

"Ready, honey?"

"Almost."

She scanned the room one last time, making sure nothing was out of place. Then she grabbed her pocketbook off the hallway bench and retrieved the garment bag that held her dress. She draped it across her arm, careful not to crease it.

"All right." She smiled. "Now I'm ready."

Sam rested his hand on her shoulder and squeezed as he followed her out, then pulled the door shut behind them.

2

The ship was massive, a white monolith at least a thousand feet long with as many tiny windows dotting the sides. It reminded Caroline of a whale. Bright colors swirled across the hull, and near the rear of the boat, an enormous black triangle pointed straight up in the air, like a dorsal fin. Maybe twenty lifeboats, their shiny tops painted regulation orange, hung suspended from the ship's side. If worse came to worse, Caroline knew she'd be among the first to jump in a lifeboat, others be damned. Of course, she would try to save her roommates and Javier, but she'd be of no use to them if she didn't help herself. She remembered the drill: *Put on your own oxygen mask first* and all that.

The ride from the airport had been mercifully short, and now she fished a twenty from her wallet to pay the cabbie as they joined the long line of taxis dropping off passengers at the cruise port. When at last she stepped out onto the blacktop, it was already steaming hot in the afternoon sun. Caroline hopped from foot to foot in her flimsy flip-flops.

"You meeting someone?" the cabbie asked, unloading her suitcase from the back. He sounded worried to be leaving her by herself.

"Oh, yes," she replied. Not that it was any of his business. "My old college roommates. It's a mini-reunion." She might have added that Javier would be boarding with the last wave of passengers, around two o'clock. That was assuming his flight from Paris to New York and then Boston landed on time. But she didn't feel like getting into it with the cabdriver right now.

"Well, I hope you have a wonderful time," he said, taking the money from her with a little nod. "Thank you."

"Thank *you*." She snapped the suitcase's pull handle into place and headed for the cruise port, a stuffy warehouse where men in orange vests busily pointed passengers to various queues. Caroline had already scheduled her check-in time online between noon and one o'clock, though now that she saw the serpentine line winding its way around the dividing belts, she wondered if staggered boarding was truly swifter.

She pulled up behind a family with teenagers, their pillows tucked under their arms. Next to them sat a rolling cart piled with a small mountain of luggage plastered with stickers like BOXERS ARE THE BEST! and I NEVER MET A WINE I DIDN'T LIKE. Caroline was confused by people who packed as if they were traveling for a month. What could they possibly need aside from a few outfits and a swimsuit?

Eventually a porter approached and took her bag, then waved her over to yet another line, where she filled out a form swearing that she'd had no recent exposure to the Zika virus or any other communicable diseases. She wondered if the small rash on her elbow counted but decided not to mention it. Around her, flustered parents struggled to corral their young children while they completed their own forms. Caroline watched while one boy pulled back his arm and slugged his sister square in the shoulder, prompting a wail. Caroline frowned and shook her head disapprovingly at him.

At last she reached the check-in desk and handed the agent her forms and passport. "You travel a lot, yes?" the agent inquired. Bright blue eye shadow shimmered on her lids as she scanned Caroline's passport. *France, Italy, Greece, Iceland, Spain, India, Japan, Myanmar, Finland.*

Caroline nodded. "Yes, I'm a journalist. For *Glossy* magazine?" The woman's eyes failed to register any connection, which wasn't that surprising. Caroline was accustomed to describing *Glossy* and its mission to strangers, even though she'd helped increase its circulation to a million readers over the last decade. She'd traveled to the French Riviera, dined at charming cafés in Paris and Milan, had prayed in the temples of Myanmar, all in the name of capturing the essence of what defined today's woman. Which was how she'd pitched this trip to her editor, with an eye toward writing off the cruise as a business expense.

"Why Bermuda?" her editor, Sara, had asked. "Don't you have to sail across the Bermuda Triangle to get there?"

"I think so," Caroline said, though she wasn't really sure. "But how is that a story unless our ship goes missing?"

Sara had laughed wickedly. "Well, that's just it, isn't it? What *is* the story?"

Caroline was prepared. She'd done her homework. "As far as I can tell, *Glossy* has never run a story on cruises, and it hasn't covered Bermuda since 2008."

"But I thought cruises were for old people?" One carefully penciled-in eyebrow arched in Sara's smooth forehead.

"Me, too. But it turns out that a lot of families go on cruises these days, and so do newlyweds. Some of them are real party boats."

"Sounds more like a cultural exploration of the modern drunk woman." Sara paused. "You might have to wait till you get to Bermuda for culture."

Which was fine by Caroline. No doubt Bermudian women had insights to offer the readers of *Glossy*. What were their favorite beaches? What were the island's hidden gems for restaurants? What did they think of American women?

"Smile for the camera!" the agent suddenly commanded.

Caught off guard, Caroline flashed a crooked smile, and her face, a cross between startled and pained, appeared on the screen behind the agent. "Your photo is electronically tagged to your room key," she explained as she stamped Caroline's documents. "So, it's important that you keep your key with you at all times." She handed over Caroline's passport and key card. "Especially when you're leaving or boarding the ship in Bermuda. It's the only way for us to know that you're an Aequor Cruise passenger."

Caroline nodded. "Got it. Thanks." Though once the crew got a good look at her photo, she thought they might have second thoughts about letting her back on board. The agent slid a handful of brochures about Bermuda across the counter, and Caroline dropped them into her handbag.

"Happy smooth sailing," quipped the agent, who'd clearly recited this exact line a million times. Caroline smirked at the reference to *aequor*, which she'd googled before the trip. It meant "smooth sailing" or "of the sea" in Latin.

She followed the signs pointing to a gateway that connected land to ship. As she drew closer, she saw bright red and yellow balloons dancing from the boat's railings, and her heart did a little skip. Somewhere calypso music played. On board, porters dressed in dapper whites greeted her with rich Bermudian accents. It was, she thought, like crossing over to her very own tropical island.

Inside the ship's lobby, Caroline allowed her eyes to adjust to the light and laughed when she saw how luxurious it was. Surrounding her were gilded pillars, a floor-to-ceiling glass elevator, crystal chandeliers, a duty-free shop a stone's throw away. It was a sailboat hopped up on steroids. She locked her knees, waiting for the rocking sensation beneath her feet, but felt nothing. Maybe so long as the ship was tied to the pier there would be no swaying? Passengers swarmed around her, pulling their small bags and children behind them. When an elderly couple sailed by on their motorized scooters, Caroline had to quickly duck out of the way.

She knew that there were miles and then there were nautical miles—a nautical mile was equal to 1.2 land miles. From Boston to Bermuda, it was roughly 673 nautical miles. It would take them two full days to get there and two days and change to return. Of course, Caroline didn't need to understand nautical terminology to set sail (she wasn't driving the boat, after all), but, as a journalist, she liked to have a firm grasp of the facts. One of her coworkers had likened a cruise ship to a limousine on the sea, but Caroline wasn't taking any chances. She'd almost forgotten: she fished the Dramamine box out of her purse and swallowed the tiny orange pill, then went to join the line for the elevator.

While she waited, her phone chimed in her purse. A text from Abby: *On our way!* To which Lee had already responded: *Us too! See you soon.* Caroline texted back: *Ship is amazing! See you on top deck, front and right for the sail away.* She was pretty sure the bow was the front and the stern was the back of the boat, but she didn't dare mix them up for the sail away.

When the elevator reached the tenth floor, Caroline threaded her way through the crowd and navigated down a long hallway to her cabin. A few swipes with the key card and the door swung open onto a room about ten feet wide and eighteen feet long. Everything was so small and quaint! There was a double bed, a small love seat, two stools, a table beneath a television, and a closet. Multicolored striped beach towels, rolled up like fat sausages, sat atop a white comforter. The adjoining door—locked when Caroline checked it—connected her cabin to the next room, where supposedly Lee and Lacey were staying.

A mere seven steps led to a wisp of a balcony, big enough for two chairs. Caroline slid open the door and breathed in the salty air. Below, a crew was busy lifting crates of food onto the ship. She wondered how many eggs got packed for the roughly two thousand passengers and one thousand crew members—and made a mental note to find out.

Back in the cabin, she freshened up. Even though her roommates would be arriving within the hour, Caroline didn't see any reason to wait in her cabin. She grabbed her room key and headed for the top deck, where a flirty bartender took her order. A reggae band played near the poolside cabana where a small group danced, the ship's photographer buzzing around them and snapping pictures.

Caroline wandered over to the ship's railing for a better view of the city. She'd seen the wide expanse of the Himalayas, the elegant stretch of the Eiffel Tower, the translucent walls of an ice castle in Finland. But she'd never seen Boston quite like this before, from this vantage point, the orange sun blazing overhead, the windows of the John Hancock building twinkling back at her. In the distance, the twin peaks of the Zakim Bridge hovered like two pointy hats. "Cheers," she said softly, toasting the skyline, the sound of tinny steel drums beating nearby.

Suddenly she couldn't wait for her girlfriends to arrive. Couldn't wait for Javier to circle his arms around her waist and tell her how much he'd missed her. And at that moment, Caroline Canton, previously wary, decided that this would be a fabulous trip, perhaps her best yet.

⸺

All Lacey could think when they pulled up to the boat was "Holy cow. It's huge!" She might have said "Holy" something else, but she'd been swearing like a truck driver and was trying to cut back. That, plus her mom would be on her case if she started cursing around her aunts. The fact of the matter was that the ship was immense. Perfectly enormous. She couldn't understand how all that heavy metal could possibly float. She didn't want to think about it. Every week thousands of people sailed to Bermuda. What were the odds that their particular ship would sink? It seemed improbable.

Like pretty much everyone else who lived in a port of call, Lacey had waved to passing cruise ships from Waterfront Park in Charleston, an ice cream cone dripping in her hand. But even then, she couldn't have imagined how massive the boats were up close. Her mom paid the cabbie, and they headed for the cruise port, a gray formidable-looking building. Lacey followed a few safe steps behind her mother, as she had since they'd left Charleston this morning. To an onlooker, she might appear to be traveling with the woman ahead of her—or she might not. Lacey hoped the relationship remained ambiguous.

A quick look around revealed a handful of teenagers and college-age kids, enough to suggest that the trip might be remotely fun. When her mom had first mentioned the cruise, Lacey had been reluctant. As much as she loved her aunts, Abby and Caroline were, well, *older* now, and the thought of hanging out with them to celebrate Abby and Sam's twentieth wedding anniversary struck Lacey as anything but romantic. More like corny and, quite possibly, boring.

But then she'd talked with Tyler, who pointed out that if Lacey went along, her mom could hardly pester her about finding a summer job—and that in and of itself would be worth it. If Lacey heard about one more person her mom had bumped into at the grocery store who knew so-and-so, who happened to be looking for help this summer, she was going to lose her mind. Her mom didn't get that she needed to relax, that college was stressful. None of her friends had jobs this summer, so she didn't know why Lee was making such a big deal about it. "Really, Lacey, you should have figured something out months ago," her mother had scolded after a particularly rough day with her preschoolers.

And then there was the whole guilt thing. Abby and Sam were her godparents after all, and they'd asked her to come along. It also occurred to Lacey that on such a big boat, it might be difficult for her mother to actually *find* her. Lacey pictured herself on a lounge chair in a remote spot on deck, where she could hide behind her Jackie O sunglasses and get a killer tan. She was furthermore counting on her aunts to keep her mom entertained—and Lee's mind off Lacey. It wasn't that her aunts were bad people; they were actually quite nice. Plus, Lacey hadn't seen Abby's boys in about a hundred years. It might be fun to hang out with them after all this time.

She tried to think when she'd last seen them. Maybe in New York? No, it was on the Cape, when the boys were probably eleven or twelve. Now Chris and Ryan were teenagers. Fifteen or sixteen, maybe? Lacey wondered if Chris was still cute. He'd always been the self-assured one, but Lacey had a soft spot for Ryan, who was sweet and empathetic beyond his years. Once, when she'd cut her foot on a piece of sea glass at the beach, it had been Ryan who'd offered her his shoulder to lean on while she limped back to the house. Ryan, who had found the antiseptic and bandages for her foot. Chris, meanwhile, had hung back at the beach to play football with his dad.

Lacey and her mom wove their way through check-in and hurried over to the ship. Eventually, they arrived on the tenth floor, where they dropped their bags in the cabin (small but nice) and knocked on Caroline's cabin next door. No answer.

"I didn't think she'd be there. Just checking. She texted she was on the top deck earlier. Let's go find her," said Lee, her cheeks flushed pink.

Her mom, Lacey had to admit, was kind of cute whenever she got together with her college roommates. Lee hadn't seen Abby or Caroline since last spring, and something about their reunions always made her mom act like a goofy freshman. Abby and Caroline liked to remind Lacey that her mother had been a fox in college, but, of course, Lacey didn't want to think about that.

She could imagine that at one time Lee might have been attractive, with her long blond hair, her lean legs.

Her mother as a total knockout, however, was tougher to conjure. Judging from her yearbook photo, Lee had put on a good forty pounds since college, and her hair was now an ashy blond, cut short, with roots that she touched up only infrequently. To Lacey, her mother looked like a woman who had just barely weathered the storms of single parenthood, life crumpling her like a dollar bill.

It might seem cruel, but Lacey thought her mom had no one but herself to blame. Sometimes she wished Lee would pull her own life back together, start exercising, lose some weight, instead of trying to live vicariously through Lacey. It would make things so much easier. But anytime Lacey suggested a plan along those lines, Lee would only roll her eyes and say, "But I *am* happy, honey, with the way I am. This is just who I am now. As long as you're happy, I'm happy." Lacey made a mental note never to let her own kids feel as if her every happiness depended on them. That was just mean.

They made their way up three flights of stairs to the top deck, both of them weaving through the crush of people, many of whom already appeared to be drunk.

"There she is!" her mother shouted, rushing toward a woman in a sheer white blouse and pink shorts. "Caroline!" The woman spun around to see who was calling her name, and a huge smile crossed her face.

"Lee!" Caroline raced over and pulled her mother into a hug. "Look at you! You look fantastic!" This was something her mom's friends always did, Lacey had noticed over the years—compliment each other on their looks no matter how fat or gray or wrinkled they'd become. "And you! Come here, sweetie! You're all grown up—and gorgeous!" Caroline squeezed Lacey so hard she could feel her aunt's ribs pressing against hers.

She laughed and pulled away. "Thank you. Good to see you, too, Aunt Caroline." And she meant it. It was no secret that Lacey had a special bond with Caroline. Her aunt was glamorous and cool in a way that her mom would never be. Plus, Caroline was always sending Lacey complimentary gifts from *Glossy*, like a cashmere wrap or a new mascara.

Caroline clapped her hands together. "I'm so excited. Aren't you? I mean, at first, I was kind of worried because, you know, I don't really *do* boats." She gestured around them. "But then I thought, *What the heck?* If our girl Abby wants to celebrate twenty years of marriage on a cruise ship, then count me in. Besides, we'll be in Bermuda before we know it, right?"

Lee nodded with little head bobs. "It's going to be great. I can't wait to plant myself in a lounge chair and enjoy a cocktail."

"Oh, go get one. Look! I already have a Bahama Mama." Caroline held up a glass of orangey liquid, a pineapple wedge hooked on its side.

"Shouldn't it be a Bermuda Bellini or something?" Lacey half kidded.

"You're right!" said Caroline. "That should definitely be our next cocktail. Does it exist?"

"Hold on there," Lacey's mom interjected. "Lacey's only nineteen. She'll be drinking soda and lemonade on this cruise."

"Mom—" Lacey started, then stopped. What was the point? The only way she'd get any alcohol on the ship was if someone covered for her. No matter that she'd done keg funnels at Tyler's fraternity parties. It wasn't exactly the kind of argument you made to your mother.

"Oh, right. Forgot. Sorry, sweetie." Caroline shrugged. Just then, her cell phone dinged in her pocketbook and she pulled it out. "It's Abby," she said. "They're on the boat and headed up." Caroline began to tap out a reply.

"Excuse us while we go grab a beverage," Lee said as she pulled Lacey along with her. "Be right back."

Her mom's friends were too funny when it came to technology. Lacey felt like she was watching *Land of the Lost*. They texted each other only when they were within walking distance, as if their texts couldn't be trusted to cross the gaping miles between New York City and Boston and Charleston. For whatever reason, though, they were completely comfortable communicating through Facebook and old-fashioned e-mail, the equivalent, in their minds, of reliable rotary phones in cyberspace. Lacey pretty much kept her Facebook account active just so that her aunts could keep in touch. But whenever she mentioned a photo she'd posted on Instagram or Snapchat, their eyes would glaze over.

When she reached the bar, Lacey could see that the countertop was aglow with tiny blue and green lights. It reminded her of a trail of phosphorescent plankton, which somehow seemed appropriate given the setting. Lee ordered their drinks while Lacey watched the reggae band try to warm up the crowd: "Are you ready for more muuu-sic?" Cheers went up around the deck.

Somewhat incongruously, the band began to play "Sweet Caroline," and Lacey felt a pang of disappointment. How many times would she have to listen to the Beantown tune? she wondered. Weren't the ship's passengers more cosmopolitan than that? At least the crew was. She'd already glimpsed name tags of stewards from Hungary, Croatia, Greece, and Spain. A person could practically travel the globe just by walking past the deckhands, which, when she considered it, was pretty cool.

"Here you go." Her mom handed Lacey a glass of Diet Coke before hoisting her own glass in the air. "Cheers, honey," she said with a grin. "Here's to a fabulous mother-daughter cruise."

"Cheers." Lacey smiled, clinked glasses, and did a little groan inside. At the very least, she thought, the cruise might help take her mind off the fact that she was late. Three days late to be exact.

⌒

Abby allowed herself to breathe. They'd made it. Just in time. Of course, they'd missed the slot when they were supposed to preboard, but nobody seemed to mind. The cruise staff had whisked her and Sam and the boys through check-in as if they'd been expecting them to run late the entire time.

And now that they'd inspected their cabins—the boys over the moon to have their very own room with a bathroom and a balcony—Abby and Sam stood on the top deck, awaiting the sail away. Lee, Lacey, and the boys had gone down to the pool area to join in the Sail-off/Dance-off competition, and Caroline was at customer service, trying to straighten out matters with Javier's room key. He'd nearly missed the boat, and in the commotion to get him on, he'd been mistakenly assigned to the wrong cabin. Abby had no doubt that Caroline would set matters straight. That was her specialty, after all. Once in college, when Abby had wanted to drop an astronomy class after the cutoff date, Caroline had marched down to the registrar's office and demanded that Abby be allowed to switch classes. Caroline was a good friend to have in such times. Reliable, persistent, a charismatic bulldog accustomed to getting her way.

For the moment, Abby was just grateful that the twins were behaving themselves. Even among teenagers, it appeared that the "third-party rule" still applied—introduce new people to the playdate and suddenly everyone was friends again. Both Chris and Ryan seemed genuinely pleased to see Lacey after all this time. Abby took a deep breath and tilted her face toward the sun, soaking in its warmth. She'd forgotten how much she loved the summertime when the light lingered till eight o'clock most evenings. The longer days were a welcome change from the chilled, rainy spring they'd had. True spring, when the flowers actually bloomed, lasted about one week in Boston.

Sam wrapped an arm around her and pulled her close. "Nice view, isn't it?"

"Mmm . . . the best."

"This will be good for us," he said. "To get away."

"I think so, too," she agreed.

More than anything, Abby wanted this trip to be a break for Sam, nine blissful, relaxing days when he could stop worrying about her, about them. They were going to be fine, regardless. So what if life had gotten a little more complicated these past few weeks? They'd been tested before. They would get through this, too. She was sure of it. The wind whipped her hair in front of her face, and she tried to tame it, pulling it behind an ear.

"I guess I should have worn my head scarf." She laughed. "Do people wear those anymore?"

Sam smiled, his eyes crinkling. He never appeared more like the kind professor than when he was smiling. Abby had fallen in love with that smile. "I don't think so, but you'd look great in one."

"You better watch it, honey. Keep buttering me up and you might find yourself a lucky man on this cruise."

"Don't be fresh," he said and squeezed her. At that moment, the captain's voice came on over the intercom to announce that they'd be setting sail in a few minutes.

"Look. They've already untied the moorings." Sam pointed to the front of the boat, where previously a thick, taut rope had held ship to shore. As the ship started to shift ever so slightly, a wave of cheers traveled around the top deck, capped by three boisterous blasts of the horn.

"And we're off!" Abby clapped and turned to get a better view of the Boston skyline. "It's so pretty, isn't it? All that wonderful architecture. I sort of take it for granted, but when you see it from a distance, it's breathtaking." She leaned back into Sam's arms and watched the handful of people onshore who were waving goodbye. A few carried briefcases, their shirtsleeves rolled up in the summer heat. "Oh, those poor souls," she lamented. "They all have to go back to work on Monday."

Sam tilted his head, studying her. "Should I be worried that my wife seems to take a perverse pleasure in other people's misery?"

She laughed. "Not at all. I've plenty of misery to share with them, if they'd like." Sam only squeezed her tighter. He knew exactly what she meant, of course.

A tugboat pulled up alongside the ship, helping it turn around to face the wide-open sea and sending them sailing past colorful freight containers, piled high like building blocks on the shore. As the boat pulled farther away, Abby turned and wrapped her arms around Sam's neck, kissing him full on the mouth and surprising them both. His lips tasted salty, like his margarita, but she didn't mind. For once, she felt content, as if everything would be okay after countless days of worrying and not knowing. Now she knew.

And with that knowledge came relief, however small.

3

~

When she woke the next morning, Lee was ravenous. Lacey was still sleeping, so Lee dressed quietly in the dark and let herself out of the room to go in search of breakfast and coffee. *Definitely coffee.* Last night, after dinner and drinks, their gang had retired to their cabins, and Lee had more or less passed out. Which was surprising, given that she typically didn't sleep well anywhere but in her own bed. But the flight from Charleston and the excitement of seeing her friends had left her drained. Her body felt stiff and creaky, her brain foggy. *Coffee,* she thought again.

When she reached the twelfth floor, the savory smells of breakfast greeted her. Her flip-flops squeaked on the cafeteria's tiled floor, the sound all the more pronounced in the early-morning quiet. Soon, dozens of cruisers would be lining up for omelets and French toast, but right now, the only people awake were the health-conscious, grabbing a glass of juice after a workout, or the health-be-damned, smokers sneaking an early cigarette just beyond the cafeteria doors. Lee helped herself to a generous serving of scrambled eggs, toast, and coffee—and a chocolate muffin for good measure—and planted herself at a table.

A heavyset woman carrying a tray filled with pastries passed by her. "I'm in my glory now," she said with a wink. Lee smiled. It was a well-known fact that the buffet was open around the clock, a food lover's dream. Last night, their entire group had stopped by to investigate and had been overwhelmed by the possibilities. There was an unlimited salad bar (as if anyone would want to eat healthy food on vacation!), a Mexican bar with tacos and burritos, sandwiches of every imaginable combination, a "hot food" selection with fish, roast beef, chicken stir-fry, and three kinds of potatoes. And a dessert island that stretched for miles, including custard tarts topped with caramelized apples and pies bursting with berries. There were brownie bars the size of her fist and a soft-serve ice cream machine where the kids could help themselves. And for the virtuous—a fruit bar.

One of Lee's coworkers had warned her that the typical weight gain on a cruise was anywhere from five to ten pounds, which (considering they'd be sailing for a week) seemed both ridiculous and entirely possible. Of course, Lee had been meaning to lose a few pounds before they set sail (when *hadn't* she been meaning to?), but then life had gotten in the way. If she'd thought to step on the scale, chances were she would have discovered that she'd even gained a few pounds.

What she was looking forward to the most, though, even more than the unlimited cookies and brownies, was the luxury of not having to prepare a single meal for an entire week. To her mind, that alone justified the expense of the cruise. For lack of a better expression, Lee was "cooked out." Every recipe in her recipe box had been tasted and tweaked, and she was sick of trying to come up with flavorful, original dishes. Besides, all Lacey ever did when she came home was pick at her food, and when Lee was by herself there hardly seemed to be any point in cooking at all. Usually, she'd boil pasta, throw on some sauce, and finish it off with a pint of ice cream.

When Lee had visited Lacey for parents' weekend in October, she'd found only grapes and a carton of skim milk in her fridge. "Honestly, honey," she'd teased. "How are you supposed to put on the freshman ten if this is what you're eating?" Lacey had shot her a look and said, "That's kind of the point, Mom. I don't *want* to put on ten pounds." Sometimes, Lee worried that her daughter might have an eating disorder, but then she'd spy Lacey enjoying an ice cream cone and would let the worry slide.

Lee took a bite of her eggs, sipped her coffee. Out the window, she could see the precise line of the horizon where the dark blue of the ocean split a dawning blue sky. She marveled at the color of the water, trying to recall where else she'd seen water so vibrantly blue, and then realized she'd only glimpsed this particular shade in a crayon. Yes, that was it: the water so far out to sea turned a breathtaking Crayola blue. She tried to think where they might be on a map. Perhaps somewhere off the Carolina coast? Soft waves lapped at the boat, rocking it like a child to sleep.

On the table sat the ship's bulletin, aptly named *The Smooth Sailor,* and Lee scanned the day's list of activities. *Bingo. Trivia. A fruit-carving demonstration in the lobby at noon. A basketball tournament on the upper deck at three.* The spa was offering a special two-for-one massage. Beyond that, a person could sign up for shuffleboard, check out books from the library, join in poolside games, or escape to a corner where one of several taverns awaited. Later in the day, there was musical theater, a magic show, karaoke. And on and on. The choices were endless, verging on the preposterous. Lee didn't understand what more people could need than sun, a good book, and pleasant conversation. So many activities struck her as window dressing, daytime soap operas for the unimaginative.

She shoveled the last bite of eggs into her mouth, swiped her plate clean with a wedge of toast, and drained her coffee. When she rose to clear her tray, a steward magically appeared at her side to take it. "Why, thank you," she exclaimed, momentarily wondering if she was supposed to tip him. Being treated like a queen, she thought, was certainly something she could get used to.

On her way out, she spotted Abby waving from across the cafeteria.

"You're not leaving, are you?" Abby was already in

her bathing suit, the black strap poking out from underneath a pink cover-up. A floppy sun hat dangled from her hand.

"I was just heading back to the room to change into my suit," said Lee. "Where's Sam?"

"Still sleeping. How about Lacey?"

"Same."

"How did you sleep?"

"Great. I was exhausted. You?"

"Like a baby. Sailing is so soothing, isn't it?"

Lee nodded. "So far so good. How about I meet you back here in ten minutes?"

"Perfect." Abby grinned. "I'll be the girl sitting in the corner with a pile of waffles and whipped cream. Come find me."

⌒

When Lee got back to the cabin, Lacey's head was tucked behind the bedside table. "You have got to be kidding me," she mumbled.

"What's the matter?" Lee asked.

"Our room has only one outlet for charging?"

"Oh, I'm sure there are more." Lee bent down on her hands and knees to peek behind the bureau and beds, but after extensive searching, it appeared that Lacey was correct. Their first full day on the boat, and Lee was beginning to wonder if they were part of some larger science experiment, such as how long could family members remain civil to each other in cramped quarters? If so, providing only one outlet to a room was a great accelerator to the social experiment.

Lacey sighed and crawled onto the bed. A moment later she held up her phone, waving it in the air. "I don't know why I even bothered charging it. We've officially lost all contact with the rest of the world. Zero bars."

"Sorry, honey, but you're going to have to learn to survive without Wi-Fi for a few days." Lee tried to sound sympathetic, but she doubted that it came off as genuine.

"Chris says you can pay to get on the ship's Wi-Fi system if you want to."

"Yeah, and it costs a small fortune. Be my guest, if you'd like. But don't you dare charge it to our room," warned Lee.

Lacey shrugged and tossed the phone down on the bed. "Guess I can manage without it for a few hours." Lee understood that the cruise presented a formidable challenge for her daughter: Could Lacey survive without being in constant contact with Tyler? It frustrated Lee that the girl whom she'd raised to be a self-sufficient woman was so clingy, so dependent, so *needy*. What had college done with her daughter? It was as if the young woman she'd sent off freshman year—sweet, idealistic— had been kidnapped and locked in a closet in her dorm room, while this other Lacey was staring back at her from the bed.

"C'mon," she said now, swatting Lacey's foot as she

went to pull back the curtains from the balcony window. Sunlight flooded the cabin. "It's a beautiful day, and you're already missing out." Lee cracked open the glass door, letting in a rush of warm air. Last night they'd cranked the air conditioner so that their cabin was now the approximate temperature of a refrigerator. "Abby and I are going to go sit by the pool. Why don't you join us?"

Lacey stretched her arms above her head and yawned. "'Kay. After I get something to eat. And shower."

Lee was about to point out there was no need to shower if Lacey was headed to the pool, but she held her tongue—she didn't pretend to understand the workings of her daughter's mind. Instead, she dug into the top dresser drawer for her navy bathing suit from last summer, which had a flouncy skirt that conveniently hid her hips. In the bathroom, she disrobed, banging her elbow on the shower stall.

"Ouch!" She opened the flimsy bathroom door to give herself a few more inches of room, but when she stepped into her suit, she realized she had bigger problems than her elbow: her suit was stuck halfway up her body.

"Uh-oh."

"What's wrong?" Lacey called from the other room.

Lee stepped out of the bathroom and gestured to her body, her boobs protruding from the top, the swimsuit not quite hiding the rolls of tummy fat below. "It doesn't fit." Had she really put on that much weight since last summer?

"Oh, Mom." Lacey shook her head. "Here, let me help you." She pushed up from the bed. "How," Lacey continued, pulling on the strap, "did this possibly fit you last year?" She tugged until finally she got one strap up over Lee's right arm, leaving only the left to contend with.

"Hey, we can't all have teensy-weensy bodies." Lee tried to think. Maybe she'd dried the suit on hot cycle by mistake and it had shrunk? She couldn't possibly be bigger than a size 12, could she? She *might* have put on ten pounds. It was possible. What a cruel irony, though! Her daughter had gone off to college, and Lee had packed on an empathetic freshman ten. She thought back to when she'd been fixing Tom & Jerry drinks for a holiday party, the recipe calling for one pound of butter—or the equivalent of four sticks. Lee did the quick arithmetic in her head: if she *had* gained ten pounds, then strapped to her very middle-aged body were forty fresh sticks of butter. She moaned.

"Here, let me get around on your other side," Lacey was saying as she circled to Lee's left and tugged again. "Hold your stomach in, Mom."

"I *am*," Lee said through gritted teeth. Lacey pulled some more, stretching the strap out beyond Lee's elbow until, like a rubber band, it snapped into place on her shoulder. "Ow!" Lee howled, but Lacey had collapsed on the bed in a fit of giggles. Before she could stop herself, Lee was laughing, too. She had to admit: it *was* a little funny. Plus, it felt so nice to be sharing a light moment with her daughter that Lee couldn't resist, even if it was at her own expense.

"Just don't ask me to help you get out of that thing," said Lacey.

"I swear it shrunk in the dryer. I have *not* put on that much weight."

"Whatever you say, Mom."

Lee batted Lacey in the leg with her beach towel. "I'm leaving. Come join us by the pool when you're ready." She stuffed her bag with sunblock, a book, and her room key. When she turned to leave, a flash of scarlet on the bed caught Lee's eye. She stopped to look. It was Lacey's teensy red bikini, big enough to cover maybe Lee's elbow. Lee rolled her eyes and went off in search of her friend.

⌒

When they stepped through the sliding doors to the pool, a blast of heat hit Lee like a slap. The abrupt change in temperature from the air-conditioning inside made her sunglasses fog up, and she had to wipe them on the hem of her cover-up before placing them back on her nose. The air was heavy, thick with humidity. She followed Abby to the pool, where flocks of teenagers were already strategically positioned along its edge. *Like birds preening their feathers for mating season*, thought Lee. And the amount of bare skin! It was shocking, really.

Even the girls in one-piece suits had the middles sliced out, exposing their pale, taut bellies. It made Lee want to spray sunblock all over their perfect little bodies.

"Let's check the other side for chairs," Abby said. Earlier, they'd bumped into Caroline, who'd promised to join them later, which meant they needed at least four chaise lounges. Abby and Lee located two amid the sea of chairs already claimed by passengers. It hadn't occurred to Lee to pack chair clips to stake their territory poolside, but apparently the more seasoned cruisers already knew this trick. Seat after seat had a towel clipped to it with a fastener that seemed to shout, *Taken!* A few aisles down, she found two more chairs and scooted them over, making an even four. "There," she said, triumphant, hands on her hips. "That ought to do us."

"We'll have to remember to get here early tomorrow." Abby shook out her towel and laid it down. "Apparently, these seats are prime real estate."

"That or we're going to have to invest in some chair clips." Lee settled into the chaise lounge beside her.

"Seriously. So, which one?" Abby waved two bottles of sunscreen in front of her. "I'm allowing myself one day in the sun, then it's back to my solar shirt."

"For the first day? Definitely seventy." Lee pulled off her cover-up, an awkward kind of striptease to hide her jiggly bits.

Abby narrowed her eyes at her beneath her hat. "Cute suit," she said.

"Thanks. You should have seen what it took to get me into it. The good news is: it's on. The bad news is: I don't think it's coming off my body for the entire trip."

Abby laughed and squeezed a zigzag of sunscreen into her palm, infusing the air with the scent of coconut. "Yeah, well, mine has a nice little tummy tuck built into it. Welcome to middle age."

"It suits you." Lee grinned at her own bad pun. "Really, you look great. Maybe even a little on the skinny side?" Lee had debated about saying anything, but since it had come up naturally in the conversation, she figured, *Why not?* Both she and Caroline had been surprised to see Abby, typically thin, looking even thinner. Maybe, Lee reasoned, Abby had lost some weight for the vows ceremony.

"Ladies, may I get you something to drink?" A cabana boy, his tanned skin the color of honey, interrupted her train of thought.

"I'm all set with my orange juice, thank you," said Abby. "How about you, Lee? Want anything?"

Lee considered. "Is it too early for a Bloody Mary?"

"No ma'am. It's never too early for a Bloody Mary." Lee smiled at him. He was adorable in that way that any man who was twenty years younger than she was adorable.

"Well, in that case—" She dug into her bag for her room key and handed it over. It was wonderful to be able to charge everything to the room. With the whisk of a card, she could charge her meals, her drinks, spa treatments, any item at the ship's gift store. At least she could *pretend* it was free money until she got the bill at the end of the trip. Lee wished there were a few other items she could put on her room key. Like liposuction, or several weeks of good therapy for Lacey, or Lacey's entire college tuition. Those would be handy. At the moment, though, she'd gladly settle for a Bloody Mary.

Her eyes safely hidden behind her sunglasses, Lee took a moment to study the other passengers on deck. As far as she could tell, there were three types of cruisers: those who'd come to sunbathe and see Bermuda; those who'd come to drink themselves into oblivion; and those (mostly of the senior set) who intended to take full advantage of the onboard activities, never once stepping foot on land. She'd once read an article in *Good Housekeeping* that categorized the majority of cruisers as "newlyweds, overfeds, or almost deads." She'd laughed when she read it, but now she had to admit it had a ring of truth.

A mother nearby hollered at her young son to stay out of the hot tub, prompting a sigh from Lee. Moms with young children were their own special tribe, and Lee didn't miss it one bit—not that she'd ever really fit in. Before she started teaching, being a single mom had sometimes felt as if she brandished a scarlet letter on her chest. How many times had she tried to brush off the judgmental stares at parents' night at Lacey's school? Word traveled fast in their small southern town, and the only thing ostensibly worse than being a divorced parent was being a single parent. Especially a single, never-married (read *unwed*) mom.

Fortunately, she'd found her own small tribe of mothers to hang out with, women who were funny, sarcastic, and not at all afraid to admit that mothering was *hard*. And, well, if Abby and Caroline hadn't been just a phone call away, Lee might have packed her bags and left young Lacey to fend for herself. It was Abby, in fact, who'd helped Lee through those first few weeks when Lee would call late at night in tears, her hormones surging. Even though Abby didn't yet have the twins, she was the most natural mother of them all. "No one enjoys the first weeks of motherhood. *No one.* And anyone who tells you she does is either high or crazy." Lee had laughed maniacally—they were the most comforting words she'd ever heard.

She smiled at Lacey, who had arrived and was now easing herself into the adjacent chair.

"Why is it that almost everyone under forty on this boat seems to have a tattoo?" Lee asked. She felt the same way about tattoos as she did about wearing jeans in middle age—neither seemed worth the pain and suffering. Why waste time with zippers when there were pants with elastic waistbands? To Lee's mind, yoga pants were one of the most ingenious inventions ever, on par with airplanes or coffeemakers. "Don't they know they can get hepatitis from needles?"

"Mom," Lacey said in a chastising tone that suggested Lee should know better. "Since when did you become such a prude?"

"Since I saw all this bare skin." Lee gestured around her, though her eyes were laser-beamed on Lacey's chest, which was just barely contained by her red bikini top. Why hadn't Lee insisted on approving her daughter's wardrobe before they left? *Because Lacey would never allow it. Because she is in college now.* Sometimes Lee had to remind herself.

Lacey shrugged, her breasts rising like two very plump tomatoes. "Tattoos are the pierced ears of today's generation."

Lee forced herself to look away. "But tattoos are so *permanent.* It's not like you can just let your pierced holes close up if you get tired of them. You're stuck with that shamrock or the name of your lover—who will probably cheat on you anyway—on your ankle for the rest of your life."

Lacey gawked at her. "How very optimistic of you."

"Well, it's true," Lee countered.

"Whatever." Lacey pulled a spray bottle from her bag and proceeded to coat her body with sunblock, leaving behind a shimmering globe of incandescent drops floating in the air. It seemed such a waste of sunblock. Lee was about to suggest she switch to the lotion variety, but her daughter had already plugged in her earbuds and shut her eyes, an all-too-familiar routine—Lacey's unceremonious way of saying that she was done talking.

Abby shot Lee a searching look, but Lee just shook her head. Trying to have a conversation with her daughter these days could be so unfulfilling. No, that wasn't the right word. *Frustrating. Maddening.* She contemplated tugging out an earbud and whispering an admonishment in Lacey's ear, such as *Would it kill you to talk to your mother and your godmother for a few minutes before tuning us out? Oh, and by the way, cover up!* But then she thought better of it. Why poke the bear if the bear didn't want to be poked?

Lee was on vacation, too. She intended to enjoy herself.

She dug through her bag for her book, a self-help title she'd checked out from the library the day before they left. When she cracked it open, a musty scent wafted up. She read the first sentence: *You can either choose to be encouraged by what you see in the world or you can choose to be dismayed. It is your choice.* The lines swam through her mind. Usually Lee bypassed the self-help shelf, but lately things had gotten so tense with Lacey that she'd plucked up a few titles in hopes that one might help smooth the way.

You can either choose to be encouraged by what you see in the world or you can choose to be dismayed, she read again. It was a nice sentiment, along the lines of all those motivational shows that told you to focus on the positive. It sounded easy enough, but that was precisely why Lee was wary. Anything that was too quick a fix couldn't possibly work, could it?

61

She glanced over at Lacey, whose head bobbed slightly to the beat of whatever song she listened to. What could it hurt to try? thought Lee. What if, as the book suggested, Lee chose to be encouraged by her daughter's behavior instead of dismayed? She tried to concentrate on something positive—maybe the fact that Lacey had joined them by the pool in the first place. That her daughter wasn't embarrassed to sit with her? That felt like some kind of small victory.

She shut the book, set it on the table next to her, and closed her eyes. After a minute, she moaned, "I could get used to this."

"Me, too," said Abby. "No one fighting. Sunshine. All the time in the world to read a good book."

"This is the life, Abs. Thanks for inviting us."

"I wouldn't have it any other way."

It occurred to Lee that she should wait for her Bloody Mary to arrive before she napped, but perhaps the kind waiter would set it down gently and leave it for her. As her eyelids grew heavier, she thought about how nice it was to have no bigger decision to make than which cocktail to order or what level SPF to use. *First world problems,* Lacey called them. Not a single preschooler to demand an extra snack, no tantrums to be defused. The sweet little cherubs, bless their hearts, were back with their parents till the end of August.

Come September, Lee knew she'd be ready to return to the classroom, but right now, lying in the sun, surrounded by perfectly reasonable adults, she was more than content—she was *encouraged*. By all the vacationing families around them, by this rare opportunity to enjoy a trip with her best friends (and, possibly, her daughter), by something as simple as today's glorious weather. It was her choice, she reminded herself.

And, with the gentle rocking of the boat, she drifted off to sleep.

At the health club, Caroline found her way to the stationary bikes lining the panel of windows that looked out over the water. Earlier, she'd tried running on the track that looped around the top deck, but the combination of the boat's rocking and the sharp corners had made her stomach lurch. She'd come to the club in hopes of finding a more level playing field; Javier, never big on exercise, had gone off to enjoy his coffee and a book at the cafeteria.

For the first morning of vacation, the gym was surprisingly packed, and Caroline was lucky to get the last free bicycle. She climbed on, slipped in her earbuds, and began to pedal slowly, all the while envisioning the breakfast buffet she would gorge herself on later. She figured if millions of calories were going to lay siege to her body over the next several days, then she would fight back as best she knew how. By pedaling hundreds of miles.

As she cycled along, the odometer ticking off the distance, she imagined herself biking across the ocean to Madrid, maybe to Paris, with Javier—and dreamily thought back to last night. Sex was always better when they'd been apart for more than a few days, and last night had been no exception. There was something almost primal about it, as if their bodies couldn't be satiated, Javier's tongue licking the salt from her skin. It was an instinctive, crazy love. The kind that kicked all the sheets off the bed in a sweaty mess.

Afterward, Caroline had wrapped a sheet around her waist and gone out on the balcony, where the dark water swirled below. Moonlight fell in ropes across the ocean, forming a shimmering ladder that climbed out to the horizon. When Javier came up behind her and nuzzled his chin against her neck, she could feel the rough stubble of his midnight shadow tickling her skin.

"That was amazing," he mumbled into her neck.

"Yep. Pretty good," she agreed, giggling at the scrape of his whiskers. Her eyes were on the orange moon above, just shy of full. "Look." She pointed. "Isn't it beautiful?"

Javier lifted his head, then rested his chin on her shoulder. "A *Star Wars* moon."

"What's that supposed to mean?" she asked.

"You know, like the moons of Tatooine? In the movies?"

Caroline turned around and took his face in her hands. "Sometimes," she said, placing delicate kisses along his jawline, "you are so little. It's adorable."

"What?" He seemed surprised and pulled back. "You

don't remember the three moons that Luke would see in the night sky? There was always one that was a vibrant orange, like tonight's."

"Just be quiet, okay?" Caroline's lips found his, and she could taste the Cabernet that they'd brought back to the room after winning at the blackjack table earlier. *Beginner's luck*, Javier had teased when Caroline raked in more than a hundred dollars. Whatever he wanted to call it, the money, the wine—it all tasted good to her. Caroline's body pressed against the warmth of his; she hadn't realized how much she'd been craving him.

"I missed you," she said at last.

"And I missed you." He stroked her hair, and she buried her head in his shoulder, feeling the steady beat of his heart through bare skin.

"Maybe we don't have to miss each other so much?" She peered up at him.

Javier met her gaze. "What do you mean?"

She bit her bottom lip, worried it with her teeth. She'd hinted earlier that she and Javier should figure out the next steps in their relationship, but should she get into it now? On their first night, when everything had been so perfect? That she wanted what they already had, only more? An official proposal. A wedding, nothing huge, but a ceremony that would bind them together till death do them part. She toyed with the idea of how best to make him understand. She knew his freedom was important to him, but it wasn't as if Caroline was trying to hold him back, was it? He could travel as much as he wanted, as much as he needed for work. And Caroline wasn't sure she even wanted kids. In her forties, she didn't know if it was possible. So, what would be the big deal if they tied the knot?

The thing was, the argument she wanted to make to Javier—that marriage was no big deal—was contrary to the very reason she wanted a ring on her finger in the first place. Marriage *was* a big deal. A lifelong commitment. Which was exactly why she longed for it.

"Nothing." She shook her head and took a step back, grabbing on to the railing. No, she wasn't prepared to parse their relationship on their first night back together. Why spoil a good evening? They had plenty of more days on the boat. Ample time for her to make her case, if need be, though she was secretly hoping it wouldn't be necessary.

"It's just nice to have you back," she said finally. She gazed out at the night sky, the graceful arc of the Big Dipper cutting through the dark. "You know, whenever my mom used to travel, she'd tell me to look up at the Big Dipper at eight o'clock, my bedtime," Caroline explained, smiling at the long-ago memory. "She told me she'd do the same, wherever she might be, and that if we looked at the same time, the stars would flash brighter. It probably sounds silly, but for a little girl missing her mom, it meant the world. Of course, I had no idea about time zones then."

"And did they ever flash?" asked Javier.

"To me they did. All the time."

"What a marvelous memory," he said. "Did your mom travel a lot?" A few months after they'd started dating, Caroline had shared that her mom was a flight attendant, and, as a result, Caroline had spent much of her childhood missing her. That this important piece of her personal history had slipped Javier's mind was surprising, but forgivable.

"She was a flight attendant."

"Oh, right. You told me that. Sorry, I forgot."

Caroline fell quiet for a moment, considering. "To think she'd only seen Long Island before she became a stewardess. I suppose I have a little bit of her wanderlust in me. I wanted to be just like her when I grew up. She was so glamorous. She would wear this crisp blue skirt and a white blouse with a tiny pair of silver wings pinned to the pocket. I thought she looked like royalty."

"She sounds lovely," said Javier. "Just like her daughter. I wish I'd met her."

"Me, too," said Caroline wistfully. Her mom would have adored Javier; she was sure of it. He was a good man to the core. But then again, her mom had also been unfailingly practical. Caroline was fairly certain that Marjorie Canton would have grown impatient with a suitor who, after dating her daughter for three years, had yet to propose. In her own graceful way, she would have pushed Javier to get his act together. And yet, Caroline also liked to heed her father's favorite piece of advice: *Good things come to those who wait.* Like a grape on the vine, Javier just needed a little more time to ripen.

Half the fun (she was sure Javier would tell her later) was in the anticipation, the suspense of not knowing when a proposal would come. Why rush it? She couldn't ask for a more perfect setting—a cruise to Bermuda while celebrating her best friend's wedding anniversary.

Now all she had to do was wait.

She finished up her final minutes on the bike, then slowed to a more leisurely pace. Eventually, she eased off the seat and helped herself to a water bottle and a towel that had been spritzed with something heavenly—maybe eucalyptus? She planned to grab a quick shower and a muffin before meeting Abby and Lee at the pool. When she pushed through the doors of the fitness room, however, Javier was coming up the stairs from the cafeteria.

"Perfect timing!" he exclaimed. In his arms was a tray brimming with juice and croissants, fresh fruit and waffles. "I thought you might enjoy room service after your workout?" He held it out to her, his eyebrows waggling above those bright blue eyes.

She grinned at him. Her very own Dionysus. How could she not love this man? More important, how could she resist? Abby and Lee would have to wait.

4

~~

On Saturday, their first full day at sea, Sam booked dinner reservations for a party of eight at the ship's main restaurant, the Blue Wave. It was Abby's idea. She thought it would be nice for everyone to come together and converse like civilized people. It hadn't occurred to her that there would be long stretches of time on the ship when she didn't see anyone else in their group. The boys, in particular, had gone missing for long periods. Which, truth be told, had been part of her original plan. Chris and Ryan seemed to have jumped headlong into all the activities for teens—the late-night dances, the trivia challenges, the basketball tournaments. Still, Abby wanted to have all the chickens in her coop together for at least one meal.

Earlier this afternoon, she'd been hit by a wave of tiredness. She'd begged off from the others to sneak in a nap. A good decision, it turned out, because tonight was sure to be a late one—there'd been talk of the casino after dinner. She clutched Sam's elbow as they walked along the corridor that led to the back of the ship, the twins following behind them. In the main lobby a man and a woman were singing "All of Me" on center stage. *Passable musicians,* Abby thought, *if not Broadway-bound.*

She and Sam exchanged amused glances. A bright pink band, about an inch wide, snaked across his forehead where he'd missed with the sunblock earlier today. They'd have to be more careful tomorrow. Sunburn aside, however, her husband was still handsome, a fact that Abby was proud of, even if she supposed it made her a tiny bit superficial. Unlike so many of their friends, Sam had held on to his thick salt-and-pepper hair, saving him from doing the odd comb-over that some of her friends' husbands were forced to do. And because Sam still liked to run in the occasional road race, he'd kept in relatively good shape for a forty-something-year-old, especially for a history professor who spent most of his days either in the classroom or behind a desk. Back in graduate school, Abby would have to drag him out of the library for a slice of pizza. Those days, she'd worried about Sam's wasting away. Now, thank heaven, he appreciated a proper meal like the rest of them.

"I didn't realize dressing up for dinner was such a big deal," Sam said.

He and the boys were wearing khakis and polo shirts, and Abby was wearing a yellow sundress with matching yellow sandals. She thought they'd cleaned up well as a family, but now, when her eyes scanned the passengers around them, she saw that their family was a tad under-dressed. Women pranced about in sleek, glittery dresses while their dates wore fitted jackets and ties.

"Just pretend we fit in, honey," Abby whispered, gripping Sam's arm more firmly.

When they reached the restaurant, the rest of their gang was already waiting. Abby exchanged hugs with the others, complimenting Lacey on her pretty blue dress and Caroline on a summery floral romper that only Caroline could have pulled off. Abby couldn't quite determine what Lee was wearing because she'd wrapped an enormous turquoise shawl around herself to ward off the chill of the air-conditioning, which admittedly felt about ten degrees cooler in the restaurant than back in the cabin.

"I think they're ready for us, if you are?" Javier gestured to their host, a young man with dark hair and thick eyebrows, who stood with menus in hand.

"Yes, please," said Abby, marveling at the grand room as she followed their party to a long rectangular table. The dining room itself looked as if it had been teleported out of the 1920s and dropped into their ship. Rich blue carpeting stretched from wall to wall. Long white pillars rose up from the floor, and teardrop chandeliers hung from the ceiling. Each table sported a crisp white tablecloth. The air was vibrating with the hustle and bustle of waiters and the sound of glasses and silverware clinking everywhere.

"I feel like I'm on the *Titanic*," Abby said. "All I'm missing is my gown."

"Yeah, that and an iceberg," Sam joked.

"Oh." Abby laughed. "I don't mean that, of course. Just that it's so fancy. Bad comparison, though, you're right. Sorry."

When they reached their table, a waiter pulled out a chair for her. Javier did the same for Caroline, then Lee, and Ryan hurried to help Lacey with hers.

"Your boys have become such gentlemen," said Caroline, giving Sam an appreciative smile.

"All their mother's doing. I'm afraid I can't take any credit." He sat down next to Abby and unfolded a napkin in his lap. "If they listened to me, they'd still be in their boxer shorts." Caroline laughed, but Abby caught Ryan blushing across the table and kicked Sam under the table. "What?" Sam demanded.

"Shhh . . . you're embarrassing Ryan," she scolded.

The waiter took their drinks order, and Lee, not missing a beat, swiveled around to Abby. "What? No wine for you tonight?"

Abby shook her head. "With all the sun I've had today, I should probably go easy. Ice water sounds perfect."

"Oh, good," Caroline said, the lines in her forehead relaxing. "For a second there, I thought you might be pregnant."

"Ha!" They all shared a good laugh. "Those days are

over, I'm afraid," Abby said, then hurried to add, "At least for me." She wasn't sure what Caroline's plans were exactly, but she knew that her friend was hoping for a proposal. *And if a proposal didn't come on the cruise?* Abby had inquired earlier by the pool. "If we're serious about this relationship, then we should both be able to commit," Caroline had told her and left it at that.

In other words, things were still murky. Abby liked Javier. He was nice, intelligent, a man who could actually pass Caroline's extensive checklist of requirements for a potential partner. He read the *New York Times* and enjoyed the odd art film. That he and Caroline had stayed together for three years was further testament to the fact that Caroline really liked him (she broke up with most guys after a few short months). And he was handsome in an Antonio Banderas kind of way, hardly a weakness. Abby just wished she knew what his intentions were for her friend. Was he the settling-down type?

"I'm so glad that we didn't sign up for the drinks plan," Caroline said now, peering at the menu through her reading glasses. "I can't imagine how we'd get our money's worth." She was referring to a special deal from the cruise line for guests who planned to imbibe generously. The deal had sparked a flurry of e-mails among the roommates, complete with mathematical calculations of how much they would have to drink in order to get their money's worth—somewhere between seven and ten cocktails each per day. That was a bit rich, even for their group.

"Thanks to your good math, Caroline," Abby acknowledged.

"Speak for yourselves, ladies," said Javier and tipped his wineglass to his lips.

"Javier." Abby leaned in closer. "I haven't had a chance to ask you yet: How was your trip to Paris?"

He shrugged, set down his glass. "Good. I found some nice Cabernets for the store. But, of course, Caroline wasn't there, so how romantic could it be?" He slung an arm around her, and Caroline smiled agreeably.

Still, Abby wondered: How much effort would it have taken for Javier to fly Caroline over for the weekend? Yes, he'd been gone for a week, but wasn't that kind of the point? Javier had spent seven days alone, footloose in the City of Light. Abby had been to Paris once, shortly after she and Sam were married. She'd fallen in love with the architecture, the foamy cappuccinos in mini-tasses, the sweet, lingering taste of *croissants du chocolat* that they'd bought from a street vendor each morning. The city practically begged a person to run back to her hotel room and make love.

She was about to suggest that next time Javier traveled, he consider inviting Caroline, but Caroline cut her off. "Speaking of romance," she began, "I think it's high time we toasted the couple of honor. Congratulations to Abby and Sam on celebrating twenty years of marriage!"

She hoisted her glass in the air, prompting clinks and declarations of "Hear, hear!" around the table.

"That reminds me," Sam added, setting down his glass. "My brother owes me a Ben Franklin. I'll have to claim it when we get back to Boston."

"What on earth are you talking about?" Abby asked.

Sam gave her a sheepish look. "We kind of made a bet. On our wedding day? Jake bet me that if you and I made it to twenty years, he'd give me a hundred bucks."

"What?" Abby exclaimed. "I don't know which is more insulting—the fact that you thought twenty years of marriage was worth only a hundred dollars or the fact that you agreed to a bet in the first place." She was only partly joking. Caroline and Lee were both laughing, however.

Sam shrugged. "I fainted. I think he just wanted to make sure I got through the ceremony okay."

"Wow, all the truth is coming out now, isn't it?" Abby said with a pointed laugh.

"Wait, what? You *fainted* at your own wedding?" Lacey, apparently unfazed by the bet revelation, stared at Sam. "I never knew that! What happened?"

"I'm not proud of it," he admitted, "but it was a really hot day, and, well, the next thing I knew, my brother was holding me up in the church basement."

"What can I say, Lacey?" Abby leaned back and crossed her arms. "Love knocked him off his feet that day."

Sam laughed and said, "Yeah, well, something like

75

that," and then, just as quickly, the conversation turned to the topic of deep-sea fishing and whether or not their group should charter a fishing boat once they docked in Bermuda. Abby glanced over at Lee, who was deep in conversation with the boys. Lee had always been gifted at getting kids engaged. She was a natural teacher—animated, effervescent. Maybe she wasn't the same gorgeous girl she'd been in college, but none of them were. Lee, Abby thought, had actually aged the most gracefully of them all. In school, there'd been an edge to her, as if she'd had to prove there was some substance behind all that blinding beauty. But Lee had grown into herself. She was lovely and comfortable in her own skin and Abby envied her that confidence.

When their food arrived, Abby stared down at her pan-seared shrimp, nestled together like plump quarter moons, and suddenly realized she wasn't hungry. Lately, her appetite had been waning. Sam's hand found her knee under the table and squeezed.

"You all right?" he asked quietly. Abby nodded while everyone else around them ate greedily.

"This swordfish," proclaimed Javier, his mouth half-full, "is for the gods."

"The prime rib isn't half-bad either," added Chris.

"Though why someone would order prime rib on a *cruise*," Lacey said, pointing out the obvious. But Chris hardly seemed to notice the insult. To the contrary, he laughed in that easy manner that Abby had come to think of as his trademark. She watched while he leaned toward Lacey, as if sharing a private joke, and Lacey nodded, a smile skirting her lips. *Yes, Chris would be just fine,* she thought. But then she noticed Ryan's eyes darting to Lacey, a faint blush creeping back into his cheeks. *Oh, Ryan!* she thought. *Don't worry. Lacey already has a boyfriend. Chris can't steal her from you.*

Once, when Chris and Ryan were in the third grade, they'd shared a crush on the same girl, Molly Samuels. Abby could still recall Molly's sweet face, round with deep dimples and blond pigtails. One day Chris caught Molly at recess and kissed her right in front of his brother. Abby took a heartbroken Ryan out for a milk shake at the mall later that afternoon. "You know," she told him over her own vanilla malted, "there are going to be plenty of girls in your future."

Ryan looked at her, his expression both doubtful and hopeful.

"You're going to have girls fighting over your telephone number," she added.

Abby felt her eyes well up at the memory. She was doing exactly what she'd promised herself she wouldn't do on this trip—dredging up the past. No, she was absolutely not going to pine over memories. She forked a shrimp into her mouth—*delicious.* Her eyes swept across all the faces at the table, these people who meant the world to her. How she hoped they'd forgive her, still love her, when she told them her secret. But it could wait. Until they were headed back to Boston, maybe even until the moment they disembarked.

Until then, she wanted everyone to enjoy every second of vacation. She was counting on it, perhaps a little too much.

5

Lee agreed to go only with severe arm-twisting. Casinos weren't her thing. But Lacey was headed off to a show with Ryan and Chris, and, well, what else was she going to do? Sit in her cabin by herself? So when first Abby, then Caroline, started pushing her to go, she made them promise that they wouldn't let her lose more than a hundred. A hundred dollars seemed like a fair amount, enough to justify the entertainment and maybe just enough to get lucky.

On the way to the casino, Abby leaned toward her and whispered, "Don't worry. I'm just as lost as you. We'll watch first, and if we want to play later, we can."

"Famous last words," quipped Lee, "before I end up blowing through my entire savings."

"Aw, we won't let that happen," Abby reassured her. "We'll protect you."

"Yeah, right. That's what you said the night of the Halloween dance sophomore year."

Abby swatted her arm. "That's not fair, and you know it. You could not be stopped." They were referring to their dorm's annual costume party. For whatever reason—maybe it had something to do with the liberal mix of alcohol and disguise?—students seemed to lose all their inhibitions at the annual Halloween fete. Lee was hardly shy to begin with, but she'd had a huge crush on a football player, a senior, at the time. Colin Overby. Only with the bravado that her Catwoman mask provided was she able to screw up the courage to talk to him that night. One thing led to another, and, despite her roommates' best attempts to pull her away, Lee had insisted on leaving the party with Colin, her arm slung through his. The next morning, she'd performed the "walk of shame" back to her dorm room.

"Oh, God. I forgot all about that night. Don't you dare tell Lacey."

Abby grabbed her hand and pulled her into the casino. "Don't worry, your secret's safe with me. At least that one is."

"Hah. Touché." Lee blinked and struggled to get her bearings. All around her, bright lights flashed and buzzers beeped. The air was thick with stale smoke, and she waved a hand as if to clear a path. What stretched before her was not unlike a small, sprawling city—coin machines, blackjack tables, roulette and craps tables—and those were only the games that she recognized. Lee groaned. She felt like a freshman showing up for her first day of orientation all over again.

Sam and Javier steered them to a blackjack table with

three empty seats, where Caroline joined them. A dealer whose name tag read ALEXANDRIA, CROATIA had just cut a new deck, and before Lee could inquire about the game, her friends were exchanging money for little red chips that they stacked into tidy piles in front of them. Abby attempted to explain the rudiments of the game to Lee.

"The idea is to get twenty-one or as close to twenty-one as you can," she said. "If you beat the dealer, then you win. But if you lose, all the chips you put forward go to the dealer." Lee nodded, half listening. How quickly the cards were dealt around the table! Lee was still counting up the value of Sam's hand when the dealer moved on to the next person, inquiring if he wanted another card. The man tapped his finger on the table for another. The next player, a woman with peroxide blond hair and canary red lipstick, sighed as the dealer flipped over her new card, a bust, and raked in her chips. "She went over with her jack of hearts," Abby whispered. "She should have stayed at fifteen."

Beyond third-grade math, Lee had never been especially gifted with numbers. She'd heard about those MIT kids who'd won millions in Vegas by counting cards, and hadn't one of their classmates gone on to win big? Harry something? He'd come up in conversation at their last roommate get-together because he'd married a famous model. It was funny, they'd all remarked, how a person could go from geek to most-wanted bachelor in no time at all.

"Sam has low cards." Abby pointed to Sam's hand: a two, a three, and a five. "He'll want to hit." Just as Abby predicted, Sam tapped the table for another card.

"Nice!" exclaimed Javier, when the dealer laid down a queen. "Twenty!"

"But," Abby whispered to Lee, "it all depends on what the dealer gets. She could still get twenty-one." Lee had forgotten about the dealer's cards and glanced at Alexandria's hand. So far, she had a six, a two, and an ace, which could count as either a one or an eleven. Before Lee could ask Abby why the dealer wouldn't just stay at nineteen, Alexandria flipped her card. A two of hearts.

"Man!" Sam slapped the table. "I can't believe you got blackjack with that hand." The dealer smiled and said "sorry" as she pulled away everyone's chips.

The table played on in silence for a while, the chips seeming to go in the wrong direction.

"This is crazy," Javier said finally, eyeing his shrinking piles. "I think I've won maybe four rounds total."

"I've never seen anything like it," agreed Caroline. "Maybe we should try another table?"

Sam nodded. "Yeah, good idea. Let's just finish off this deck."

A cocktail waitress delivered a fresh round of drinks, and between the fizzy feeling of the vodka tonic making its way to her head and the hazy smoke, Lee was having a difficult time concentrating. Her eyes scanned the room. Some of the players looked as if they'd spent the entire day at the casino. One young woman, who appeared to be wearing her pajamas, sat next to a large bucket of change. Lee watched while she pulled out a handful of coins, slipped one in the slot machine, pulled the lever, and repeated the process all over again.

Before long, their group was gathering up their chips in search of a new, luckier table.

"Ready to give it a try, Lee?" Sam asked.

She wrinkled her nose. "That depends. If Abby will, I will."

"Sure," said Abby, joining Sam at a new table. "Why not? Who knows, we might get lucky. And nothing could be worse than that last table."

Lee hesitated. "Okay, but you guys have to help me."

"Of course." Caroline sat down beside her. "Relax. It'll be fun."

Lee handed the dealer a one-hundred-dollar bill and hoped like hell that she'd see it again.

⁓

An hour or so later, a man in faded jeans and a button-down white oxford shirt joined their table. He was about fifty, with graying hair that had been buzzed short to hide a receding hairline and nice hazel eyes. A few cocktails in already, Lee confessed to him that she knew nothing about the game.

"Looks like you must know something." He gestured to her chips. "Either that or you're extremely lucky."

Lee glanced at her piles of pretend money and was surprised to see that they'd grown considerably since she sat down. When she counted them all up, it appeared she actually had two hundred dollars.

"Hey, when did that happen?" She turned to Abby and pointed at her newfound loot. "Did your chips get mixed in with mine?"

Abby grinned. "That's all you, girlfriend. You're our lucky charm."

Lee was amazed. Something was actually working in her favor. Things seldom worked in her favor. Not since college. Not love, not marriage, not a daughter who appreciated her. She had a long, storied past of being *un*lucky. The nice gentleman next to her smiled encouragingly. Maybe, she thought, this was all it took. A little roll of the dice, a shuffle of the cards.

"I'm Lee," she said, suddenly feeling brazen, and held out her hand.

"Nice to meet you. Thomas. Hope some of your luck rubs off on me." He took her hand and shook it—and proceeded to win the next four hands.

At the end of the night, Lee walked away with four hundred dollars. A windfall! She couldn't believe it. Thomas, who hadn't done so badly himself, suggested a celebratory drink at Gatsby's Lounge. There was a part of her that said she should go back to her room and crawl into bed. But there was another part that screamed, *That's what the old Lee would do.* So, she went with Thomas.

She learned that he was from California, a divorced dad with two daughters who attended college in Boston.

"That must be so hard for you. The long distance and all."

"It is, or it was, I should say. It's actually easier now that they're in college. They don't feel like spending time with me *or* their mother," he kidded. "But now that I'm retired, I can fly out to see them on a moment's notice. Like this cruise—it was a last-minute thing."

"What a good dad you are." Her mind flitted to Lacey, whom she'd more or less had to light on fire to persuade to come along.

"What about you?" he asked. Lee hesitated, then gradually, as she talked, she began to feel herself opening up. She hadn't shared her story with anyone in such a long time. She tried to weigh the risks in her mind, but she couldn't see any reason *not* to tell. What were the odds that she'd ever see this nice man again beyond this night, this boat? She figured a cruise was like a trip to Vegas—what happened on the boat stayed on the boat.

"Well," she began, as his finger boldly began to trace the knuckles of her left hand. "It just so happens that I have a daughter in college, too."

"You're kidding. What are the odds of that?"

"Probably pretty good," she admitted with a laugh. "Considering we're both, I think it's safe to assume, middle-aged." He smiled, and next thing she knew, the floodgates opened. She told him her entire life story—or at least as much as seemed pertinent. That she'd grown up in Charleston and never thought she'd return after college in New England, but then Lacey came along, and suddenly Lee was living back home with her own mom. How when her mom passed away, Lacey only six, Lee quickly had to learn how to be a single parent all over again. How much she adored Lacey but how lately they seemed only to fight, and how she wondered what the future held now that her daughter had flown the coop. Before long, Thomas was leading her by the hand back to his cabin.

"But what about your daughters?" Lee demanded. She had enough sense to know that it was a terrible idea to go back to a cabin with two daughters in the mix.

"They have their own cabin," he explained, coaxing her along. When they reached his door, he kept trying the key card backward.

"Here, allow me," she said, taking the key from him. He took it as an opportunity to kiss her. "Hmm," she said, pausing. "You're a good kisser. I'll give you that." She struggled to get the lock to unlatch, and finally the door swung open. Before she knew what was happening, Thomas was kissing her up against the wall, his lips pressing on hers.

"I want you to know," she started to say as he began to pull off her dress, but the words got lost in the muffle of fabric. "I want you to know," she tried again. "I'm not that kind of girl," she managed at last, her sundress falling to the floor around her ankles, "who usually does this."

"Oh, I know," Thomas murmured somewhere around her belly button. "I can tell." And with that, he lifted her onto the bed, and she was unzipping his fly.

Suddenly, her hands stopped his. She wasn't going to make the same mistake twice. "Do you, you know, have something?"

"Do I ever." He grinned, and Lee worried that he'd mistaken her veiled reference. But he fished in his jeans pocket to pull out the foiled protection, then placed it between his teeth and ripped it open. "Grrr," he said, and she laughed.

It wasn't long before Lee thought, *Well, then. This is what I've been missing. I almost forgot.*

Later, when she woke, the room was dark, and she had a momentary fright that she'd somehow stumbled into the wrong cabin. Then it all came flooding back. Lee rolled over to find Thomas on his back, sound asleep and snoring. Her head flared with pain. How much had she had to drink? Here she was telling Lacey to be responsible in college, and Lee herself had gone off on a drunken bender that would have put her college self to shame. She pushed up from the bed, bright streaks of light darting before her eyes, and stumbled into the bathroom. She flipped on the lights. When she glanced in the mirror, she hardly recognized herself. Eye makeup ran down her cheeks in black streaks, and the skin beneath her eyes puckered. Her hair stuck out at funny angles. She was a wreck.

She splashed cool water on her face, then used the toilet. Lee considered searching for paper to leave a note, but it was dark. And late. And her head hurt. She could go on with the excuses. It was better if she just left. And so, she gently slipped out of Thomas's room, allowing the door to click softly behind her. She carried her strappy sandals and her purse (her purse that held all her winnings!) as she made her way back to her cabin. Two girls, chattering about their night, passed by, and Lee momentarily wondered if they were Thomas's daughters.

When she reached her room two flights up, she tugged off her dress and crawled into the crisp sheets that room service had thoughtfully turned down. From the other bed came soft puffs of air from Lacey, sleeping like a purring cat. Lee rolled over onto her back and stared up at the ceiling. Without warning, a laugh escaped from her throat, and she slapped a hand across her mouth. Lacey stirred but didn't wake. *Oh my word,* thought Lee. *What on earth have I done?*

Maybe—she allowed herself to consider the possibility as she tumbled into sleep—just maybe, her luck had changed.

6

It was easy for Caroline to tell the serious cruisers from the first-timers. The veterans came armed with pink and yellow highlighters, ready to tag their favorite activities in the ship's daily bulletin. They stuck whiteboards to their cabins' magnetic doors so they could post their exact locations on the boat, hour by hour, for their families. They carried extra towel clips. At the cafeteria's juice dispensers, they gripped their personal water bottles, not wasting time with the tiny plastic cups that the ship provided for the same purpose. They were getting their money's worth.

Caroline tapped out notes on her digital notepad from her lounge chair, a traveler turned social anthropologist. Javier and Sam had gone off to hit golf balls on the top deck. It was wonderful and unexpected all at once, an anniversary cruise for her friend that was turning out to be fabulous article material as well. Already, she'd e-mailed her editor in chief a few highlights. *Did you know* . . . she began, followed by a laundry list of facts:

Roughly 20,000 eggs are consumed on board.

1,000 gallons of ice cream are packed for each cruise.

The ship sets sail with 7,000 *pounds* of potatoes.

That if a person falls overboard, the ship can detect his exact position with sonar.

On average, passengers guzzle 20,000 bottles of beer per sail.

She could not have imagined the conversations she'd overheard—or some of the things she'd seen—if she'd tried. Like the woman who promenaded around in a tiny bikini that revealed her C-section scar, a prominent white zigzag across her tanned stomach. Or the newlyweds who seemed to think that displays of affection on deck were entirely appropriate, even expected. Or the guy who sat by the pool with a bucket of beers and worked through them one by one. What was absolutely clear was that no one cared what anyone else might think. Beer bellies and wiggly thighs, saggy asses and lumpy arms, all were on full display. Lewd comments about the occasional voluptuous woman and idiotic conversations about the current state of American politics were thrown about with abandon.

On the one hand, it was refreshing to be in a place where people clearly didn't give a hoot what others thought of them. On the other, Caroline couldn't quite get over the lack of self-censorship. People seemed to say whatever came to mind, wore whatever they pleased. She wasn't sure if it said something about the types of folks that a cruise attracted or if it was a larger commentary on American society in general.

She watched while a big man with an enormous belly danced across the pool stage to "YMCA," throwing up his arms to form the letters. Who, she wondered, was happier? This man or a woman grabbing her skinny latte before rushing off to her Very Important Job in Manhattan? In an effort to be successful, Caroline wondered, had her fellow New Yorkers become tone-deaf to the siren call of good food and fun?

Caroline shut down her computer and gulped the last of her iced tea. Later today, around dinnertime, they'd be docking in Bermuda. Passengers weren't allowed to step off ship till tomorrow morning, but just to see the island would be exhilarating. Already, there was a list of places she wanted to explore: the Swizzle Stick Inn Pub. The popular beach at Horseshoe Bay. The quaint shops and churches of downtown Hamilton. Maybe the Crystal Caves on the other side of the island, where stalactites supposedly dangled from the ceiling like chandeliers.

She glanced up to see Lacey walking by and gave a little wave. Lacey's body was all sinew and muscle, which made Caroline sigh wistfully. A long time ago the measure of her hips had been nearly the same as that of her rib cage, but she'd had the misfortune of developing childbearing hips over the years without the benefit of having children. Fortunately, Javier appreciated her curves.

"So, what happened with that Thomas guy last night?" Caroline asked. Lee was stretched out reading a magazine in the chair beside her.

"Oh, you know. We had a drink. He's nice, semi-retired. Has two daughters in college."

"Then you two must have had plenty to talk about." Caroline flipped over onto her stomach and waited for Lee to continue.

"Mmm . . . hmm." But Lee couldn't get into it right now. Maybe later. The scent of alcohol still leaked from her pores, and if she moved too quickly, a sharp burst of pain galloped across her brain, despite the aspirin she'd taken this morning. If today was any indication, she was too old to party like that ever again.

"Tell me about Javier," she asked instead. "How are things?"

A small ladybug landed on Caroline's arm and she flicked it off with a finger. She shook her head. "I'm afraid I don't have much to report on that front. Trust me, you and Abby will be the first to know when and if there's any news. He has six days left to propose. Seven, if you count Saturday morning when we disembark. Not that anyone's counting."

"Ha!" Lee snickered. Leave it to Caroline to treat romance like a magazine assignment. Everyone had deadlines, even poor Javier. "You can't mean you're going to give him the boot if he actually fails to propose on the cruise?"

Caroline narrowed her eyes at Lee. "Watch me."

"Wow," said Lee, still trying to gauge if Caroline was being serious. "Doesn't that seem a little—I don't know—harsh for someone you love?"

Caroline shrugged. "Probably, but he's had three years. It's not like I'm rushing him into anything. If you know, you know." Lee stared at her. "What?" Caroline demanded.

"And I'm assuming you know. That Javier's the right guy for you?" Lee pressed.

Caroline made a *pftt* sound. "Of course. Don't be silly."

Lee squirmed in her chair. Did Caroline realize how ridiculous she sounded? "I'm sorry," Lee said, shaking her head. "It's just that you seem so sure everything will go according to plan, when this is *romance* we're talking about. You love Javier, but you're going to break up with him if he doesn't propose on the cruise? You know that's crazy, right?"

Caroline shrugged. "Well, it's not like I haven't hinted. He knows I'm expecting something on this trip. And besides, *someone* has to draw a line in the sand. I'm not getting any younger. I want a grown-up house. I want to enjoy the benefits that come with marriage—you know, like tax deductions, shared real estate, security.

All that stuff." She waved a hand in the air as if it were obvious.

"Wow. How very romantic of you," Lee teased. Lee hadn't always been Javier's biggest fan (he was a little too handsome, a bit too debonair for her tastes), but she was beginning to feel sorry for him as it dawned on her what Caroline's expectations were for this trip.

"And you're certain Javier knows that you want a ring?"

Caroline shrugged again. "He ought to. I mentioned something the other week about figuring out the 'next steps in our relationship' in Bermuda. I assume that's pretty much code for: *I'm waiting for a proposal*, right?"

Lee frowned. "Not necessarily. It could mean a lot of things." She was pretty certain that when a guy heard the words *next steps*, he either thought of a front porch stoop or tuned out entirely. But that was Caroline's way: once she set her mind to something, it had better happen— or there would be consequences. "Maybe he thinks you want to get a dog."

Caroline grunted. "If he's that dense, I'm not sure I want to marry him."

Lee considered the situation for a moment. Was Caroline setting herself up for disappointment? "What's wrong with enjoying what you have?" she asked now. "You guys are practically married anyway. You already live together in that gorgeous loft apartment."

Caroline rolled her eyes. It was no secret that, of all

the roommates, Lee was the most dubious about marriage. Yes, it had worked out nicely for Sam and Abby, but Lee could list on a single hand the number of friends who were happily married. Most of her girlfriends had separated, divorced, or stayed in their marriages for the sake of the kids. Caroline's sudden focus on tying the knot struck Lee as misguided, slightly troubling. Was Caroline worried that Javier wouldn't stick around otherwise? Should she or Abby give Javier a heads-up?

After having lived together for four years in a cramped dorm room, Abby and Lee knew Caroline probably better than anyone. They understood, for instance, that she needed to be handled with kid gloves when it came to personal matters. She could be defensive, protective, inscrutable. Once in college she'd dropped ten pounds in a week. Only after Lee inquired if she was feeling okay did Caroline confide that she'd broken up with her boyfriend. Despite her tough exterior, Caroline grew weepy at sad movies, always stopped to pet a dog, and never missed donating to the Salvation Army bucket during the holidays.

"Anyway, I'm going to talk to him," Caroline said now. "Make it clear that I think it's time we move things forward in a definite way. It just hasn't been the right time."

"What hasn't been the right time?" Abby asked, rejoining them, a plate of mozzarella sticks in her hand. She lowered herself into the chair beside Lee and set the plate on the table.

"Oh, nothing." Caroline laid her head on her hands, as if to say, *This conversation is over.*

Javier, Lee mouthed silently before dipping a stick in the marinara. She took a bite and moaned with pleasure. "Do you remember how many of these we used to eat at the grill?"

"Probably a million?" Abby guessed. "How on earth did we not graduate weighing three hundred pounds?" Abby thought back to when they'd befriended the guys who ran the downstairs café—a.k.a. the Grill—in their dorm. It was a friendship cemented in cheese and grease, in other words, the kind that lasted a lifetime.

"Speak for yourselves," Caroline said. "Some of us did not frequent the Grill every night. We were busy studying."

Lee rolled her eyes. "Oh, c'mon, Caroline. You're going to play the studious card again? You were just as bad as the rest of us."

"Not true!" She shot up in her chair and pushed her sunglasses onto her head. "Do I need to remind you that only one person in our rooming group graduated with honors?" Abby knew she was only half kidding. Caroline took great pride in this distinction.

"Yeah," Abby teased. "In sociology."

"That's a hard major!"

Lee and Abby started laughing. It was kind of fun that they could still raze Caroline about her major after all these years. In college, Abby had been jealous that, for

Caroline, school seemed to come so easily, when it was all Abby could do to keep her head above water. She'd even spent a semester on academic probation. But then Abby had discovered art, and something clicked. She would be an art history major, and that had been what saved her. That and Sam, of course. Her eyes skimmed the pool for the boys.

"Hey," Caroline asked, "has anyone else noticed that lady over there?" She gave a nod toward an older woman a few seats away who appeared to be sleeping with her sunglasses on, her mouth agape.

"Wow, very tan," Abby said.

"No, not that." Caroline lowered her voice. "I'm worried about her. I've been watching her for about half an hour and she hasn't moved. I think she might be dead."

Lee half laughed, half snorted.

"Stop it!" Abby swatted Caroline. "You're terrible."

"I'm serious. Do you think one of us should poke her? Maybe drop a book?"

As if the woman had overheard them, she suddenly let out a loud snore and shifted onto her side.

Abby dissolved into giggles. "Well, I guess that answers your question!"

Caroline shook her head. "One of these days, that's going to be us, ladies, so you'd better stop laughing."

"Never. No way. I will never allow my skin to turn that dark." Lee shuddered. "That cannot be healthy."

Abby spotted the boys off in a far corner of the pool.

They were trying to get a game of water polo going with Lacey, but they kept hitting strangers with the ball. Abby was about to call out that they might want to consider another game but then thought better of it. The boys were sixteen, for goodness' sake. They ought to be able to figure it out for themselves. Plus, if she intervened, someone might need her. And Abby did not want to be needed right now.

She settled back in her chair and closed her eyes. To her left, a woman with a thick Brooklyn accent was bossing her husband about where to set up her chair. Abby would recognize that accent anywhere—she and Sam had lived in Manhattan briefly, before the kids, and Abby had disliked nearly every minute. She was a person who needed wide vistas to look out on, long sweeps of land, preferably with a lake or an ocean nearby. Whenever she found herself in the city, she'd look up and experience a profound sense of vertigo, all those buildings stretching to the sky. In the summertime, the air conditioners from the apartments above would drip down on her arm as she walked by. That sensation—an unexpected *ping!* of condensation on her bare skin—and the smell of baking nuts mingling with hot, humid air were what she remembered most about New York summers.

Cruising was much more pleasant, indeed.

She rolled over onto her stomach. When she'd first suggested the cruise, it had taken some arm-twisting to get Sam on board. It was a vacation that sounded idyllic in theory but could easily go haywire. Eventually, however, she'd convinced him it was the perfect anniversary getaway. Sam was a traveler, a journey-goer. She was more of a nester, inclined to escape to a summer home, someplace quaint and swept by an ocean breeze. On a cruise, Sam would get his journey, while Abby could plant herself poolside. She didn't necessarily have to move; the ship would move *her* to their destination, and the boys would have nonstop entertainment.

She felt a hand brush across her shoulder and lifted her head to see Sam. "Hi there. I'm going in search of refreshments. Anyone want anything?" Abby shielded her eyes with her hand to better see in the sun's glare. She had to stifle a laugh because her husband was dressed in khaki shorts, a red and white Hawaiian shirt, dark glasses, and a Red Sox cap.

"No thanks, honey. You look like you're on the *America's Most Wanted* list, by the way."

"Really? That bad?" He held out his shirt and stared at it. "I thought I was channeling my inner vacationer. Your boyfriend, incidentally, is quite the golfer, Caroline."

"I'll bet you let him win," said Caroline. "Sam the Saint."

"Ah, we were just hitting balls." Ever since college, the roommates had tagged Sam with this moniker, largely because he seemed to always be rescuing people, popping up unexpectedly on campus. Need a few extra dollars? Ask Sam. No place to go for winter break? Sam will invite you home. When he'd first asked Abby out (sophomore year, the holiday dance, over a bowl of spiked punch), she'd assumed he was drunk (he was). But when he actually showed up at her door the next day for a date, she'd panicked. What if Sam Bingham was *too* good for her? No one wanted to date a guy who made you look bad.

And what would he think once he learned that she'd grown up on the Cape, a place where his family only "summered"? How could she sleep in the same bed with someone who was so self-assured, when she always scrubbed her face raw and plopped her mouth guard in before bedtime? Once Sam realized who the real Abby was, she was sure he'd call *Fore!* Fortunately, though, it turned out that her husband-to-be had a few quirks of his own: he slept with his socks on, was a book nerd, and had a snore that could wake a small village. Then, when Abby's parents died in quick succession, it was Sam who'd propped her up. He may have been born with a silver spoon, but his core was solid granite.

"Well, in that case, I shall return," he said, interrupting her thoughts. "You're sure you don't want anything?"

"Nothing," she said. "Everything's perfect."

⌒

By the time she woke from her nap, the sun had nudged its way to the west. Abby sat up and glanced around, trying to get her bearings. Sam must have wandered off in search of more lively conversation. Caroline's towel was gone. Abby dug her watch out of her bag and saw that it was two o'clock—only four hours till the ship docked in Bermuda. Next to her Lee and Lacey were chattering in their chaise lounges.

"Really, Mom," Lacey was saying. "You should care more about your environment. It's the world your grandchildren are going to grow up in after all."

"You'll be happy to know," Lee replied, "that I recycle so much that I had to buy one of those oversize recycling bins. It's as tall as a trash can."

"Whoa, you're really hitting it out of the park," said Lacey truculently.

Poor Lee, thought Abby. She was trying so hard, but Lacey wouldn't give her a break. Abby was tempted to point out that Lee had raised Lacey single-handedly (no small feat), not to mention she was teaching preschoolers how to write their names and responsibly share their Lego blocks. To Abby's mind, those things alone counted for plenty of good karmic payback. There was no need to wag an accusing finger. In fact, a big fat *thank-you* seemed in order.

She was about to say something to that effect when Lee spoke up. "If you're so intent on saving the world, honey, why don't you major in something like environmental studies or marine biology? Even the law. You could go work for the Nature Conservancy."

"Here we go again," Lacey said. "I was wondering how long it would take before the 'college' talk started."

She twisted in her seat to look at Abby. "Mom thinks I'm wasting my college education."

"I never said that, honey. I'd just like you to declare a major, settle on something you want to do with your life." Lee glanced at Abby for support. Abby stretched her neck from side to side, debating how best to get involved without seeming to take sides.

"Well, it can't hurt to start thinking about it, Lacey," she began. "Let's see. What did we want to do when we were sophomores in college, Lee? Do you remember?"

"I was going to be a lawyer."

"Oh great, so now it's my fault that you didn't go to law school?" Lacey demanded.

"No, that's not what I said. Why do you have to be so defensive? I love teaching."

"Remember how we were going to change the world?" Abby tried again. "We were so idealistic back then."

"See?" Lacey countered. "You guys didn't know what you were going to do either. Or if you did, it all changed anyway. My point exactly." She folded her arms across her chest, a tennis player who'd just won a volley.

"You know," Lee continued, "it was a different time back then. Everyone was talking about how all these doors were opening for women, and we felt a certain responsibility to take advantage of that. You know, stand on the shoulders of those who came before us. Sometimes I think you take it for granted that you have all the opportunities you do today."

Lacey stiffened. "Yeah, I get it." She stood up from her chair. "I've heard the lecture before. I'm grateful, okay?" She grabbed her towel and bag. "Anyway, thanks for the pep talk." She turned on her heel and strutted off, leaving the two of them to stare at each other.

"Was it something I said?" Lee asked, and Abby laughed.

"It's hard, but you should be proud, Lee. You've raised a smart girl who can think for herself."

"Thanks, but I'm not sure how much thinking she does. She usually just assumes that whatever position I take, she'll take the opposite."

"But that's her job. She's separating from you."

"Oh, is that what it's called? I thought it was more like torturing me."

Abby laughed. "Yeah, I know what you mean. I get that with the boys, too."

"When Lacey was little," Lee continued, "she was like this fragile flower that needed watering every day or else she would wilt. But now that she's grown up, I feel like she's turned into this prickly cactus. One that shoots darts at me without the slightest provocation." Lee groaned. "Whatever it is, I hope it ends soon. Do you think she intends to be a pain in the ass for the entire cruise or just part of it?"

Abby laughed sympathetically. "Oh, lovey," she said. "We can only pray it's the latter."

7

Lacey went in search of Chris and Ryan, far, far away from her mother. She got that her mom was worried, but seriously, she needed to lay off. Lacey would get a job—eventually. Maybe. But she was only a sophomore! And what consumed her thoughts most days was Tyler. She hated not being able to contact him while she was on the ship. Even when he was in New York and she was home in Charleston, they could text each other all the time—he might as well have been downstairs in her living room. But now, without any Wi-Fi connection for two straight days, Lacey was going slightly insane.

Ryan had told her that there were coffee shops in Bermuda where, if she paid for a latte, she could get free Internet service for an hour. It was the first thing she was going to do when they stepped onto land. Text Tyler that she missed him terribly.

She and Tyler already knew what kind of wedding they wanted—smallish with just their families and closest friends. Lacey was not the kind of girl who fantasized about her wedding day like some of her girlfriends. It made no sense to her to spend thousands of dollars on a dress and a party that would last for one day. And Tyler wasn't into that kind of stuff either. He got that marriage was about bigger things—like love and commitment and family.

They'd both agreed that two kids was the perfect number—one girl, one boy. The boy would have Tyler's deep dimples and dark, curly hair. The girl would have Lacey's brown eyes and, teased Tyler, her pouty lips. (After their first kiss, he'd told Lacey that she had Brigitte Bardot lips. That night, she'd gone back to her dorm room and googled "Bardot," failing to see any resemblance whatsoever. But if her boyfriend wanted to compare her lips to those of a blond bombshell, it was fine by Lacey.)

She was so tired of listening to her mom and friends talk about how hard they'd had to work to get to where they were in life, in their careers. It was the old "walked uphill to school and back," story, which, of course, was theoretically impossible. Lacey understood that the women's movement was important. She'd learned all about it in her women's studies course, thank you. But what her mom and Abby and Caroline didn't seem to realize was that things had *moved on*. They needed to get over the notion that Lacey should single-handedly carry the torch for all women. That she should become a U.N. ambassador or President of the United States. As far as Lacey was concerned, women were already equal. If Hillary Clinton could run for president, then what was left? Well, winning, she supposed.

Lacey was grateful for her privileges, but that didn't mean she had to dedicate the rest of her life to paying previous generations back. And, if she were being completely honest, sometimes it seemed like her mom's generation had gotten it all wrong. In their race to shatter glass ceilings, many of them had put their own families on hold. *Look at Caroline*, Lacey thought. She loved Caroline, but her aunt had dedicated her whole life to her career—and look where it had gotten her. She was still alone (well, technically, if she didn't count Javier).

When Abby had asked Lacey by the pool how she was getting along with her roommate, Lacey had said, "Great. She's really nice. From North Dakota," instead of telling the truth. Which was that Lacey hardly ever saw Grace. They had been amiable enough dining hall partners those first few weeks of school when no one knew anyone else. But Grace was on the freshman soccer team, which meant that she already had her own group of friends to hang with and that most weekends she spent on the road for games. Then Lacey had met Tyler, and a month later she'd more or less moved into his dorm room. (He'd been one of the fortunate few to get a freshman single.) So, no, Lacey didn't have the kind of roommate bond that her mom and her friends shared. It was a little disappointing, she supposed, but she didn't feel as if she was missing out on anything because, well, *Tyler*.

Lacey wanted a family so bad she could taste it. She wanted a husband and the house with the white picket fence and the two kids and a dog. She wanted neighborhood barbecues, the dads smoking cigars and the moms standing around, comparing notes on the best teachers and Crock-Pot recipes. She wanted a boy who would grow up to mow the lawn, play sports with his dad, and maybe have a soft spot in his heart for his mom. She longed for a daughter who might look a bit like her but would be sweet, not angry. Her daughter would have no reason to carry a chip on her shoulder because she'd have a dad and a mom who adored her and a brother, who, though he might poke fun at her, would defend her like a bulldog if anyone tried to pick on her.

That was what Lacey wanted, what she aspired to. Her dream. Her mom didn't get it. But did she want it all *now*? What if her dream of a family was about to begin? Before she even graduated from college? Before she and Tyler had a chance to get properly engaged and married? The thought of it both excited and terrified her. Her mom would kill her if she was pregnant.

Lacey told herself she was being silly. Girls were late all the time, and her period had been erratic before. But it was five days now, and that was pushing it, even for her. She tried not to think about it. Eventually, it would arrive, and then she'd laugh at how stupid she'd been, thinking she might actually be pregnant!

On the upper-deck basketball court, sprawled along the sidelines, she found the boys.

"Hey," she said, folding herself down next to Ryan.

"Hey," said Chris, not even turning around to glance her way. He was talking to a random girl with a tiny rose tattoo on her shoulder. She was gorgeous—and older than Chris by at least a few years.

"Hi," Ryan said, sounding relieved to have company. "Where've you been?"

"Getting lectured by my mom on the lido deck."

He made a whistling noise. "That's rough. You should have just come with us earlier."

"Yeah, live and learn." She paused and watched as one guy landed a dunk shot on the opposite court. There was something strange about having bright blue sky above and blue water on either side of them, as if they were watching basketball on a court suspended in midair.

Her mind looped back to when her friend Hannah first told her that Tyler Sharp thought she was hot, and Lacey had said, "Yeah, right." But then one night he'd stopped by the dorm when they were all watching football in the common room, and Tyler had plopped down on the armrest of the couch, right next to her. Lacey had played it cool, pretending to watch the game. "Hey," he'd said. "Hey, back," she'd replied.

After a few minutes, he'd asked, "So you like football?" Lacey didn't particularly enjoy the game (and if Tyler had pressed, he would have discovered she didn't even know what a two-point conversion was), but he was a running back on their team. So, she'd feigned interest. Plus, by that point, her heart was racing. "Yeah, sure," she'd said, watching the smile ride across his face. The next thing she knew, he was asking her if she wanted to take a walk. And the next, next thing, Tyler Sharp was kissing her just beyond the steps of her dorm, his lips sweet and tender against hers, his hands running through her hair.

Ryan flung down the book he'd been reading, *The Grapes of Wrath*. Patches of pool water dimpled the cover. "No good?"

He shrugged. "Not really. Summer reading."

"Ugh. I used to hate summer reading. As if you don't get enough homework during the school year."

"I know, right?" Ryan leaned back on his elbows. "I actually think reading the book is making me wrathful."

"Ha! Good one." Lacey grinned. She vaguely remembered slogging through the Depression-era novel during her senior year in high school. She recalled over four hundred pages of dust and wind and general misery.

"Hey, do you guys want to head to the grill?" Chris asked, extricating himself from the girl with the dark hair for a moment.

Lacey glanced at Ryan, who shrugged. "Sure," she answered for them both and jumped up to pull Ryan to his feet.

At the grill, the boys ordered burgers, and Lacey asked for a soda. Chris plopped into a lounge chair next to Tattoo Girl. Lacey rolled her eyes and followed Ryan to a table.

"What's with the girl?" she asked.

Ryan shrugged. "You know my brother. Wherever he goes, the women are sure to follow."

"Does she have a name?"

"Yeah, Trisha or Tina, maybe? Something like that. Maybe Tiara?"

Lacey snorted. Tiara somehow seemed fitting for the regal, entitled air about the girl. Not that Lacey was judging, but would it kill her to say hi? When the other kids from the basketball game joined them, Lacey scooted her chair over to make room. She had to admit, she was impressed: Chris and Ryan had formed their own little maritime clique in two short days.

Ryan bit into his cheeseburger, sending a spurt of grease down his chin, and swiped at it with the back of his hand. "So, I guess we'll be seeing Bermuda soon."

"Yeah, thank God," Lacey said. "Finally, we'll have Internet connection." She fiddled with her straw wrapper, tying it into little knots. "I mean, the cruise is fun and all, but I'll be glad to be on land for a few days." Ryan nodded, his gaze lingering a bit too long, as if she'd just said something profound. Lacey frowned, and Ryan dropped his eyes.

"Yeah, totally," he said, and his cheeks flared with color.

Only then did it dawn on her: Ryan (*little Ryan!*) had a crush on her. Lacey shook her head and laughed.

"What's so funny?" He lifted his head and met her gaze.

"Nothing." She shrugged. "You're just cute. That's all."

"Yeah, cute in a way like a little brother or cousin is cute, right?"

She smiled. "Exactly." But Ryan looked so crestfallen that she immediately regretted having said anything at all. When she thought back on the past two days, however, it made perfect sense. The way he'd helped her with her chair last night, the few times in the pool when she'd caught him checking out her boobs. It was both cute and creepy.

"Hey, Ry—" She reached out to rumple his hair, but he pulled away.

"It's okay. I get it," he said.

"No, look. I'm sorry. I didn't really catch on till just now, but I have a boyfriend. You know that, right?" *A boyfriend and possibly much bigger problems than you can imagine,* she might have added.

"Yeah." A puff escaped from his lips as if to say, *Tell me something I don't know.*

"What about you? You must have a girlfriend."

Ryan shook his head. "Nah, me and girls, we don't really mix, you know?"

Lacey wasn't sure she did. "What do you mean? Like you're gay?"

His mouth fell open. "No, nothing like that, just . . ."

He seemed to stop and think. "All the girls at my school are boring. They never have anything to talk about."

"That's probably because they're secretly hoping you'll ask them out."

"Yeah, right, that's probably it." He stood up to throw out his tray, then remembered his book, which he grabbed off the table. "Well, see ya around."

"Hey, Ryan, don't worry," she called after him. "We girls get more interesting!"

When Tiara twisted around in her seat to give Lacey a strange look, Lacey grinned, as if to say, *Isn't it the truth?*

But rather than offer a nod in sisterhood, Tattoo Girl spun back around and proceeded to run her tongue around the outer edge of Chris's ear.

Yuck. Lacey got up, in search of better scenery.

⌒

Later, on the starboard side of the ship, the slip of Bermuda came into view, blurry and far away, the first visible landmass in the last forty-eight hours. Lacey had wandered off to be by herself. Everyone was rubbing her the wrong way and vice versa—she was better off alone. She watched while the island drew closer, its bends and curves calling to mind Nantucket's boomerang silhouette. Nantucket was home to the handful of Lacey's best summer memories—lazy days spent building sand castles, digging for clams, late-night runs to the Juice Bar for ice cream. Maybe Bermuda would be her next.

As the ship rounded a rocky, craggy bend, she drew in a sharp breath. There, right before her, was the most stunning stretch of beach she'd ever laid eyes on. Bright turquoise water lapped up against wide, lambent stretches of pink sand. Dotting the lush green canopy of palm trees were dozens of white rooftops. They reminded Lacey of white butterflies flitting across a summer lawn. A breeze swept over her, a combination of salt and something sweet, like honeysuckle. *A Bermuda breeze*, she thought.

Lacey smiled, her face to the wind. For once her mom was right. Bermuda was as pretty as a postcard.

8

On Monday, their first day on the island, the morning dawned with a glorious pink sky. By nine thirty, the temperature had already climbed to eighty degrees, and the air, stitched through with humidity, shimmered in little waves. Abby was eager to get to the beach, where she could calm down and cool off in the water, then plant herself under an umbrella. She imagined herself flipping her wet hair over her shoulder just like Ingrid Bergman must have done on the beaches of Morocco.

Abby was fighting to maintain her composure as she wove in and out of the crush of passengers, all of whom appeared to be disembarking for the beach at the exact same moment as her family. Really, who could blame her? Only three days into the cruise and Chris had lost his room key twice. *Twice!* She'd just spent the better part of her morning in the ship's customer service line. A line in which a person could easily lose a year of her life just waiting to speak to the person in charge.

Sometimes Abby felt as if she was still raising toddlers. Sixteen-year-old toddlers, but toddlers nonetheless. Would the boys ever learn to keep track of their own things? *Well,* she thought as she spied Lee and Lacey off to one corner, *they'd better.* They had no choice. Soon enough, Abby might not be around to fix every little problem for them. She waved to Caroline and Javier, who were coming down the stairs.

"Sorry to keep you waiting," said Caroline, slightly out of breath. Her face was partially hidden by a white sun hat, the brim so wide it brushed Javier's shoulder. Javier carried a bag of snorkeling gear.

"That," said Lee, "is a fabulous hat. Kentucky Derby–worthy, for sure." Lee was referring to the Derby parties that their rooming group had hosted in college with Lee coaching them on southernisms like *madder than a wet hen.* It was Lee who'd taught Abby how to muddle her first mint julep, though to this day she still couldn't abide the bitter taste of bourbon.

In fact, Abby saw now that it wasn't just Caroline's hat that was fabulous. The rest of her was a stunning montage of whites as well—a white spandex top accompanied by a wraparound maillot skirt and wedge sandals. Even her toenails were painted white. Caroline appeared to be heading to the French Riviera, not to the beach with her best girlfriends and a couple of teenagers. Abby felt like asking if she had a Frisbee tucked somewhere in her Louis Vuitton bag (also white).

Instead, she said chirpily, "Is everyone ready for the beach?"

"Yes, please," pleaded the boys, who were shifting from foot to foot. Chris knew better than to complain by this point, but even Ryan had acted out of sorts at breakfast this morning, glowering into his stack of pancakes. Abby wondered if Lacey were involved. Ryan had been following her around like a puppy dog, and Lacey had been nothing if not accommodating, throwing him a treat every now and then. But it was no secret that Lacey had a serious boyfriend in college. (Abby knew that Lee was concerned and hoped the distance of summer would slow the relationship down.) The fact that Lacey already had a boyfriend, however, seemed to be doing little to curb Ryan's infatuation.

Abby fell into line behind Sam to get her passport checked and stamped. When their party sailed through customs without a ding, she was pleasantly surprised. Maybe, after a rough start to the day, things would proceed calmly after all. On land, everyone regrouped and followed a winding sidewalk that led to a clutch of taxicabs painted in bright island colors. Sam went to talk to one of the drivers, and Abby fanned herself with her hat.

"Feeling okay, Mom?" Chris asked while cabdrivers called out to them, promising the cheapest fares.

She nodded. "It's just the heat. I'll be better once we get to the water." It was a ridiculous thing to say, of course. Why else did people travel to Bermuda but to enjoy the warm weather and beautiful beaches? She just wished Sam would get on with it and pick a driver so they could be on their way. Abby didn't have the patience to haggle with the cabbies. How ironic that they'd just spent thousands of dollars on a cruise and now her husband was insisting on shaving a few dollars off their cab fare.

As if reading her mind, Sam waved them over to a minivan.

"This guy is giving us a great deal," he said, beaming. "He'll take us to Horseshoe Bay and give us a history of the island on the way." Abby didn't know if the rest of their gang wanted a lecture on island lore, but Caroline spoke up immediately.

"Great! Maybe I'll get some material for my article."

"Nice work, man." Javier socked Sam in the arm and climbed in, while the kids crawled around to the seats in the far back. Sam sat up front with the driver—probably all the better to grill him with questions—and Abby squeezed into the back with Lee and Caroline, who were busy digging in the cracks for seat belts. There didn't appear to be any, however.

Caroline shrugged. "Island time, island rules, I guess?"

"Let's hope the island gods are watching over us," Abby muttered. A friend had warned her about Bermuda's curvy roads, thin as a sliver, so she was happy to see the main road unfold smoothly enough above Somerset

Harbor, where dozens of sailboats bobbed like candied apples in the sun. But gradually, as the twists began to grow sharper and the hills steeper, Abby had to grip the armrest to keep from crushing Lee. Middle Road was *maybe* as wide as her kitchen table back home. If she stretched her arm out the window, she was pretty sure she could touch the stone wall that acted as a guardrail. It seemed a miracle that one car—let alone two—could fit, and every time a truck or taxi approached in the opposite lane, she held her breath as they squeaked by.

Thank heaven Sam hadn't insisted on renting mopeds (a suggestion he'd tried to sell them on at dinner last night) or they'd all be roadkill by now. Not to mention the whole driving-on-the-left-side-of-the-road rule—and the rotaries! It was absolutely impossible to get her head around entering them in the reverse. Abby tried to pretend it was like driving in London, but without the benefit of racing around in those cute Mini Coopers.

When they hit a particularly sharp turn, her bag dropped to the floor with a thud.

"Honestly, Abby, what's in there?" Lee demanded. "A small child?"

Abby shrugged. "Stuff?" Lee and Caroline burst out laughing, and Sam glanced back, as if to say, *What's so funny?* But Abby couldn't have explained, even if she'd wanted to. Certain things were funny only to the three of them, references that added up only if you'd been a

119

roommate in Wordsworth Hall, room 404. Like the time during freshman year when she, Caroline, and Lee had gone to a homecoming football game. The air was chilly in the way a crisp fall afternoon should be, and Lee had stuffed herself into a huge red down parka. Abby and Caroline had poked fun, calling her a soft southerner. When they'd asked what she had in her parka, Lee had grinned and replied, "Stuff?"

Not until they settled into their stadium seats did Lee reveal why she was wearing such an enormous jacket. On the inside were generous pockets in which she'd smuggled six beers. They'd applauded Lee's ingenuity that day. Ever since then, it had become a refrain for whenever one of them asked a question that the others didn't feel like answering. "What were you doing out so late?" Abby might ask, and Caroline and Lee would both shrug and reply, "Stuff?"

Abby was smiling at the memory, when Lee accidentally collided with her leg (another quick turn), and Abby exclaimed, "Ouch!" Without thinking, she pulled up her skirt to have a look.

"I'm so sorry!" Lee squinted at the purple bruise, roughly the size and color of a plum, which now smudged Abby's thigh. "Wow, did I just do that?"

"No, of course not," said Abby. "I've had it for a few days. Must have rammed into a table." She tugged her skirt back down. To be honest, though, she couldn't recall what her body had collided with.

Lee shook her head. "You need to be more careful, missy."

Abby nodded. "Yes." She stared out the window as juniper trees, frothy with green leaves, zipped by. Pink hibiscus flowers poked their heads out from the roadside. The entire island bloomed with a lushness that complemented its stucco homes, all painted in delightful pastels—pink, yellow, and blue. The houses reminded Abby of colorful macarons, and the white stucco churches, which seemingly popped up every mile, of wedding cakes. Abby chuckled to herself. Apparently, piety got you paradise.

"Why are all the roofs white?" Sam was asking now as the car accelerated up another hill. Abby grabbed the seat in front of her. "To reflect the sun?"

"Good guess," their driver replied. His voice was threaded through with lovely Bermudian and British accents. "But it's actually because of the material they're made of—limestone that's whitewashed. It helps to catch the rainwater from the roof. Our roofs are made of gutters, you see?"

Abby leaned toward her window for a better view and saw that it was true: small gutters lined each roof in horizontal grooves. "That is how we collect our water in Bermuda. Almost half of our drinking water is from rainwater."

"Amazing." Caroline scribbled in her notebook.

They careened along for another fifteen minutes, up

and around bluffs with magnificent water views, before the car finally pulled over to a dirt road leading off the main highway. "Here you are, my friends," their driver announced. "Just follow the path down to the beach."

"Whoa, think I need to catch my breath after that roller-coaster ride," Lee said as she climbed out, looking slightly pale, while Sam paid. "Next time remind me to pop a Dramamine for just the cab ride."

Abby agreed; the ride had been unexpectedly hair-raising. Her stomach felt queasy, too, but nothing that a little ocean air wouldn't remedy. She fell into line behind the kids, who led the way down the long, winding path. When they reached the beach, Abby propped her sunglasses on top of her hat.

"Oh, wow." Her breath caught in her throat. "That's what I call stunning." Out on the horizon, a cobalt sea gave way to a pale blue sky. Closer to shore, the water turned a turquoise so clear that she could make out a submerged boulder with bright yellow fish darting around its edges. Abby walked over to where the waves eddied along the sand and pulled off her flip-flops, stuck in her toes. The water was indeed warm (the whiteboard that welcomed them said eighty degrees). Here, where the surf kicked up the sand, the water turned a rich café au lait color. It looked, frankly, good enough to ladle up and drink.

"I'll be darned," said Sam. "The sand really is pink." He reached down to cup a handful, and Abby did the same. She'd read that because of the strong waves in Bermuda, millions of seashells were pulverized into bits, and it was the pearlescent insides of the shells that lent the sand its color. She rubbed a few grains between her thumb and forefinger and couldn't recall ever touching sand so soft. If her eyes were closed, she would have sworn she was cupping flour.

"Hey, check it out! The sand isn't even hot!" shouted Chris, who'd wandered further down the beach. It was true, Abby noted with surprise. A person could walk barefoot on the sand, which didn't appear to absorb the sun's heat. Abby meandered a few yards up from the water and shook out her towel over a smooth stretch of beach, making sure not to intrude on anyone else's space. (It was a personal pet peeve whenever perfect strangers plopped their towels down right next to hers, as if there wasn't an entire beach to enjoy!)

She sat and waited while Sam and the others rented umbrellas and chairs from a nearby stand. Sam turned her way and waved. *Paradise,* she mouthed, her arms stretched out behind her. It was the first word that sprang to mind. He nodded and shot her a thumbs-up. Abby was surprised by how easily her mood had lifted. Here she'd been ready to strangle Chris a few short hours ago. And now, well, it was hard not to be grateful for every little thing.

Caroline liked to think of herself as adventurous, except when it came to water pursuits. In sixth grade, she'd failed the gym swim test, and, ever since, she'd had a tenuous relationship with the water. She managed to get along, by either sidestroking or using some combination of the front crawl and breaststroke, but no one would ever mistake her for a strong swimmer. She'd only barely passed the swim test in college. Yet somehow Javier had managed to twist her arm to go snorkeling with him today. All in the name of research for her article.

"Snorkeling isn't swimming," he'd assured her. "You just kick with your flippers. Besides, we're not going out deep. Just breathe normally with your air tube."

So now, in a small cove off the beach, Caroline swam along next to her boyfriend, the only sound in her ears that of her own breathing. In her right hand, she clutched a small underwater camera. Yesterday Javier had been so excited about going snorkeling that she'd begun to wonder if he had something up his sleeve—maybe a diamond ring hiding in the coral reef? But now, gliding along the cove, she realized how ridiculous that was.

The entire sensation of snorkeling, she thought as she swam along, was an odd one. After a few tries, she'd mastered the mouthpiece, but her breathing sounded like Darth Vader's. And now she realized that her mask cut off her peripheral vision so completely that she had no idea who—or what—might be swimming beside her.

When her elbow brushed up against something, her mind instantly darted to *Shark!* But when she turned, she saw that it was only Javier. She waved her arms, trying to explain to him about the imaginary predator, but realized too late that talking broke the seal around her mouthpiece. Water came rushing in, sending her sputtering and choking, till she lifted her head out of the water and spat out the mouthpiece, gasping for air.

"Your feet!" Javier, whose head popped up, called out. When Caroline lowered her legs, she was surprised to find that it was shallow enough to stand. She shoved her mask up and spat a few more times, her mouth salty and tangy-tasting.

"You scared me," she said between breaths. "I thought you were a shark. Or a ray."

Javier grinned, his mouthpiece dangling beside his chin. "No worries! I told you, no sharks here. We're entirely safe in the cove." Caroline nodded, unconvinced. She struggled to catch her breath. "Ready for another run?" he asked.

When she hesitated, he said, "Here, follow me this time."

She took a couple of deep breaths, stuck her mouthpiece back in, and dove under, this time reaching for Javier's hand. They swam further out to the reef's edge, where plumes of purple fan coral waved in the current. Bright yellow coral globes, like miniature suns, clung to the rocks. Javier was right—the underwater fauna was its own exquisite world, and Caroline soon forgot to be afraid. A long green fish, the size of a thick steak, gently glided past, and she snapped a picture.

They drifted along, Javier pointing to a shimmery blue fish ahead and then a cluster of orange fish with vibrant spots. A few yards further up, a silvery school darted in and out of the coral in what Caroline imagined was an elaborate game of hide-and-seek. She snapped photo after photo. These would be great for the article; her boss would be pleased. But when a wisp of darkness shot in front of her mask, she startled, pulling back abruptly. Was it a jellyfish? She waited for the searing pain she'd read about to bubble across her forehead, but there was nothing. When another wisp darted before her, she realized her mistake: the jellyfish "tendrils" she'd seen were, in fact, strands of her own hair drifting in front of her. She would have laughed, if her heart weren't pounding.

Enough was enough. Who was she kidding? Caroline was a landlubber, unsuited to exploring the mysteries of the sea—except for maybe from the comfort of her own living room, where she could watch Jacques Cousteau documentaries. She had plenty of photos for her article. There was little point of prolonging the dive—or her discomfort. She motioned to Javier and pointed back to shore. He shot her a thumbs-up before holding up ten fingers to indicate he wouldn't be much longer. She waved before kicking off.

They liked to joke that the Kahlil Gibran saying about maintaining "spaces in your togetherness" was the key to any good relationship. But Caroline believed in it, just like she believed in the restorative power of summer vacation or the medicinal punch of a red sauce for a cold. She and Javier enjoyed many of the same things, but it was also fine—and necessary—that they had their own interests. Snorkeling, Caroline decided as she flippered back to shore, was one hobby that Javier could keep for himself.

9

~

Abby dug her toes into the soft pink sand and wondered if she'd ever grow tired of Bermuda. It was hard to imagine. The abundant sunshine, the slower idle of island time, and that marvelous turquoise water. She tried to envision herself as a lady of leisure, drifting in and out of her days, no schedule to hew to, no children to take to and from sporting events or orthodontist appointments. It sounded tempting. But, as with all good things, there would inevitably be something to complain about—maybe the unrelenting heat or how there was seldom a rainy day. The chance of a rogue hurricane sweeping through.

She dug out the novel she'd brought along, one of her all-time favorites, George Eliot's *Middlemarch*. It was, admittedly, a bit of an odd choice for vacation, but Abby was revisiting the classics this summer. Already, she'd polished off *The Great Gatsby* and *To Kill a Mockingbird*. Next up was George Orwell's *Animal Farm*.

She opened the book and began to read: *Miss Brooke had that kind of beauty which seems to be thrown into relief by poor dress.* What a wonderful opening line! Abby kept reading, perfectly content to be alone while Sam body-surfed with the boys. Every so often, they would race out to pat the salt water from their eyes, and Abby would offer a small wave of acknowledgment. It seemed to be all that was demanded of her at the moment. *Heaven.*

She continued reading, but found herself growing impatient with the book's main character. Even after all these years, Dorothea Brooke was making the same dumb mistakes when it came to men. Intellectually, Abby understood that this was the same novel she'd read in college, and so nothing, really, could change. Intuitively, though, she thought of Dorothea as a friend (as she did all her favorite characters), and so there was a part of her that had expected Dorothea to learn from her past mistakes, just as any smart woman would. That Dorothea was falling for the stuffy Casaubon all over again was disheartening. Abby wished she could reach through the pages and centuries and shake some sense into her.

Just as she was about to set the book aside, a shadow fell across her page. She glanced up to find Caroline, standing in front of her and shaking her hair out. She dropped her snorkeling gear in a heap on the sand.

"Well, hello there. How was it? Have fun?" Abby marked her place in the book and tucked it back in her bag.

Caroline gave her hair a final wring, sending a small ripple of water down onto the sand. "Well, I survived."

She grinned. "We actually saw some beautiful fish. Javier's still out there. Where's the rest of the gang?"

Abby's eyes skimmed the water. "Let's see . . . Lee and Lacey went in search of snacks. Sam and the boys are those three little heads bobbing in the waves over there." She pointed, and Caroline squinted in the same direction. "They're bodysurfing."

"If you say so," Caroline said with a laugh. "They look like gulls or maybe buoys to me."

Abby patted the towel next to her. "Here, come sit with me. Keep me company." Caroline collapsed beside her. Abby waited a moment before diving in. "So? How are things with you and Javier? Good?"

"Ha!" Caroline held one arm out in front of her and stretched it across her chest, as if snorkeling had given her a cramp. "I knew it was a trick. Invite me to keep you company and then grill me about Javier."

"Got me," Abby conceded. "But that doesn't change anything. I still want to know how things are between you two."

Caroline pulled her knees up to her chest and rested her chin on her hands. "Honestly? It changes from day to day, hour to hour, even. We're having fun. The cruise has been so nice—it's good to hang out with you guys and get away from work. We're relaxing, you know? Beyond that? I'm not really sure."

Abby leaned back on her elbows. "What are you going to do? Any more thoughts about the 'getting married' part?" Caroline had confided to her before the trip that if Javier didn't propose over vacation, she was going to suggest they take a break. It struck Abby as an odd time to suddenly declare an ultimatum, but then again, she understood her friend's impatience. Three years seemed ample time for Javier to know if Caroline was the One. What was he waiting for? Apparently, Caroline had dropped a few hints before the cruise.

"Not really," Caroline said after a moment. A huge wave crashed onto the shore, and Caroline watched the surf tumble back out to sea, leaving behind long, winding twists in the sand. She'd been so sure that this would be the trip where she and Javier would lay the groundwork for their lives ahead together. But Javier had yet to make any reference to tying the knot, and Caroline was beginning to resent the fact that she might have to be the one to suggest it. Ironically, she'd written an article for *Glossy* about how, if a man was dragging his feet, a woman should feel free to propose to him. But Caroline realized now that it was different in practice. She didn't *want* to be the one to initiate a proposal. A part of her was still old-fashioned; she was waiting for Javier to ask.

She thought back to when she and Javier had first met. At an art show in Manhattan. His company had been supplying the wine, and a writer friend of Caroline's whose husband owned the gallery had invited her. The paintings had been truly awful, abstract splashes of paint that Caroline could never make sense of, except

132

these had seemed unusually forbidding. Huge canvases of gloomy blacks and moody grays, as if the artist had been working through an argument in his studio.

Caroline stood in front of a painting, her head cocked in mock contemplation, when Javier came up beside her. He leaned in, fished his glasses out of his coat pocket, and read: "*Mother with Child.*" For a moment he was quiet before stepping back and saying, "I don't see it, do you?" Caroline stifled a laugh and shook her head. It was exactly what she'd been thinking, searching for any suggestion of a mother *or* a child in the bold splashes of paint.

"Not really. But I never was good at art."

"But no one is good at art, per se, right?" he challenged. "It's all about the *effect* of a painting on the viewer. If it doesn't resonate with you, then the painting is not a success."

She'd never really thought of it that way before, that it was up to the painting to evoke a meaningful response and not the other way around.

"In any case, do you think it's supposed to be a picture of a woman *with* child or of a mother and her child?"

Caroline peered more closely. "I hadn't thought of that, I mean, that the woman might be pregnant." She'd been searching for a small child, holding her mother's hand.

Slowly, she let her gaze wander over to the talkative stranger and was surprised to see that he was handsome, with thick wavy hair, olive skin, and some of the bright-est blue eyes she'd ever seen. Men hit on Caroline often, largely because that was what men in New York did—it was part of the urban caveman culture, as if securing a woman's interest branded a capital *M* for *Masculine* on their chests. Caroline understood that she was pretty enough, but certainly not stunning in the way that so many Manhattan women were—tall, blond, waifish. She allowed herself to be starstruck for a moment until another thought hit her.

"Uh-oh," she said, panicking suddenly. "You're not going to tell me you're the artist, are you?"

His eyes crinkled. "Not a chance. It's not my thing. Wine, however, that I could probably tell you a thing or two about." And he lifted his glass, as if to bid farewell, and walked away.

Later in the evening, after she had enjoyed a few more glasses of wine, he found her again, sitting on a window bench with a view of Central Park and wonder-ing how much longer before she could leave without appearing rude. He sat down next to her. "The paint-ings? So-so. But the wine?" His eyebrows danced above his bright blue eyes. "Delicious, right?" It made her laugh. Even back then, he'd been charming. He con-fided that his company was furnishing the wine for the gallery show that night.

"Really?" she asked, suddenly emboldened. "In that case, you'll have to teach me about a proper vintage."

"How long do you have?" he teased.

"As long as it takes."

A few weeks later, they were officially a couple.

She turned to Abby now and sighed. "I was so sure that he was going to propose on the cruise, and if he didn't, I was going to bring it up."

"But he still can! It's only Monday," said Abby. "Have you? Brought it up, I mean?"

Caroline's shoulders lifted in a shrug. "Not really. What's that saying, again? You can't hurry love?" She traced lazy circles in the sand with her finger. "I just keep hoping that he'll do it without prompting. I mean, if he can't get his act together now, when will he? Lee thinks I'm being unreasonable. That I can't expect him to read my mind. But, honestly, if the man hasn't figured out I want to marry him by now, then maybe *he* doesn't want to get married. At least that's my worry for today." She laughed. "I'm sure by tomorrow I'll have a different one."

Abby didn't know what to say. It did concern her that Javier hadn't asked her what kind of engagement ring Caroline might like. But then again, Caroline was the kind of person who'd probably already drawn him a diagram of the exact ring she wanted. It was possible that Javier was one of those guys who wanted to spend his life with Caroline but was averse to getting married. Abby knew a handful of men like that.

She sighed. "I'm sure you guys will figure it out," she said finally. "There's still plenty of time left in our vacation. And, hey, if he doesn't propose this week, maybe he will when you're back in New York."

"So you're saying I should give him an extension if he doesn't propose on the cruise?" Caroline secretly wondered if she'd be brave enough to end things if Javier didn't meet her deadline.

Abby thought back to the loving way that Javier had placed his hand on the small of Caroline's back at dinner the other night, or the way Caroline lit up whenever he walked into a room. Javier had done countless sweet things for her friend, like filling their apartment with tulips, her favorite flower, on her birthday last year. "I think it's worth considering," Abby said finally. "I also think you might want to talk to him sooner than later. Just in case he doesn't know that you're, you know, expecting a proposal."

Caroline was quiet for a moment. "It's funny," she said. "When I was talking with Lee about it earlier, I was so sure of myself. Javier better propose or else . . . But now talking with you, I don't know. Maybe I'm missing the whole point of this companionship thing." She dug her toes into the sand. "I guess I sound pretty pathetic for a modern woman, huh? Why should I care so much about getting married?"

Abby arched an eyebrow. She so wanted Caroline to be happy. The question was, What exactly would make her happy? "Maybe because you love Javier so much," she said now.

There was an awkward lull in the conversation, and Caroline swiped at her eyes. "Yeah, well, hey," she said, changing the subject. "Two more days and we'll be back here for your vows ceremony. Do you need help with anything?"

Abby exhaled, happy to table the Javier discussion for later. "Thanks, but we should be all set. Nothing fancy, just a little ceremony on the beach at noon. That should give us plenty of time to enjoy lunch and still make it back to the ship before the sail away at five."

Caroline flipped over on her stomach and gazed out on the ocean. "You've found the perfect spot for it, Abby. Truly. The ceremony will be beautiful."

But as she sat there, conjuring up a picture of her best friend and Sam on the beach, Caroline's vision kept getting interrupted. She couldn't help it—it was an image of herself in a flowing white gown, her hair done up with tiny island flowers. And Javier, tall and tanned in a pale linen suit, standing across from her.

10

When they returned to their cabin, the room had been miraculously transformed. Dirty towels had been whisked away, the beds turned down with mints on the pillows, and the lights dimmed to evening setting. The air smelled faintly of cleanser with a hint of lavender. Abby threw herself on the bed, a princess who needn't lift a finger.

It felt good to be spoiled for a change. It used to drive her nuts when the boys were little and Sam would walk by their discarded toys or shoes in the living room, as if they were invisible. As if she was the only person in the house whose eyes could focus below waist level. In the scheme of things it seemed trivial now, laughable even. But it had stuck with her all these years. If only life could grant her a kind of quid pro quo—the number of times she'd bent down to retrieve a toy truck or an abandoned sneaker from the floor rewarded by an equal number of years to live. Surely, it would stretch into the hundreds, if not the thousands.

Sam had stepped into the bathroom, and she could hear the tepid spray working in the small shower stall. Abby stretched out on the bed, exhausted. Every pore in her body ached. The sand in her swimsuit itched. Her doctor back in Boston had cautioned her not to overdo it, but she hadn't given a second thought to a slow, relaxing day under an umbrella at the beach. Fortunately, all that was demanded of her for the remainder of the day was a shower and a quick trivia challenge before dinner.

She rolled over and flipped on the television with the remote. The kids had already complained about the paltry choice of stations, and Abby saw now that it was true. There was Fox News, a few other stations, and a movie channel that appeared to be stuck in the eighties. At the moment, *Footloose* was playing. She unwrapped a mint and popped it in her mouth while Kevin Bacon strutted across the floor of a high school gym. He was cute in a way that guys in high school who were cool but not necessarily handsome were cute. *My boys still have so much to look forward to!* The thought ran scattershot across Abby's mind, making her heart contract into a tight little fist. Would she get to see it all?

So much had already rushed by! From those first days of kindergarten, when Ryan had stood outside the front door and cried until the principal took him by the hand and led him to class (Abby still had a special place in her heart for that kind woman, Mrs. Henderson), all the way to fifth-grade graduation. Abby's mind swam with the myriad rites of passage in between: the struggles over recorder practice and multiplication tables in third grade. The state capitals in fourth. Robotics in fifth. Though she'd hardly noticed each individual passage at the time—she'd been too busy living it.

Her breath caught, her thoughts spiraling down the rabbit hole that she desperately tried to avoid these days. The boys were sixteen now! Who would make sure the twins' boutonnieres matched the colors of their dates' dresses? Who would help them plan a "promposal," those ridiculous public displays of affection that boys were now responsible for? Who would their dates be? Chris wouldn't have a problem—he had a different girlfriend every few months. But Ryan? Ryan struggled to be himself around girls. What if he couldn't find anyone? What if no one said yes?

She climbed off the bed and went to the dresser, searching for the cream leather journal that she'd tucked beneath her T-shirts. She'd yet to open it this vacation, but her intention had been to write things— important things—down as they came to her. Stuff that the boys might need to know. Just in case. She fiddled around the desk for a pencil and landed on a pen in the top drawer. She flopped back down on the bed, flipped open the book, and began to write. *If you go to prom (and know that it's OK if you don't!), please remember these few things . . .*

In some ways, she felt as if they'd already left her and

she'd taught them all she could. But on other days, in her weaker moments, she worried that she still had so much knowledge to pass along. Would there be enough time? They'd graduate in two more years, and then they were off to college. Did they know right from wrong? Had she taught them to value kindness over all else? To help those whom they could and encourage those whom they couldn't? Did they know what love was and what it was to be loved?

Yes, those things she thought they carried with them, whether or not she was there to remind them. But what about the other stuff? The ups and downs of jobs, of life, the disappointments and joys of marriage, the unspeakable love that came from being a parent. How could she list all that here? She sighed. Those were life lessons, she supposed. Things they would have to learn for themselves, over time. She prayed she'd given them the courage to get through them with grace.

She was still writing when she heard the shower click off and then back on, as if on second thought. Abby waited and cocked her head toward the door. The bathroom door opened a sliver. "Honey?" Sam called out. Little tendrils of steam spiraled toward the ceiling. "Did you want to get cleaned up?"

Abby checked the clock: only twenty minutes till they were due in the lounge for trivia. "Oh, yeah. I'd better," she said. "Just a sec." She jumped up and tucked her journal back into the dresser drawer.

Only when she stepped into the bathroom did she see her husband, still standing in the shower, naked and dripping wet, his hands lathered up with soap. For her.

"I can assure you," Sam said with a smirk, "that my intentions are pure." And for the first time in what Abby had come to think of as the Long Break, they found their way back to each other, one sudsy wash at a time.

⌒

Javier and Caroline were supposed to meet everyone for trivia at Hawthorne's Pub at 6:30. Caroline checked her foldout map of the boat. The pub was located on level six, and she punched in the number on the elevator keypad, watching the floors zip by.

"I didn't know Hawthorne had a pub," she said absently. She was standing on her tiptoes, shoulder to shoulder with Javier, trying not to collide with the woman next to her. "Shouldn't it at least be named after someone who had a *reputation* for drinking?" Caroline pressed.

Javier shrugged. "Isn't every writer a drinker?"

"You have a point. Still, Hemingway's Pub, maybe? Or, Tolstoy's Tavern? I don't know, somehow those strike me as more right."

Javier laughed. "More right? I don't think you're helping your case for literature. Maybe you mean *better*?"

Caroline rolled her eyes. "Yes, I guess that would be *better*." When they arrived at the lounge, the others were already waiting. Lacey and the boys were huddled in conversation at a table in the corner, while Lee, Abby, and Sam sat at an adjacent table. The bar was packed. Javier and Caroline found two extra stools and scooted them over to the adults.

Their master of ceremonies, a pretty young woman who introduced herself as Athena from South Africa, welcomed everyone and proceeded to outline the rules of the game. Since no more than four players were allowed on a team, Javier amiably slid his chair over to join the kids. Caroline stayed with the adults.

For the first few questions, Caroline's team did tolerably well. *What is the capital of North Dakota? Which artist sang the Piña Colada Song? Name a country that borders Libya.* Caroline was pleased that she knew these: Bismarck; Rupert Holmes; Egypt. When the questions grew increasingly difficult, though, she sat back and gulped her soda. She was miserable at trivia. Her group volleyed possible answers back and forth. Thank goodness Sam appeared to know something about everything—history, geography, telekinesis.

"Okay, gang," Athena announced, flipping her long dark braid over her shoulder. "Next one's tricky." Javier pointed at Caroline in mock challenge. "Who was Dolly Parton's first husband?"

"Oh, I know this one!" Lee whispered to their circle. "It's Carl Thomas Dean. He also happens to be her *only* husband."

Caroline stared at her blankly. "How do you *know* this stuff?"

Lee shrugged. "A lot of spare time on my hands during preschool nap time?" She scribbled the answer on their little white card.

Next was a question about the order of the planets.

"I have a trick for that." Abby fanned her fingers out in front of her. "It's that acronym. You know the one: Please Excuse My Dear Aunt Sally?" She began to rattle off the planets one by one. "So that would be, let's see— Pluto, Earth, Mars . . ." They held their breath while they waited for her to figure it out. "Wait a second. What the heck is *D*?" Lee was the first to burst out laughing. "Lovey, I think that's an acronym for something else."

Sam furnished the order of the planets, a list that flew off his tongue like a foreign language he was fluent in, and eventually it was Lee who remembered that the Aunt Sally acronym applied to the order of operations when solving math problems: parentheses, exponents, multiplication, division, addition, subtraction.

"See? I knew it was useful information I'd stored away," Abby quipped.

"Less useful, though, if you can't remember where to apply it," Sam kidded, and everyone laughed, including Abby.

"Last question." Athena cleared her throat for emphasis. "What does the Italian word *coriandoli* mean?"

145

Everyone groaned. "I'll give you guys a hint," Athena said. "It's something that you find at weddings."

Caroline shrugged. "Cake, maybe?"

Since no one could think of a better answer, they went with it.

They exchanged cards with a group who were wearing matching red T-shirts that said, I'M WITH EDDIE.

"Let's hope we did better than Eddie's crowd," Caroline whispered. As Athena read off the answers, Caroline checked Eddie's card, which happily had a preponderance of wrong answers matched by an equal number of beer smudges. Remarkably, Caroline's group had gotten all correct answers through question nine. But when Athena announced the last answer and another table let out a whoop, Caroline knew they'd lost.

"*Coriandoli* means *confetti.*" Caroline shook her head. "Not in a million years would I have guessed that."

"Me either," said Sam.

Athena had later hinted it was something people throw at weddings, prompting one passenger to call out, "Rice!" The crowd chuckled.

Athena, however, was bemused. "Rice? Really? You throw *rice* at weddings? Not in South Africa." She wagged a finger in the air. "In South Africa, we would never throw rice. That would be wasting food." And again, everyone laughed, as if in bonhomie.

Her words struck Caroline, though. Here she and her friends were eating and drinking to their hearts' content, some passengers already beginning to slur their words. What must the ship's staff think of all these rowdy Americans living to excess? It was the first time on the cruise that Caroline had considered the dichotomy, and she felt embarrassed, ashamed. The crew must think they were ungrateful gluttons. She would make a point of talking to some of the stewards for her article.

As the game wrapped up, Caroline took Javier's hand in her own. "C'mon, let's go get some air," she suggested. She needed a break from all the noise, the nonstop revelry. They waved good-bye to their friends and stepped out into the cool night.

11

~

When Lacey walked out on deck, a red glow about ten yards away flickered in the dark. She approached the light, thinking it might be Ryan. But when she drew closer, she saw it was a crew member, probably in his twenties, watching her.

"Got an extra I can bum off you?" she asked.

He shook his head. "My apologies. This is my last one." He hesitated. "Would you like mine?"

Lacey desperately wanted it but knew she shouldn't take it for a whole host of reasons. "Maybe just one puff," she said finally. He handed it over and she inhaled. The burn that crept down her lungs felt good, oddly cleansing. She'd forgotten the appealing rush of nicotine in those first few seconds.

"You mustn't tell anyone, though," he said, suddenly mysterious.

"Okay."

"I'm Victor. From Namibia." He held out his hand.

"Nice to meet you, Victor from Namibia. I'm Lacey, from Charleston, South Carolina," she added.

"The pleasure is mine, I'm sure."

It felt a little weird to be speaking so formally, but she supposed part of it was in the translation. She'd dumped Chris when his little posse of admirers had shown up tonight. She didn't feel like hanging out at the arcade and was seriously considering curling up in her cabin with a book. Her mom had brought a stack of paperback romances—maybe one of them would be decent.

"Do you know where Namibia is?" Victor asked, interrupting her thoughts. "On the west coast of Africa?"

"Yes, I know where it is," Lacey said quickly, though she hoped he wouldn't ask her to pinpoint it on a map. "I still don't understand why our shared cigarette has to be a secret, though."

He hesitated before answering. "The crew is not supposed to fraternize with the passengers." He puffed on his cigarette.

"Really? Huh." She considered that for a moment. "Why not?"

Victor shrugged. "Captain's orders. Typically, we hang out in crew quarters down below. But I needed to deliver something to the captain, so here I am, catching a smoke before I return to my bunk."

"Well, don't worry. Your secret is safe with me."

"Do your parents know you smoke?" he asked softly. "You seem very young."

She flung her hair over her shoulder. "I'm twenty-one," she lied. "But thanks for your concern. No, my mom doesn't know I smoke, but there are a lot of things she doesn't know about me." Technically, Lacey didn't think of herself as a smoker, but she liked to light up from time to time.

Victor exhaled and was quiet for a moment. "Such as?"

Lacey was surprised by the boldness of the question. There were probably too many things to list out here in the middle of the ocean to a perfect stranger. Like the first time she'd fooled around with Todd Larson her freshman year in high school (in the back of his car and totally unglamorous) or the time that she and her best friend, Ellie, had snuck off to go skinny dipping in the harbor. Or how she'd stolen a sweater from Macy's on a dare from Jane Kellen when they were in middle school. But the big one was the one that probably counted the most.

"Like I already know who I'm going to marry." Lacey inhaled sharply. There. She'd said it out loud. She'd promised herself that she wouldn't let the words slip out on the cruise, not even if her mother held her by the hair overboard and threatened to feed her to the sharks. Not that she would, but Lee had been known to go to insane lengths in search of the truth when she suspected Lacey was hiding something. Tyler had already given her a promise ring with a tiny diamond; it was hidden in her top drawer at home. Even if she'd told her mom, though, she doubted Lee would believe her. Her mom was big into denial when it came to inconvenient truths.

Lacey refrained from saying anything more. Like the fact that she was now six days late. Almost a whole week.

Victor raised an eyebrow at her. "Ah, yes? Who is the lucky man?"

"His name is Tyler," said Lacey. "He's amazing."

"My congratulations then," said Victor. "That's big news. Most people don't fall in love like that until much later in life. Myself included," he added with a wink.

"Yeah, well, my mom might choose another word than *congratulations*," Lacey muttered. They both turned to gaze out at the water, a slate of black with a shimmering triangle cast by the moon. A lattice of stars pinpricked the dark sky above.

Victor said, "I take it she's not happy with your boyfriend then?"

"She's only met him once!" Lacy found herself automatically launching into a defense of Tyler, but stopped. Her mom was definitely unhappy with her choice of boyfriend. That was putting it mildly. And if it turned out that Lacey was pregnant, well, Lee would probably be the first one to hunt him down and kill him.

Victor nodded, as if carefully processing the information Lacey was passing along.

She felt a wave of embarrassment rush over her. "Sorry, too much information, right? And you don't even know me!" What was she thinking? Confiding in someone she'd just met?

Still, it felt good to talk about Tyler. She'd been missing him so much, and the current circumstances were hardly helping. The possibility that she might actually be pregnant was starting to take hold. *Six days late.* In the back of her mind, Lacey knew that during finals week she hadn't exactly been diligent about birth control. This morning she'd even checked the ship's little sundries store, surreptitiously combing the aisles for a pregnancy test. But there didn't appear to be any, and Lacey would rather die than ask the salesclerk.

Victor smiled at her. "You know, where I come from, true love is cause for celebration, not for secret keeping."

Lacey let the notion sit with her. Victor was right, of course, but he didn't understand her circumstances, that her mom wanted Lacey to become a doctor or an astronaut before she even thought about guys. Lee thought she knew what was best for Lacey, but her mom had never been in love. How could she possibly understand how Lacey felt about Tyler? It was so hypocritical!

"I know what you're saying makes sense. Really. That's the way it's supposed to be in America, too. But my mom's different. She wants me to become president or something before I fall in love, get married."

Victor shook his head. "Sometimes you Americans confuse me. You have so much at your disposal. So many riches, and yet it's never enough. Someone wants you to do one thing; you want to do something else. When the world is your oyster, why make clam chowder out of it?"

Lacey laughed at the mixed metaphor, but she had to admit: Victor had a point. There were worse things in life than worrying about what your mom thought of your boyfriend. Or whether or not said boyfriend had gotten you pregnant. Even if her mom would consider it the ultimate screwup. Lacey had the perfect comeback for that, though: How could Lee accuse her of being stupid when Lacey had been conceived out of something less than love? Just the pure lust of a one-night stand? At least Lacey and Tyler loved each other. At least they planned to get married.

A loud cackle from the other side of the boat suddenly interrupted her thoughts. When she glanced over, a small group of passengers, their arms slung around one another, were slowly making their way across the deck and singing loudly.

"You know that none of this is real, right?" Victor asked, gesturing widely. "It's an illusion. In a few more days, the captain will wave his wand and this—the ship, the partying, the beautiful beaches—will all be gone and everyone will go back home. But that is precisely why they come, so they can leave their lives behind for a little while." He pursed his lips around his cigarette, making it bloom orange in the night. He shrugged and exhaled. "Who knows? Maybe they have a broken heart or a job they hate—but on the ship they can forget about all that and become someone else entirely. That's the magic. When they get home, though, their real lives are still there. Waiting for them."

Lacey nodded, uncertain what he was driving at.

"But *you*, you see." He pointed, as if he suspected she hadn't quite understood. "You have something to look forward to. True love. Marriage one day. Perhaps a family," he added.

Lacey felt herself blanch at the mention of family. Was it that obvious? But then she smiled. Victor might be a little dramatic and dreamy, but he was right: Lacey wasn't so much trying to escape her life as she was hoping to embrace it.

Victor dropped his cigarette on the deck and stubbed it out with the sole of his shoe.

"You don't just throw it overboard?" she asked, surprised.

"No." He shook his head. "Too risky. You never know with this wind, it might get blown back onto the ship."

"Oh, that makes sense." She turned her face away from the wind. "Well, thank you, Victor from Namibia. It's been a pleasure talking to you." She held out her hand for him to shake.

"Yes, a pleasure." He smiled, the whites of his teeth flashing in the dark. He took her hand and kissed it. "Maybe I'll see you around the ship another time?"

"I'd like that," Lacey said.

She watched him walk away. And at that precise moment she felt a stitch in her abdomen. She held her breath, waiting for more, but none came. Was it a kick? But that was ridiculous! A baby the size of a poppy seed couldn't kick. *Oh my God,* she thought, *what if there really is a baby in there?* It hadn't seemed real until just that instant. Being late was one thing, but that unfamiliar zip across her stomach, almost like a flutter kick? She'd never felt that before.

Lacey shook her head. She was freaking out. She needed to get back to the cabin, where she could pull herself together. If only she could remember which way led to the front of the ship, it would be so much easier to get home. She started off in search of a sign, any sign, really, pointing the way, and tried not to panic.

12

On Tuesday, their group decided to split up. Javier and Caroline wanted to explore the Swizzle Stick Pub on the other side of the island. They'd rented a moped, and Lee walked over to wish them good luck. "Watch out for the rotaries," she warned. "Remember to turn *left* into them."

"Don't worry. I'll take good care of her." Javier patted Caroline's knee. She was behind him, clasping his middle, her lips pulled into a tight line. A bulky orange helmet rested on her head, and Lee was taken aback for a moment. It was the first time she'd seen Caroline appear anything less than glamorous.

"Consider yourself my sole executor," Caroline told her, then added, "I'm not kidding, you know that, right?" Lee laughed and shooed them out of the parking lot.

Since the kids were not about to wait one more nanosecond to get online, everyone else was headed into downtown Hamilton this morning. As much as they'd enjoyed Horseshoe Bay yesterday, it had been like pulling teeth trying to get everyone back on the ship. There had been pleas, whining, outright bargaining of souls, so that the teenagers might go into town to check their e-mails. But the adults had been firm: tomorrow. So, now they were keeping their promise. Chris, Lacey, and Ryan hovered near the front of the ferry as they pulled up to dock, eager to be the first to step off the boat.

Abby nudged Lee. "Look at them. They're like a bunch of bloodhounds. No amount of pepper spray could throw them off the scent."

"Let's hope they turn back into cute puppies once they get their fill of the Internet."

When the ferry docked, relief washed over Lee. The ride had been unexpectedly rocky, and she was grateful to step onto terra firma. They checked the ferry's return schedule posted outside the main terminal, then crossed over to Front Street. Quaint cobblestone sidewalks meandered through a neighborhood that included Louis Vuitton and other stylish vendors. Lee did her best to dodge the sun, which was intense, blistering even, without a sea breeze. Already, a bead of perspiration was winding its way down her chest, and she held her shirt away from her skin to allow for air. A little bell chimed, and a local man, dressed in a polo shirt, khaki shorts, and knee socks, sailed by them on his bicycle.

"Hey, I forgot about the long knee socks with the Bermuda shorts. It's a good look," Abby said. "Maybe you should get a pair of socks, Sam?"

"Be careful what you wish for," he teased. "I might buy a whole case of them in different colors." Lee laughed and tried to picture her friend's husband in knee socks, unsuccessfully. Even professorial Sam wasn't quite that nerdy.

Eventually Lacey came up to join them. Lee noted the small constellation of freckles that had taken up residence on her daughter's nose. It reminded her of when Lacey was little and they'd spent hours at Folly Beach, Lacey piling sand into her pail, her fair skin turning darker by the minute, her hair bleaching in the sun. Those had been blissful days. Lee turned to her now.

"Doesn't it seem like you *have* to be happy if you live here? Almost like it's required?" She fanned an arm out around her daughter. "I mean, look at this place. How can you be depressed when the stores are the color of sherbet?"

"I think you're right, Mom."

Lee glanced at Abby and grinned. She was secretly thrilled by her daughter's affirmation and mentally filed it away as a win. After the college discussion, when Lacey had clomped off, they seemed to have reached an unspoken agreement. So long as Lee steered clear of college and careers, her daughter was willing to remain in her company. Sometimes (it depended on the hour, of course) Lee even allowed herself to think Lacey might like her again. That it could be like old times. Still, Lee knew she shouldn't hold her breath. She was like one of those comic book characters with a little bubble floating above her head. One that inflated or deflated depending upon her daughter's fickle moods.

"So," Lacey began, unlocking her arm from Lee's, "when do you think we can find an Internet café?"

Lee sighed. Such a fragile bubble.

She knew her daughter had been living in adolescent purgatory, severed from the Internet and her boyfriend for four excruciating days. Every time Lacey complained—about a million so far, if Lee had to guess—Lee had pointed out that people used to *write* letters to each other. *You know, the kind on paper*, she'd amended when Lacey had stared at her blankly.

"I don't know, Lace. As soon as we see something," she said, trying to hide her irritation. "Why don't you grab a postcard while you're at it? You know, reach out to Tyler the old-fashioned way?"

Lacey groaned. "That is so lame, Mom." And she scurried off to join the boys ahead.

Abby cut a sideways glance at Lee. "Stop being so lame, Mom," she mimicked.

Lee smiled but felt a skewer of longing. She didn't like to think of herself as one of those parents who struggled to fill the hours in the day when her only child went off to college. In truth, though, Lacey's leaving had been harder than she'd expected. The days went by quickly enough—her job kept her busy. But the nights were lonely, and Lee had been looking forward to spending some quality time with her little girl this week. Easier said than done.

She and Abby crossed over to the shady side of the street, where a souvenir shop with a wooden sun nailed to its front door lured them inside. Thanks to a blasting air conditioner, the store was an icebox. Lee made her way through the rows of assorted island bric-a-brac. There were miniature bottles of rum with recipes for rum cake; conch shells, their pink insides polished to a fine sheen; dish towels stamped with pictures of the beach; and woven baskets filled with wooden pirate swords.

A number of their fellow cruisers seemed to have stumbled onto the tourist haven as well, and Lee squeezed past a small crowd to reach the books along the back wall, where she pulled out a photo journal of the island and thumbed through its pages. Gorgeous pictures of the water and pink beaches stared back at her. The album, she decided, would make a nice addition to her coffee table back home.

As she wound her way through the aisles to pay at the register, a familiar voice called out.

"Lee!" When she turned, she recognized him immediately. His face was more boyish than she'd remembered, one eye slightly more narrow than the other. "Hello, there," he said, stuffing his hands into his pockets. "Didn't expect to bump into you off the ship."

It was Thomas. Thomas, whose room she'd slunk away from without so much as leaving a note. Whom she'd avoided seeing on the boat since. She'd been embarrassed to think how blithely she'd followed him back to his room. And, if she were being completely honest, she didn't remember a whole lot about that night. There had been drinks, heavy petting, followed by sex. She was pretty sure it had been good. But now here he was, standing before her fully clothed, with two young women who appeared to be his daughters.

Lee tugged at the hem of her shirt self-consciously. She felt exposed, a similar feeling to the time she'd gone to bed one night and had mistakenly left the garage door open, all her junk and trash in plain view for the neighbors to see.

"Oh, wow. Hello," she said. "Funny running into you here." Her eyes darted to the girls, who looked from her to Thomas and back to her, their foreheads pulled into tiny lines. "These must be your daughters." She held out her hand.

"Yes, let me introduce you to Tyra and Heather." Thomas's eyebrows knitted together, as if he were trying to get a read on Lee's takeaway from the other night. His girls were pretty, tall with long dark hair, around the same age as Lacey. Lee noticed a small tattoo darting around Tyra's shoulder.

"I'm Lee. Very nice to meet you. Your dad couldn't stop talking about you two the other night."

"Dad, we told you not to bring us up when you're on a date!" scolded Heather.

Thomas chuckled. "The girls insist I have a knack for scaring women away."

The taller daughter nodded. "It's true. He isn't used to dating. We apologize for whatever he might have said. He usually talks too much about himself."

Lee laughed. "Don't worry—he wasn't that bad." She winked at Thomas, unsure why she was pretending to share a secret camaraderie with him. Her eyes skimmed the store for Lacey, who appeared to have vanished into thin air. "I'm sorry," she said. "My daughter was here just a minute ago, but I'm afraid she's gone off to look for an Internet café."

"Oh, I don't blame her. We almost died without it on the ship," Tyra said.

Thomas folded his arms and rolled his eyes. "Almost *died*? Such hyperbole from this generation."

Lee smiled, wary of entering into another family's generational fray. "I'm pretty sure my daughter feels the same way."

The cashier rang up the book and handed Lee back her credit card. "Well, it was nice bumping into you," she said.

"Yeah, it was great to see you again. Hopefully, I'll see you back on the ship."

Lee offered a wave over her shoulder. It was all she could do not to tell him that *hopefully*, in strict usage, meant "in a hopeful manner." It would have been better to say, for instance, "I hope I'll see you back on the ship." But Lacey was constantly telling Lee to stop correcting people's sloppy grammar. Apparently, it wasn't an attractive quality for a single, out-of-shape, forty-something mom. Still, old habits died hard for a reason, didn't they?

～

Later, she and Abby caught up with Sam and the kids, a block further down at the Color of Joy Café. It struck Lee as a fitting name for an island café, and if it was meant to convey the look of adulation on her daughter's face when they walked into the store, then the color of joy was spot-on. Lee approached Lacey, who clutched her phone.

"Finally! I feel like I'm living again!" exclaimed Lacey. Sure enough, tiny fluorescent bars danced along the top of her phone. It occurred to Lee that her daughter was like a drug addict who'd been denied meth for too long. She was finally getting her fix.

"Sweetie, you *have* been living these past four days." Lacey's eyes flitted to her for a split second, then back down to her cell. "This other stuff?" Lee continued, undeterred by her daughter's disinterest, "it's all an illusion." She telegraphed a look at Abby, who shrugged as if to say *What's the point?* while Sam went to order their drinks.

Was the irony really lost on her daughter? Lee wondered. Here they'd been sailing the seas, feeling every brush of wind and slip of sunshine, living in the moment, and only now, in this dinky café while she checked her texts and e-mail, did Lacey feel truly alive? It verged on the comical. No, there was a better word for it—shameful. That's what it was. Had Lee done nothing to teach her daughter the value of experiencing the real world?

Abby pulled Lee aside to help with the drinks. "Hey," she whispered at the counter. "Don't be so hard on her. Remember when we were her age? Remember what it felt like to be in love?"

Lee shook her head. "Not really, I'm afraid."

Abby's eyes fluttered. "Oh, yeah? What about Tim Coughlin? Remember him?"

At the mention of the name, Lee felt her face grow warm. She hadn't thought of Tim in years. He'd been her first crush in college, during freshman year, and she'd made Abby stalk him to ask if he'd go out with her. Turned out he already had a girlfriend. "I totally forgot about him," Lee said. "You're right. I was crazy in love with him."

Abby shrugged again as if to say, *See?* "Don't worry. It's just puppy love." Lee nodded and gratefully accepted the iced coffee that Sam handed her. She hoped her friend was right. As her mom had been fond of saying, *If the creek don't rise . . .*

"Speaking of which." She grinned wickedly at Abby. "Guess who I just bumped into at the souvenir shop?"

13

~~

Caroline kept reminding herself that maybe this was it—maybe the moped adventure was part of a larger undertaking. Though, she'd assumed that if a proposal *was* forthcoming today, it would have already happened at the Swizzle Stick Pub or in the depths of the Crystal Caves. Now *that* would have been a proposal to tell her roommates about. *And then we were walking across a bridge surrounded by these stalactites that have been growing for hundreds of years—it looked like a cathedral of organ pipes—and Javier got down on one knee* . . . Except at the moment, Javier was driving around the island like a lunatic, and Caroline was clutching her arms around his middle, holding on for dear life. They were headed back to the ship. It was hard to imagine when or where he might squeeze in a proposal now.

She dug her fingers into his stomach. She'd never liked motorcycles—or any of their brethren, for that matter. Every time she shouted to slow down, though, Javier screamed that he couldn't hear her. Caroline wasn't sure if it was the actual words he couldn't make out or if he just didn't care to listen. She was beginning to worry it might be the latter.

Their waitress and bartender at the Swizzle Stick had plied them with all sorts of information about the island, and if Javier wasn't going to propose today (which was looking more and more likely), then Caroline wanted to tap out some notes before she forgot everything they'd told her. She was confident that she had the beginnings of a strong story in her Bermuda piece. Now if they could just make it back to the ship alive.

After endless zigs and zags, the ship's hull came into view. Javier pulled up alongside the booth where they'd rented the moped earlier this morning and, as if to signal a victory lap, gave the engine a final rev. Caroline allowed herself to breathe. Javier held the bike for her while she unstuck her bottom from the sweaty leather seat and hopped off. She felt as if she'd been riding a horse for the last half hour. Her stomach rocked. Her hair was a witch's nest of tangles, and she worked to shape it into a ponytail with the spare elastic that was twisted around her wrist.

On the pavement she did a funny little dance, stamping her foot up and down.

"Foot fall asleep?" Javier asked.

"I guess." But Caroline couldn't bear to look at him. The truth was—she was mad. Mad that Javier had insisted on renting a moped rather than hitching an air-conditioned taxi ride like any normal tourist would have done. "It'll be fun," he'd promised her, the same refrain he'd used when he wanted to go snorkeling. Mad that she'd been fooled again into thinking that today might be the day. She could kick herself! For a smart woman, Caroline was amazed by how incredibly gullible she could be.

Javier took her bag and amiably slung it over his shoulder, while she rested her hands on her lower back and began to rotate her trunk in a slow swivel, not caring how she looked. She twisted a second time, left to right. The thing was, when they were in New York and Javier suggested doing something outside her wheelhouse, it was almost always fun. But here on this sun-soaked island, she was starting to feel as if Javier and she were experiencing two separate vacations. The "space in togetherness" that she'd been coveting earlier had tilted toward pure separation. He was clearly enjoying the adventure of their getaway while Caroline was so focused on getting a proposal that she could barely think about anything else.

She made a final swivel and exhaled. Javier grinned. "Better?"

"Not sure." She wasn't willing to give him even that much. Maybe she was just tired and dehydrated, but it felt like something more. She'd been beyond patient with him. If these last few days were meant to be a tease leading up to a proposal, then she'd had enough. She felt deflated, completely defeated. "Please don't make me ride on one of those things ever again," she snapped.

Javier stared at her, surprised. "Okay? I thought it would be fun."

"I know you did," she said. "And it wasn't." They walked back through check-in, and Caroline gratefully accepted the cool, damp towel and small cup of water that the porters offered her.

"You look like you might want to rest?" Javier was still holding her bag while they waited in line for the elevator.

"Yeah, I think I'll head back up to the room."

"All right." He hesitated, as if uncertain whether he should follow. "Maybe I'll go look for the others, then?"

"Fine." She held out her hand for her bag just as the elevator doors pinged open. "I'll catch up with you later." She was only too happy when the doors slid shut.

⌒

Back in the room, Caroline showered, changed into her sweats, and stretched out in her favorite yoga position— child's pose. The cabin was so small that there was barely enough space, but if she angled her body just so—her arms reaching under the desk—she could manage. Deep breath after deep breath. *Wasn't there at least one fight in every happy vacation?* It was good for her to let off steam, she reasoned. But she was done with tiptoeing around the marriage topic. *Enough!* She resolved to talk to Javier later today. Either he was in this relationship one hundred percent—or he was out.

Armed with a plan and a steady breath, she felt her blood pressure drifting back toward normal. She lifted her head and pulled her body upright into a sitting position. After a few more soothing breaths, she climbed onto the bed, turned on her notepad, and began to write.

A few minutes later, there was a knock at the door. "Hi, do you mind if I come in for a minute?" Lee asked when Caroline propped it open.

"Of course not." Caroline stepped aside. "What's up?"

"It's Abby." Lee went over and sprawled out on the bed. "I'm worried about her."

"Huh." Between Javier and her article, Caroline hadn't given a single thought to Abby. After all, they were on the cruise to celebrate Abby and Sam's anniversary. Aside from the fact that Abby appeared to have lost some weight, what was there to worry about? "You think she's getting cold feet about the ceremony?"

Lee shook her head and tugged at a loose thread on the bedspread. "No, but doesn't she seem—I don't know—a little off to you?"

Caroline fell onto the bed and replayed the last few days in her head. "Not really. I mean, I haven't noticed anything out of the ordinary. How so?"

"I'm not sure, exactly. But she's been awfully quiet." Lee hesitated. "And obviously she's lost a lot of weight. Too much, if you ask me."

"Come on—we'd all want to look our best if it was our twentieth wedding anniversary. We can't fault her for that, can we?"

"I know, but then there's that bruise on her thigh."

"And? So she banged into something." Caroline stretched out on the bed and slid her elbows under a pillow. "I bang into stuff all the time."

"That's what I thought, too, but then there's other stuff. Like have you noticed she's forgetting things?"

Again, Caroline searched her mind. "I know she was upset when Chris lost his room key for the second time in a row. But that wasn't her fault."

"Right, but the other day we were talking by the pool, and she didn't remember that she'd already ordered lunch. I had to stop her from ordering another tuna sandwich."

Caroline shrugged. She thought Lee was making a big deal out of nothing. "That seems pretty normal when you're on vacation. Maybe she'd had a few cocktails."

"No! That's just it. I don't think she's had a sip of alcohol since we've been on the boat."

Caroline had noticed Abby wasn't drinking, but since when had turning down a glass of wine meant something was wrong with one of them? She said as much.

Lee nodded, but Caroline could tell she was still concerned. She watched while Lee worried the stray thread a minute longer, then snapped it off with a tug. "I suppose you're right. It just seems weird to me. And Sam's been acting strange, too, now that I think about it. He's been pretty somber for a vacation that's supposed to be a raucous celebration."

"Look at us," Caroline said, reaching over to squeeze Lee's arm. "Did you ever consider the possibility that we're just getting older? We can't party like we used to, and, hey, my memory isn't what it used to be either. Half the time I go searching for something and then can't remember what it was."

Lee's breath escaped slowly, like air fizzing out of a tire. "Yeah, I do that, too." She shrugged. "So, I guess we should chalk it up to middle age? That and we can't party like we did in college?"

Caroline gave a small laugh. "That sounds about right to me. So now what?"

Before Lee could answer, there was another knock at the door.

Lee stole a glance at Caroline. "Javier?" Caroline shrugged and got up to see. She'd almost mentioned their fight to Lee but then had thought better of it—she wasn't sure her friend would be sympathetic.

"Don't you have a key?" she demanded when the door opened on Javier, but Lee was already brushing past her.

"Hi, Javier. Good to see you. Catch you guys later tonight?"

"Sure." Surprise darted across Javier's face, as if he

couldn't quite fathom why Lee was in their room. In his hands were two very large margaritas. "Am I forgiven?" he asked once Lee had gone.

"That depends." Caroline stepped aside to let him by. "Normally forgiveness follows an apology. I don't think I've gotten one of those yet."

He set the drinks down on the table and came over to her, circling his arms around her waist. His head dipped down toward hers, his nose brushing hers. "I'm sorry," he said. "I shouldn't have made you ride a scooter if you didn't want to. I thought it would be fun."

Caroline felt something soften in her. He sounded so sincere. It probably *was* his idea of a good time. "I know," she said, "and usually I *do* like an adventure, but sometimes it's too much, and I need you to listen when I say I'm afraid. I'm not as tough as I look, you know."

He kissed her forehead. "You mean even the great Caroline Canton is sometimes afraid? I didn't know this." She stepped away to help herself to the margarita, which tasted like icy, delicious pineapples.

"Yes, I am, as much as I hate to admit it." She sat down on the bed, across from him. "Speaking of which," she began, "I think we need to talk."

14

⌒

Abby hadn't said anything to the boys, not yet. Only that she'd been feeling tired. Somehow, she and Sam had managed to keep the doctors' appointments secret from them, Abby going in for visits during the school day. On the night that they biopsied the lymph node, Abby had fibbed and said she was staying over at her friend Marie's because Marie wasn't feeling well and needed help with the baby. Abby didn't like lying to the boys. But as soon as they heard the news, she knew they would worry, and she wanted to protect them for as long as she could. In her mind, they were still her little boys. Why burden them unnecessarily until they were certain about what they were dealing with?

The doctor had mentioned options. "Something else will probably get you first," he'd said in a grim attempt at levity, she supposed. There were pills she could take—was taking—a whole array of them in a variety of colors that were supposed to make her body stop attacking itself. And once her body adjusted to the medication—

maybe in a few weeks, a few months—she'd start to feel more like herself, perhaps even put on a few pounds.

But the looming question was one that she and Sam had yet to discuss: Would she try the next step? The only true cure for what she had—a very rare type of leukemia—was a bone marrow transplant. Just the thought of such an invasive procedure made her want to crawl under her bed. That compounded with the slim odds of finding a match (especially since Abby didn't have any siblings) made her less than sanguine. And, to tell the truth, she wasn't confident that her body could withstand the procedure. She'd been feeling so tired lately. On the other hand, even without the transplant, she might still live another twenty years. People had. Abby had read the literature. Twenty years was plenty of time to see the boys graduate from college, get married. And really, who of them knew how much time they had left on this earth?

She slipped a book of poems she'd been reading into her bag while she waited for Sam. There were two that she wanted to include in tomorrow's ceremony. Sam wouldn't mind. As far as he was concerned, Abby could order up a mariachi band and it would all be fine. *So long as we renew our vows, honey, I'm good.* She sipped her gin and tonic, the tang of it delicious on her tongue. It had been so long since she'd had a cocktail! Not since the doctor had suspected something might be amiss. And now she was under doctor's orders to abstain from

alcohol while on the medication. But what could one little G & T hurt? A person didn't get to celebrate twenty
years of marriage every day. The way Abby saw it, the
gin scrubbing at the edges of her anxiety, was that she'd
earned it. If she couldn't celebrate now, then when?

She was satisfied with her poem selection and with
her brief meeting with the ship's chaplain earlier today.
She'd wanted to make sure everything was set for tomorrow's ceremony at noon at Horseshoe Bay. Lunch would
follow at the Reefs Resort. The chaplain, a portly fellow
with a mop of gray hair and an easygoing manner, had
been just as Abby had imagined him when she spoke with
him a few weeks ago from Boston. The ceremony would
be a simple affair—a couple of readings, an exchange
of vows. The chaplain seemed to understand. Better yet,
he supported her wishes to keep the whole affair under-
stated. In the Bermuda heat, short and sweet was best.

Abby searched the crowd again. Still no sign of Sam.
For the hundredth time, she checked the screen above
the bar that listed the forecast for tomorrow: Wednesday
would be in the eighties and filled with bright sunshine.
The ceremony would be lovely, and also, quite possibly,
as hot as a fried egg. Thank goodness the Reefs Hotel
had offered to pitch a modest white tent and chairs on
the beach for the affair. It would protect them from the
sun—and lessen the chances that someone would col-
lapse from heatstroke.

Abby thought of her dress, a shimmering Badgley

Mischka made of the softest ivory chiffon. The top was a simple halter that tied at the neck, and the skirt cascaded out from the waist like a waterfall. Wearing it made Abby feel like the most graceful woman in the world. She couldn't wait to put it on tomorrow, to feel the drape of the chiffon against her skin, and, most especially, to see Sam's expression when he laid eyes on her for the first time.

More people were beginning to gather on the ship's dance floor, and Abby wondered if Caroline or Lee had found her way up yet. It was the night of the White Hot Party—which their cruise director, Simone, had been talking up all day. Above the parquet floor, a spinning disco ball threw off diamonds of light that illuminated passengers' white shirts and dresses in a strange neon purple. It occurred to Abby that she had no idea where the kids were. Probably off at the karaoke bar or the arcade.

Forty-six was still young, which worked in her favor. And her particular kind of chemotherapy could be taken in pill form—the wonders of modern science! The doctor had mentioned she'd likely keep her hair, and for that she was grateful. She worried, though, that she would lose her mind before anything else. Sometimes she could sense little bits of information slipping away from her, Post-it notes ungluing from her brain, and Sam would give her a look as if she'd just told him to pour salt in his iced tea. Evidently, there was even a name for it—*chemo brain.*

Plenty of time to think about it, the doctor had said. *Let's see how the medicine treats you first.* So, that's where Abby stood, on the precipice of waiting and seeing. Of course, if the rogue cells in her body didn't respond—or grew resistant—well, twenty years suddenly got whittled down to ten or five or two. But Abby pushed that thought out of her mind. When the test results had arrived two weeks prior to their sail-away date, the doctor had handed her the green light to go on vacation, as planned. She was fine to travel so long as she promised to get her blood work done the moment she returned home—something about counting the blasts and platelets darting around inside of her. The pills, of course, were meant to manage that, knock the blasty things down to a more reasonable level. Her body, it seemed, had a disturbing preponderance of white cells—big, muscular bullies (she imagined them sporting tattoos) that were crowding out the healthy red ones. Sometimes she liked to imagine the chemo pills giving the bullies a swift kick in the nuts.

She flagged the bartender for an ice water. The revelers were warming up now, and she watched as people began to swing their hips with a more suggestive vibe. One man had already yanked off his shirt, and it now looped around his head like a turban. It was shocking, really, the things people felt free to do on vacation. *What do they do for their day jobs?* Abby wondered. Was the bare-chested man, for instance, the CEO of a very important company? Was the woman whose breasts threatened to break free from her halter top with every shimmy in fact the president of a prestigious Manhattan philanthropy board? It was hard to imagine.

Abby tried to think back to six months ago. Had her own body shown signs of turning on itself? Were there inklings, other than some weight loss and general fatigue, that had escaped her notice? She'd just assumed it was all typical premenopausal stuff. The trick of leukemia, of course, was that it rarely introduced itself in obvious ways. Instead of forming a palpable lump, the infected cells coursed through your body, masquerading as blood, that life force. Abby had even boasted to friends about how rarely she was sick. *Must be good genes*, she'd joked. How strange to think that a year ago she was moving through her typical days, ushering the boys to sports games and appointments, meeting friends for lunch, without a clue that her body would soon be under siege.

Even harder to imagine was some unnamed technician "reading" her cells in a faraway lab. Were her sick cells dramatically different from her healthy ones, she wondered, somehow bent or misshapen? Did the technician consider what kind of person might provide a home to such cells? Did he conjure up Abby's auburn hair, which hung just above her shoulders, or her hazel eyes? What about the more abstract things? Did he (or she, Abby reminded herself—it could be a woman technician) see a hologram of her, the wife of

Samuel Bingham and the mother of two boys? A woman who loved her family deeply and wanted her life to stay exactly the same? How much could a person intuit from another person's DNA?

The doctor had tried to reassure her, a flop of gray hair brushing over his eyes. "This is not a death sentence, Abby. Now is not the time to despair." And Abby had remembered her first thought: *what a cliché*. Of all the ailments to take her down, it had to be cancer? Why couldn't she have a rare disease, something exotic maybe, one that could be caught only in the wilds of India? Something that would get people's attention for its rarity without instantly invoking their pity. Yes, Abby had been mad at her cancer not because it threatened her life but because it seemed so blasé, another statistic in her doctor's day. If she were going to be taken out of this world, then she wanted a touch of drama, at the very least, a good story.

And then she'd gone online to read about her particular brand of cancer (precisely what the doctor had ordered her *not* to do) and learned that roughly four out of one million Americans were diagnosed with her type of leukemia each year. She'd called out to Sam to recite the astonishing statistic. *Four in one million.* They'd shared a perverse chuckle over that—"I have a better chance of getting struck by lightning, don't you think?"—and the abrupt realization that her diagnosis was plenty unique.

Abby's thoughts were interrupted by a woman, probably in her mid-sixties, blond hair and heavy makeup, who collapsed in the empty seat next to her. She ordered a Coke and tossed a smile Abby's way. "Let me guess. Waiting on your husband?"

Abby raised an eyebrow. "Is it that obvious?"

The woman laughed. "You'd be surprised how many women on this ship find themselves in the same position." She smiled. "Myself included. My husband's mistress is the casino. I'm Nancy, by the way."

"Nice to meet you. Abby." They clinked glasses. "Where are you from?"

"Originally? Canada, up near Toronto. But these days, the ship is my home."

"Oh, you travel a lot?" Abby asked.

"You could say that. My husband and I actually live on the *Bermuda Breeze*."

Abby straightened in her seat, surprised. "Really? Do you work on the ship?"

"Heavens, no. We're retired. It just so happens that we chose to retire on a big old boat instead of in a condo in Florida. This way we get to see some of the Caribbean and meet interesting new people every week. We love it."

Abby cocked her head, considering the cruise in a fresh light. Could it be a balm to call such a floating house her home? She wasn't sure that she'd ever get used to the idea of making it permanent. Casinos and shuffleboard were not her thing. Plus, Abby liked having her feet on solid ground as opposed to drifting on water with no discernible bottom. Still, she could see how the simplicity of it all, of having someone cook and clean for you, could be appealing. And when she kicked the bucket, a burial at sea sounded easy, peaceful even.

"You should look into it," Nancy encouraged. "I'm sure they have some brochures at the front desk. It's a good gig."

Abby nodded. "It does sound pretty nice, actually."

"Ah, the prodigal husband returns," Nancy kidded as a man with a shiny bald head and a loud Hawaiian shirt approached them. "Did you win big, Larry?" she asked as he wrapped an arm around her.

He held up his fingers to form a zero. "Nada. Not my lucky day."

"Too bad." She shrugged. "Maybe tomorrow. Can I buy you a drink?"

"The answer to that question, my dear, is always yes." He winked. "How about a martini?"

After introductions, Abby confided that she was celebrating her twentieth wedding anniversary, and Larry insisted on ordering her another gin and tonic. "Next year is our fortieth," said Nancy. "You should come back. It's going to be a real party!"

But before Abby could construe an enthusiastic answer, Sam materialized by her side, a book in hand. She introduced him.

"I was just telling your wife how great it is to live on

the boat. You meet tons of people, from all over the place." Nancy clapped her hands together. "Let's see . . . There was a couple from Holland, another from Brazil. Oh, and that nice young man from Tennessee. Who else? Think, Larry." Abby caught Sam's gaze, slightly pleading. After a few more minutes, the cruisers excused themselves for dinner, and Sam dropped into Nancy's empty chair.

"Wow, do you think the cruise line hires her to get people to sign up for life?"

Abby laughed. "It's possible. They do seem to like it, though." She turned her face to catch the breeze. "Can you imagine? Nothing to do but sit by the pool during your retirement years? You wouldn't even have to step off the boat."

Sam shook his head. "No way. I'd be bored to tears."

To tell the truth, Abby thought she would, too. But there was something to be said for getting away from it all. Was it possible, she wondered, for the ocean air and salt water to cure her particular brand of sickness? Maybe fighting her illness was simply a matter of mind over body, warm sunshine over punishing, gray springtime.

"Oh, look, there's Lee." Abby pointed as Lee made her way toward them through the throng of dancers, a water bug fighting the current.

"How on earth did you guys ever manage to get seats? This place is packed," Lee huffed when she finally reached them, her cheeks flushed pink.

"It's crazy now, but it was empty earlier." Abby flagged down the bartender and ordered Lee a strawberry margarita.

"Have you seen the kids?" Abby asked. "I don't think I've spotted Chris or Ryan in hours."

"Nope," replied Lee. "And I'm not going to worry about it. I'm sure they're off having fun somewhere."

"You're probably right. How about Caroline? Any sign of her?"

"Last I saw the lovebirds, they were sharing margaritas in their cabin."

"Aha," said Abby and winked. "Perhaps tonight is the night then."

"Perhaps," said Lee slyly. Sam shook his head.

"You ladies," he began, "are ridiculous. I say let Javier propose on his own time."

"Do you know something we don't?" Abby asked.

"No, nothing." Sam held up his hands, feigning surrender. "As a guy, though, I have to say probably the last thing that would make me want to propose is knowing I was *supposed* to propose."

Abby sipped her cocktail. "You have a point. But still," she continued, "don't you think it's about time Javier sealed the deal?"

"You two are really all about the romance, aren't you?" Sam teased.

Abby sighed. She only wanted her friend to be happy. She scanned the crowd to see if Caroline and

Javier might be dancing, but instead her eyes landed on a young couple whose bodies appeared stuck together like mating dragonflies. She clicked her tongue.

"Honestly, don't young people have any manners these days? There, over in the corner, look."

Lee and Sam peered into the dimly lit area. "Hey, Abby—"

But Abby realized it at the same moment as Lee. "Honey? Doesn't that look a little like Chris?" Before Sam could answer, the boy glanced in their general direction. Abby gripped Sam's arm. "Oh my God. It *is* Chris. Honey, do something!" She nudged Sam hard enough that she could feel her elbow land in the soft flesh between his ribs.

"Ow! Go easy there, would you, killer?" He pulled back, squinting in Chris's direction.

Abby huffed. Sam was hopeless in these kinds of situations, as if he needed to read the entire book before drawing a conclusion based on a mere chapter. If anyone was going to stop the scene unfolding in front of them, it would have to be her. Abby felt her body practically levitate out of its seat. As she marched toward her son, the thought crossed her mind that these men—her boys—would need someone else to save them from themselves when she was gone.

But she'd deal with that later. Right now, she was on a mission.

"Christopher Matthew Bingham," she shouted over

the music. It took a few seconds, but eventually the girl lifted her head from his shoulder, and Christopher's gaze followed hers, settling on his mother. Tiny diamonds of light from the disco ball danced across his face. "What on earth do you think you're doing?"

"Geez, Mom, can't you give a guy some space?"

"*Space?*" Abby felt a cackle race up her throat. "Oh, really? You want some space? I'll give you space. What are you *doing* with this girl? Woman?" Abby flapped her hands in the air as she searched for the appropriate nomenclature. She turned to the girl. "Hi, dear," Abby quipped. "I suggest you find someone closer to your own age. This happens to be my son, who is only sixteen."

The girl took a step back, the pink liquid in her cup sloshing over the side and puddling on the floor. "Sixteen? But I thought you said you were twenty-one." Sam, suddenly at Abby's side, rested a firm hand on her arm, as if readying to corral a rabid dog.

Abby shot him a look. "Oh boy, this is getting good now, isn't it?"

"Mom—" Chris began, but she held up her hand.

A wave of heat whooshed up her face, just as she caught a whiff of alcohol. She leaned in closer and noticed that her son's eyes were rimmed with red. "Are you *drunk*? You've got to be kidding me! You have a lot of explaining to do, Christopher Matthew Bingham."

Sam ushered Chris off the dance floor, and Abby followed. "What were you thinking?" she hissed. She found an empty chair and shoved him into it. "How can you be so, so—" She sputtered, searching for the right word. "Stupid!" A spray of spittle flew through the air as she spat out the word.

"God, Mom, calm down. I'm not drunk, okay? I just had a few sips of her drink."

"Oh, really? Now you're going to lie to us, too?" She glowered at Sam, who stared at her blankly. "You're not going to back me up here?" she demanded.

"Of course I am, it's just that we're on a cruise. It's vacation, honey."

"And what? That makes this"—she gestured with a wide sweep of her arm—"all okay?"

"Seriously, Mom, chill."

"*Chill?* Is that your entire verbal wingspan?" Chris stared at her as if she were a lunatic. "Well, excuse me, but last I checked, twenty-one is still the legal drinking age. Not to mention that Miss Thing on the dance floor looks old enough to be your teacher." She shot Chris her best I'm-very-disappointed-in-you look.

Sam blew threw his teeth. "Okay, let's all just try to breathe for a minute. Maybe it's not as bad as it looks. Chris, do you care to explain yourself?"

Chris shrugged. "What do you want me to say? So, I had a few sips of her drink—big deal. We were having fun. Remember what that feels like, Mom? Fun?"

Abby stepped back as if he'd slapped her. How dare he accuse her of not having fun! He didn't know the half of it. It was all she could do not to tell him right there, spill all the beans. *It just so happens*, she wanted to say, *that I'm sick. Very sick.*

As if sensing an imminent eruption, Sam wrapped an arm around her. "All right, I think we could all use some time alone. Chris, I'm taking you back to your cabin, where you should consider yourself grounded until further notice."

Chris's eyes lit up. "Grounded? You can't ground me on a ship. It's like a, a, an oxymoron."

Abby was about to congratulate him on his clever use of an SAT word but caught herself. "Sure he can. *We* can," she amended. "And we *are* grounding you. Back in your cabin. No more arcade or movies or karaoke lounge for you until further notice."

"C'mon. Get up," Sam commanded. When Chris didn't move, he yanked him out of the chair by his elbow. "I said, *Let's go. Right now.*"

Abby watched them leave, then fell into a chair, ready to weep. Lee, who'd witnessed the whole scene unraveling, came over to give her a hug. "There, there," she said. "It's not as bad as you think."

"That's the thing," Abby said. "What if it is?"

15

"You know that movie with Diane Keaton and Jack Nicholson?"

Lee was sitting across from Thomas at the Starboard, sharing a plate of chicken wings while, just beyond the deck railing, a brilliant orange sun was setting.

"Oh, what's the name of it again?" She snapped her fingers in the air, as if for instant recall.

Despite Lee's best intentions to avoid him for the remainder of the cruise, Thomas had kept popping up unexpectedly, like a drifting buoy at sea. When she'd gone to walk on the treadmills at the gym after their excursion in Hamilton, there he was, offering her a bottled water. When she'd snuck a brownie in the cafeteria, there he was, waving to her from the crepe line. And shortly after Abby had gone to check on Chris tonight— and Lee was wondering what to do next—who should cruise by but Thomas?

"It must be kismet," he'd joked.

So now they sat together, discussing their favorite

movies. A smudge of barbecue sauce hovered on his chin, and she watched it while he talked, a little goatee of grease moving up and down. "Oh, I know the one you're talking about," he said. "*As Good as It Gets?* No, that's not right. That was the one with Helen Hunt and Nicholson." He hesitated a moment. "Oh, wait, I've got it—*Something's Gotta Give.* That's the one, right? Loved it."

"Yes, that's right." Lee nodded, pleasantly surprised that he'd come up with it. "It's one of my favorites."

"I was dragged to that movie back in, let's see, around 2003, if I'm not mistaken." Thomas chuckled. "Wasn't Nicholson a riot? That scene in the hospital when he's all looped up in his hospital johnny—I lost it."

Lee was laughing now—it *was* funny. "Was it really that long ago?" She moaned. "It doesn't seem possible."

"I know, right? And Diane Keaton was awesome, of course." He wiped his mouth, making the goatee vanish. "All those white turtlenecks. Must have been a year's supply. At least I think that was the movie where she wore all the white turtlenecks at the beach?"

"That was the one," Lee confirmed. "And collected white rocks."

"That's right. I remember now, and Jack gave her a jar filled with white rocks and a black stone in the middle. Now that's poetry right there."

Lee leaned back in her chair and allowed herself to reassess Thomas for a moment. That he could recall such details, let alone call it poetry, was unusual. The few men she dated usually wanted to see Arnold Schwarzenegger action films or science fiction flicks. Thomas couldn't possibly know it, but Lee had worshipped Diane Keaton in that movie. Not to mention the sweeping beach house that brimmed with books and charming window seats. It struck Lee as the way life should be: living in a grand beach house with your best friends, copious amounts of wine and good novels at your disposal. After the movie (she and Abby had gone together), Lee had confided that she wanted to be just like Diane Keaton's character when she grew up. *What do you mean?* Abby had half teased. *You want to be closed off and unavailable for the rest of your life?*

It wasn't what Lee had meant, of course, but she remembered thinking that maybe Abby had tapped into some small vein of her inner psyche. Maybe there *was* something in Lee's genetic makeup that made her unsuitable for dating. A gene, say, with an uncanny ability to detect men who were overly suave or disingenuous. Or, maybe, it was just a matter of simple mathematics and probability—she'd used up all her chances at love in college. She'd been so cavalier with her heart back then, slipping in and out of different boys' arms, always assuming there was another guy waiting around the corner. And then: *Lacey*.

Since forever, it had been Lee and Lacey against the world. But now, with Lacey off to college, their united front dwindling to only one, Lee could no longer say what she was fighting for—or against, for that matter.

"You remind me a little of her, actually." Thomas was still talking.

"What? Sorry? Remind you of whom?" Lee had zoned out of their conversation.

"Diane Keaton."

Lee snorted and gulped her lemonade. "Yeah, right."

"No, really, you do. I was trying to figure it out the other day and that's it."

"Maybe if I lost about forty pounds and actually had a hairstylist." She set her glass down and smoothed her napkin in her lap.

"Aw, come on. You're being too hard on yourself. You're a natural beauty."

Lee threw her head back and laughed. She wished she could be charmed so easily.

"No, I mean it," Thomas persisted. "There's something about you that's clever and funny and kind of flighty, too, like you're not taking life too seriously."

"Well, that would be a first. Most people tell me I have a tendency to take things too seriously, as if it's a character flaw." She was thinking maybe she'd start wearing white turtlenecks when she got back to Charleston, imitate the simple grace of Diane Keaton. But then she remembered all the small hands that pressed up against her through the course of a day. Hands demanding markers or Play-Doh or juice. No, white turtlenecks wouldn't hold up against the onslaught of all those messy fingers or the southern heat.

"Really?" he asked, surprised. "Maybe it's the setting—vacation and all—but I don't see it." He shook his head. "Nope, you might be tightly wound but not overly serious. They're two different things."

Lee nodded. She was getting confused now. She was fun and flighty but tightly wound?

"Anyway," Thomas was saying, "tell me more about Lacey. I know you told me some last time we were together, but I want to know more. What does she want to do after college?"

Lee rolled her eyes. "Don't get me started. She doesn't have the faintest idea."

"Funny, Tyra and Heather are polar opposites. Tyra wants to travel the world, maybe join the Peace Corps. She's the do-gooder, you know, the save-the-whales and hug-the-trees person in our family. Heather, on the other hand, can't wait to go to business school and make loads of money. Some days, I worry about her soul." He cast his eyes downward, thoughtful for a moment. "But you know what?" He trained his vision on the horizon. "I've decided I'm not going to worry anymore. I know, I know." He held up his hand as if anticipating Lee's objection. "I can guess what you're going to say. Easier said than done, right? But the girls are grown-up now. They can take it from here."

Lee sat back in her chair and considered this. She

wasn't sure she could let her grip loosen so completely on Lacey. Maybe it was different for fathers. They couldn't wait for their kids to turn into miniature adults, even friends, while most moms Lee knew wished that the snuggling pockets of childhood would last a few years longer. When Lacey had turned sixteen, Lee didn't think anything could be more tortuous than staying up till the wee hours of the night and awaiting the dance of the car's headlights in the driveway, her daughter home safe. But she'd been wrong. This betwixt and between, never knowing if she was dealing with Lacey the adult, or Lacey her little girl, made Lee's head spin.

"Wow, you sound so . . ." Lee searched for the word, then laughed. "Grown-up."

Thomas's eyes crinkled at the edges. "Do I? Well, it's a good front that I put up anyway. We'll see how it actually pans out." He leaned across the table and brushed something off her cheek. "Sauce," he explained. "Anyway, isn't it funny how a parent's love for a child is absolute? Nothing they do can shake it. It's a powerful thing." He fished a piece of ice from his glass and chewed on it, turning philosophical. "Spouses, though, well, they're a whole other story, aren't they? Love 'em one minute, hate 'em the next." His sentences slurred slightly, as if he were pulling a Magic Marker through the air, smudging his words.

"I wouldn't know," Lee offered. "I was never married to Lacey's dad."

"Oh." Thomas straightened in his chair. "I'm sorry, I guess I just assumed . . . something you said before made me think you were divorced."

"Nope. Single, never married. That's me." It rolled off Lee's tongue without a hint of irony. She'd grown so accustomed to identifying herself that way that it was almost second nature, an extra last name that she carried around with her. *Hi! I'm Lee Single-Never-Married. So nice to meet you!*

"Well, I can tell you, you've saved yourself a lot of heartache going the no-husband route," Thomas continued, unfazed. "Because one day you're head over heels in love, and the next, you're looking across the dinner table wondering who the heck is staring back at you." The sun had slipped almost completely below the horizon now, and hundreds of white lights strewn across the deck rails switched on like tiny stars.

Lee sighed into her glass. Why were relationships so hard? Abby and Sam were about the only ones she knew who were any good at it. They'd always been smooth and steady—straight-up vanilla. "You should talk to my friend Caroline. She's itching for a proposal from her boyfriend, who's also on the ship. You might get her to change her mind."

Thomas slapped the table with such force that their glasses trembled. "Tell her not to do it! Where is she? Let me talk to her."

Lee smiled warily. "I will." Meanwhile, her mind was

beginning to sift through options of how best to excuse herself. Thomas could keep talking all night, but did she have an obligation to stay? Should she walk him back to his cabin to make sure he didn't somehow manage to pitch himself overboard? Where did responsibility and liability lie when you accepted a seemingly innocent invitation to appetizers? She was weighing her choices when a peal of laughter followed by a clatter of shoes down the nearby stairwell shot a hole through the night.

"What the—" Thomas tried to swivel around, nearly falling off his chair in the process. From her vantage point, though, Lee could just make out the source of the noise—a group of teenagers coming down the stairs had tripped, toppling over one another. A few girls lay scattershot across the wooden deck, laughing, while the guys tried to help them up.

Lee hurried over. "Are you kids all right?" she called. When she drew closer, she thought she recognized the blond curtain of hair, the lanky legs in high heels, the sundress speckled with purple and white flowers. "Lacey?" She reached out a hand to pull her daughter up. "Are you okay?" She didn't recognize any of the other kids, probably Lacey's new friends from the ship.

"I'm fine, Mom," Lacey said, clearly embarrassed to have Lee there. But as Lee began to pull her up, Lacey squealed, "Ow, ouch! My foot!" Her daughter winced in pain as she hopped on one foot.

"Oh, honey. I think you might have sprained your

ankle. Here, wrap your arm around my shoulder," said Lee as she looped her own arm around Lacey's waist.

"Can I give you a hand there?" Thomas asked, approaching them. "Looks like you did quite a number on your ankle." When Lee glanced down, she could see that he was right. Lacey's ankle was already starting to swell beyond the strap of her sandal. Together, they helped her limp to a chair. "Let me get you some ice for that," he said before heading for the bar.

Lee reached for Lacey's foot in order to unbuckle her sandal. "Ouch, Mom. Be careful! That really hurts."

"I'm sorry, Lace. I'm trying to be gentle. I just want to get this sandal off before your foot really swells up."

"Well, can you stop it? Like immediately?"

In an instant, Lee was transported back to seventeen years ago, when she and Lacey would fight over the smallest things—picking up a toy, having the right color sippy cup, licking a crayon. *Don't you dare lick that crayon*, she'd warn, and the next thing she knew, the entire crayon, paper and wax, would disappear into Lacey's mouth and Lee would have to pry her little jaws open to fish it out. *Nonsense fights*, Lee had called them then. Well, here they were, years later, still arguing, only now it was about whether or not her daughter would allow her to remove her sandal.

"There," Lee said, finally managing to slide it off. Thomas, meanwhile, had returned with a bag of ice and gingerly laid it across Lacey's foot.

"You really should elevate it," he told her kindly.

"Okay," Lacey said. Lee watched as Thomas helpfully propped Lacey's foot up on a chair and rearranged the ice pack. Why was her daughter more obliging when a perfect stranger offered to help? Why did she refuse to let Lee in when all Lee wanted to do was make sure she was all right? Thomas ran Lacey's toes through a quick battery of tests that he claimed to know from a college football injury.

"Well, the good news is I don't think it's broken. But you've definitely got a nasty sprain. Might want to check in with the doctor on board. Pop a few Advil."

Lee was suddenly grateful for Thomas, who, even in his current state, was proving surprisingly proficient in defusing mother-daughter tension. "Thank you." She turned to him now. "You've been a huge help."

He straightened from his crouch, a little wobbly on his feet, and smiled. "You're welcome. Do you want me to help you ladies to the ship's infirmary?"

Lee exchanged looks with Lacey, who shook her head almost imperceptibly. "Oh, no, thank you. That won't be necessary. I think we girls will just sit here for a while before we try to venture any further."

Thomas shrugged and said, "All right, then. I guess I'll see you later. I'll check in with you tomorrow to see how the patient is doing."

"Thanks again," said Lee and smiled.

They watched him cross the deck and go back into

the ship's main lobby, leaving only the two of them. Lee pulled her chair up next to Lacey's.

"Wow, what a night, huh?" Lacey's head rested on Lee's shoulder, like old times. Her daughter's body shook, as if trying to hold back laughter. "What on earth is so funny?" Lee demanded. It took her a moment to realize that Lacey was crying. "Oh, honey," she said. "Does it hurt that much?"

Lacey lifted her head and swiped at her eyes. "No." She gulped. "Well, sort of. But, Mom," she said, "I have to tell you something."

Lee stared into her daughter's wet, beautiful brown eyes. "What is it?" she asked.

Lacey took a breath. "I think I might be pregnant."

16

~

The ceremony was at noon, but Abby couldn't honestly say who would show at this point. After the events of last night, the only people who seemed certain to appear were the minister and Sam. Both Lee and Caroline had promised to meet her at quarter past eleven by the cabstand, but, so far, there was no sign of them. Abby wanted the men and women to arrive separately at the beach. The element of surprise—Sam seeing her for the first time in her dress—was something that Abby still looked forward to, even after all these years. Given the current circumstances, however, her insistence on decorum seemed downright comical. A bomb might as well have exploded in their merry little band.

Last night, she'd bumped into Lee in the hallway as she helped a wobbly Lacey back to the cabin. From the looks of it, Lacey would be nursing a vicious swollen ankle this morning. Who knew if she could even walk on it? As for Caroline, she seemed to have gone completely AWOL. Aside from Lee's assurances that their friend was doing okay, Abby hadn't seen Caroline since she left on the back of a moped with Javier yesterday. Had Caroline read him the riot act? Abby wondered. Meanwhile, Chris, grounded in his cabin, had been granted release for this afternoon only.

Abby clenched her fists into tiny balls, recalling her son's bravado of last night. Sam had talked her down off the ledge eventually (well, maybe to the midpoint of the ledge), but really, had they taught their kids nothing? Chris knew better than to go off drinking. Sam excused it as a flight of fancy, nothing more than a teenager and his hormones getting the best of him. *Wouldn't you rather have him try this stuff out when we're around?* Sam had pressed. *I'd rather he not try* on *certain girls while he's at it,* Abby had huffed in reply.

But none of that mattered today. At least, that's what she told herself while she'd coaxed her hair into a bun earlier this morning in her cabin. She would not dwell on the events of the last twenty-four hours because today was supposed to be her day. *Their* day, if she were being precise. *The day that they'd all been sailing toward.* One afternoon to celebrate all that was good in their lives, to toast twenty years of marriage and friendship, and a family that, on most days, was pretty wonderful.

As she stood on the corner, holding a cab for the others, her mind flashed back to twenty years ago. Sam had fainted, and even here, standing on the steaming pavement in her white flip-flops, Abby could conjure up the dread she'd felt, like a phantom limb, when Caroline rushed out of the church to tell her the news. And yet, if Abby had learned anything during twenty years of marriage, it was that you adapted to the circumstances. You worked together to make things come together.

So, that was that. No matter what the universe threw at them today, she and Sam would reaffirm their vows. Let chaos reign—they had each other to hold on to. And even if rogue bully cells insisted on coursing through her veins, Abby Bingham was here today, fully alive and wearing a brand-new Badgley Mischka dress. *Every day is a gift,* she'd heard enough times, a sentiment that typically struck her as trite. But even she was beginning to see that there were shades of truth to such maxims.

In her hand she clasped the navy hankie that Caroline had given her so many years ago (something blue) and blotted her forehead, already wet with perspiration. The hankie, worn soft from years of her taking it out of her dresser drawer and fingering it like a talisman, was the one thing Abby had kept close by from her wedding day, whereas everything else—the dress, the dried flowers, a copy of the invitation—had either been donated to Goodwill or stuffed in a box somewhere in the attic. She liked to rub her finger across the nub of her monogrammed initials, AMB, as she had on her wedding day, a faithful reminder to stay calm.

"Just one more minute," she pleaded with the cabdriver, who didn't seem to care how long the meter ran before anyone stepped foot in his taxi. "They should be here very soon." She ducked her head into the cab for a brief moment, letting the cool air conditioner blast her skin, then pulled away and shut the door. If Lee and Caroline had any hope of seeing her, she needed to plant herself on the curb. A stray strand of hair broke free from her updo, and she tucked it behind an ear.

Despite the heat, it was a beautiful day for a wedding, the sun beaming down and a bright blue sky overhead. Weeks ago, when Abby had called the hotel to inquire about rates, the wedding coordinator had suggested an eight-piece band and a parquet dance floor set down on the sand. Abby had hurriedly explained that theirs would be a bare-bones affair, an anniversary celebration, not a wedding. *How about flowers?* the coordinator pressed. *Oh, we should be all set.* Abby thanked her. *I'll get some locally once we're on the island.* (The last thing she wanted to do was spend hundreds of dollars on flowers when they blanketed Bermuda.) She'd settled on a simple white tent and chairs on the beach with a celebratory lunch at the hotel to follow.

Abby performed a small twirl in her dress. "A breezy elegance" was how the saleswoman at Nordstrom had described the ivory chiffon, and Abby agreed. She was in love with this dress. No, *besotted* with it. Even more so than with the gown she'd worn twenty years ago. That dress, while elegant, had left angry red cinch marks across her waist, as if hinting that grace did not come naturally to her. Funny, Abby thought, how it had taken her twenty years to settle on a style that matched her very being.

At last, she spied Caroline hurrying down the ship's ramp in tight little steps, holding her dress above her flip-flops. Lee and Lacey trailed behind while Lacey limped along. Abby felt a smidge guilty about pulling Lacey off the ship with a sprained ankle. Nevertheless, everyone looked lovely. Caroline floated along in a diaphanous lime-colored dress that she'd had tailored to her specifications in New York. Lee wore a lavender sheath dress, and Lacey had chosen a simple sundress, the color of plums. Abby clapped her hands together appreciatively—the three of them could have been flowers in her bridal bouquet. Lee, the fragrant lilac; Lacey, the delicate periwinkle. And Caroline, the sturdy, green stem.

"Abby!" Caroline waved as they bustled toward her. "Sorry to keep you waiting." She leaned in to hug her. "You look gorgeous, like you're twenty-six all over again. That dress is to die for!"

"Why, thank you." Abby did another twirl and grinned. It was the first time her friends had seen her in it, and she felt as pretty as Julia Roberts. "It's kind of fun to be a bride at forty-six. Much less pressure."

"That, and you have a pretty good idea whether or not the marriage is going to last," Lee added. "That's helpful."

"Right!" Abby laughed. She stopped for a second, worried that maybe no one else in their gang was in the mood for levity, but her friends just smiled back at her, as if the calamities of the last twenty-four hours were but a dream. "You okay?" she asked Caroline quietly.

"You bet," Caroline said. "Couldn't be better." Abby was dying to know what was going on with Javier, but she didn't dare pry. She was afraid she might not like the answer. Instead, she focused on the obvious.

"Lacey, honey, how's your ankle? Are you okay to walk?"

"Of course, Aunt Abby. I wouldn't miss this." She lifted the hem of her dress to better show off her black walking boot.

"Oh, kiddo. That looks like it must hurt."

"It's not so bad," Lacey said with a shrug. "But doctor's orders that I have to wear this ugly boot. Sorry if it ruins your pictures."

"Don't be silly," Abby scolded. "I'm just relieved everyone could be here." She hesitated a moment. "Well, shall we get going, ladies?"

They piled into the car as best they could without wrinkling their dresses. Abby buckled herself into the front seat, excitement splashing over her. *Finally!* Everyone was here. She could feel the knots in her stomach untangling: all was forgiven. For the next few hours, everyone would be well behaved. They'd better be.

Abby stared out the window as the island whizzed

by. After all these years, she could honestly say that she loved Samuel L. Bingham even more than she had on that sultry summer day on the Cape. But it was a different kind of love, one that had mellowed over time, one that swam a smoother line. Abby had come to realize that they were well suited as a couple, two currents balancing each other out. They *complemented* each other. That was the word she'd searched for when trying to explain it to the boys the other day.

The girls were chattering in the backseat when Caroline suddenly called out, "Wait! Stop!" The car lurched forward, then slowed and thumped over to the road's shoulder. "Sorry, but I just spotted a flower stand back there. Abby, do you want to check it out?"

Abby twisted around for a better look. "Sure. Why not?" She'd been meaning to grab fresh flowers for the ceremony after all. The three of them made their way across the pebbled shoulder to the modest stand, which was thick with flowers stuffed into coffee cans. They reminded Abby of fireworks, only prettier.

"Oh, Abby, look at these." Lee thrust a sprig of purple blooms with tiny yellow centers into her hands.

"Gorgeous," Abby agreed. "They even match Lacey's dress. They're perfect."

"You'd like some Bermudiana?" the seller asked. He smiled, revealing a front tooth capped in gold. "Bermudiana is our national flower."

"Well, in that case," said Abby, "we'd better take a

whole bunch." She combed through the other green-
ery, landing on a cluster of tiny white flowers haloed by a
wreath of waxy green leaves. "How about this one? Fran-
gipani, I think?" The fruity scent was familiar.

"Yes, it smells like peaches, right?" he asked.

Caroline took it from Abby and inhaled. "Oh, my
gosh. That is the most delicious scent! We have to have
some of this, too. Our friend is getting married today,"
she said by way of explanation and passed him the flowers. "Could you make her a bouquet?"

The seller's eyes flickered to Abby for a moment,
and she felt compelled to explain. "For the second time.
Renewal of vows."

"Ah, different wedding, same husband, right?" he
said, as if reading her thoughts, and began to clip the
stems.

"That's right," Abby confirmed with a laugh. She
watched while he tenderly plucked the leaves and
arranged the flowers, as if filling in a paint-by-number.
It was no secret that the locals made most of their money
from tourism, but even that couldn't explain such genuine thoughtfulness, such care. A few minutes later, he
handed Abby a clutch of purple and ivory blooms. "It's
beautiful," she said, taking the arrangement from him.
"Thank you."

"And these are for your friends." He passed each a
small bouquet banded together with a thin green rib-
bon, nearly the same shade as Caroline's dress.

Lee pulled out a wad of bills from her beaded clutch to pay. "Thank you. They're perfect."

"Wait." He held up a finger. "One more thing." He plucked a lavender orchid and came out from behind the table. "May I?" He gestured toward Abby's hair.

Abby glanced at her friends and wondered if it might be best to let one of them place it but nodded anyway. With a simple sleight of hand, he gently glided the flower behind her left ear. "Now you are ready. A goddess." He nodded, pleased. "God bless."

"Okay, thank you!" Caroline called over her shoulder, suddenly in a hurry to get them back to the cab. "Hustle, hustle, ladies! We don't want to be late." Abby had completely forgotten about the time. She grinned as she cradled her bouquet in one arm and held up her dress with the other hand—Caroline still had a little bit of the wedding coordinator left in her after all.

17

Below the cliffs, Lacey could spy the shimmering beach, the white thumbprint of a tent set on the pink sand. *Thank God*, she whispered to herself. She was wedged against the car door and, at the moment, solely focused on keeping the contents of her stomach—a bagel and coffee—firmly in place. Tossing her cookies all over her periwinkle dress would be a decidedly uncool way to start the wedding. But Bermuda's winding roads, like a corkscrew, were pushing her luck. Also, her foot ached. Oh, and the fact that she might be growing *a baby* inside of her wasn't helping either.

If nothing else, Lacey knew she should be grateful for the distraction of the vows ceremony this afternoon. She was happy for her godparents—twenty years of putting up with someone else's crap and managing to stay in love was pretty remarkable. She wondered if she and Tyler would make it to twenty years, assuming they got married. When she'd texted him on the island yesterday, it had been only to say, *Having a great time but I miss you sooo much!* It was too complicated to delve into anything deeper in a text. Besides, she wasn't totally sure yet that she had any news to report.

Today's ceremony also meant that her mother couldn't scream at her for at least a few more hours. This morning, Lee had handed her a glass of water and the painkillers that the ship's doctor had prescribed. "Here, take these. They should help your foot."

Lacey had replayed last night in her mind a million times, but she still didn't know what her mom was thinking. After she'd confided that she might be pregnant, Lee's eyes had widened, and Lacey had thought she might slap her. But then she'd pulled Lacey into a hug. "Oh, Lacey, my dear, sweet girl," she'd said. A few minutes later, Lee had asked, "Are you sure?" and Lacey had shaken her head. "No. I'm late, though. Seven days—a whole week—and I've never been this late before."

One thing Lacey *was* sure of was this: she was grateful for what her mom *hadn't* said, like pointing out how Lacey had let her down or asking if Tyler was the guy or posing weird, unanswerable questions such as *How could you?* The only thought even more worrisome to Lacey than being pregnant was the idea of disappointing her mom. Lacey knew she wasn't always nice to Lee, but she also recognized that her mother had pretty much devoted her life to making sure Lacey turned out all right. It was a huge sacrifice—Lacey got that. In fact, she worried she couldn't possibly be as devoted a mom as Lee was.

Instead of saying what was surely darting through her mind at the time, though, Lee had sat with Lacey and watched as her foot ballooned. "Well, okay," her mom had said finally. "First things first. That ankle is just getting bigger, even with the ice, so let's have the ship's doctor take a look." And that was that.

Later, after the doctor wrapped her ankle and fitted her with the appropriate size walking boot, her mom had asked to speak to him privately in the hallway. Lacey suspected she was alerting him to the possibility that her daughter might be pregnant so he could take it into account if he were prescribing painkillers. Whatever he'd given her, the medicine had knocked Lacey out shortly after they retired to their cabin.

"We'll talk in the morning," Lee had said when she tucked Lacey in last night, like the little girl she had once been. "I don't want you to worry." But then they'd woken up late, and it had been a rush to make it into the shower and to the cab. There had been no time for a heart-to-heart.

"We'll figure everything out after the ceremony," her mom had whispered as they left the ship this morning. Lacey was surprised. She'd been expecting Lee to strangle her when she told her the news last night. At least for the moment, she supposed, they could both pretend it wasn't real. Once Lacey took the pregnancy test that the doctor had given her mom last night, though, that all very well could change. Both she and Lee had agreed: Lacey would take the test after Abby's ceremony.

When they pulled up to the beach, Lee climbed out first and came around to her side to help. "Here, wrap your arm around me," she coached, and Lacey hoisted herself out of the car, shifting her weight onto her mom's frame. Slowly, they followed Abby and Caroline down to the beach. A short, stocky man, a white collar circling his neck, was waiting for them under the tent. Already, the sun felt blistering hot on Lacey's bare shoulders.

The minister stepped out of the shade to greet them. "Well, hello! Abby, you're absolutely glowing. And your friends are as well! But goodness, what happened to you?" He pointed to Lacey's black boot.

Lacey smiled.

"Our girl had a small injury yesterday. Twisted her ankle," Abby explained. "But she's a trooper. She insisted on still coming."

"I'd say so," said the chaplain. "Well, good effort by you!"

"Is it okay if we sit till the others get here?" Abby asked.

"Oh, of course! Sorry. Here let me grab you a chair." He carried a folding chair over to Lacey and helped her get settled comfortably before checking his watch. "Shouldn't be much longer till your other half arrives. It's quarter to the hour."

"Is it crazy that I just got goose bumps?" Abby shivered in the heat.

The chaplain chuckled. "Not at all. I've had people tell me that a renewal of vows can be even more nerve-racking than the wedding itself."

"Oh, that reminds me." Abby pulled out a creased sheet of paper from her purse and handed it to Caroline. "I was hoping you could read this poem for the ceremony? Sorry not to get it to you sooner. I gave Lee's to her last night, but when I stopped by your room, no one was home."

Caroline smiled weakly and took it from her. She'd been in her cabin when Abby knocked last night but hadn't had the courage to answer. "Of course. What a nice idea."

Just then, the sound of a car horn cut through the air. When Caroline turned, she saw all the men—Sam, Chris, Ryan, and Javier—heading toward them. "Woo-hoo!" Sam called out, jogging down the beach. "Where's my beautiful bride?"

A few sunbathers turned to look, wondering what all the commotion was about. When Sam reached Abby, he pulled her in for a kiss.

"Hey, you're not supposed to kiss the bride until after the vows!" She swatted at him.

"Aww, c'mon. I couldn't help myself." He took a step back. "You look stunning."

Abby beamed. "You're not so bad yourself." It was

true, Caroline thought. Sam looked gallant in his khaki pants, white linen shirt, and pink paisley tie. Javier and the boys were similarly dressed, but with blue ties.

"And you ladies are visions as well," Sam said, as if remembering his manners. "Geez, Lacey, a boot and everything, huh? I heard about your tumble last night. Are you feeling okay?"

Lacey waved her hand in the air. She *so* did not want to be the center of attention right now. "I'm fine. Really. Just a stupid trip." She could feel herself blushing. "Everyone looks great. Like a J. Crew ad."

"You're right, Lacey," said Caroline with a laugh. "They're dashing, aren't they?" She rested her hand on Sam's arm, not Javier's. Caroline was surprised, frankly, that Javier had even dared to show up. After their talk yesterday, she was pretty certain that their relationship was on hiatus. But she was not about to spoil the day for Sam and Abby. If Javier was so afraid of marriage, then let him be afraid by himself. She thought back to his response in their cabin yesterday when she'd told him she wanted what Abby and Sam had: "But why do we need to get married if we're perfectly happy as we are?" he'd asked.

"But that's just it, isn't it?" Caroline had pressed. She *wasn't* happy as they were and she'd told him as much. "I want to be *married* to you, Javier. I want to spend the rest of my life with you. If you don't feel the same way, then you should tell me." To which he'd replied, "But I do feel the same way. You know this. I just don't need a ring or a piece of paper to confirm it."

Caroline's eyes had welled with tears. "No, Javier, I don't know it. In fact, since the whole idea of getting married seems to terrify you so much, I can only conclude that you don't want to be married. At least not to me." It dawned on her that there had been no proposal on the cruise *because there was no ring*. The realization had hit her like a sock to the stomach.

Caroline felt a twist of humiliation, remembering how, a few weeks before the cruise, she'd pointed out a ring that she thought was exquisite. It was a pleasant summer evening and she'd suggested the two of them walk home from dinner rather than hail a cab. Caroline had known full well that their stroll would take them past the Tiffany's window, where she'd spied the ring earlier that day. When Javier acted uninterested, she'd assumed he was being coy. Now she understood the awful truth—he was indifferent.

They were at an impasse. Caroline couldn't see her way around it. After their argument, Javier had left the cabin, and Caroline wasn't sure where he had gone, or where he had slept last night. She didn't care. Her eyes began to fill again, but she swiped at them with a tissue she'd brought for Abby. No, she was not going to think about it for the next few hours. *Absolutely not.* She'd promised herself. For Abby and Sam's sake. How hard could it be to fake happiness for a few hours?

"Well, shall we?" the minister asked, startling them all, as if they'd forgotten he was there.

"Absolutely," Sam said. "I couldn't be more certain than I was twenty years ago that I want to marry this woman today."

A wide smile played across Abby's face as she clasped Sam's hand and joined the minister up front, the others settling into their chairs. Caroline watched while the minister patted his broad, pink forehead with a handkerchief, then cleared his throat.

"Friends and family," he began. "We are gathered here today . . ." Caroline only half listened despite her best attempts to focus. It was uncomfortably hot, and Javier had sat down right next to her. She didn't know what he was thinking. When Abby peered over at her, she beamed back the widest smile she could muster. Luckily, the minister's homily was short, and then Lee rose to read a poem entitled "How Falling in Love Is Like Owning a Dog," by Taylor Mali. It was funny, sweet, and perfectly suited to the occasion.

When it was Caroline's turn, she did her best to recite the stanzas of her poem with genuine feeling, but a few words, like *love* and *commitment*, caught in her throat. She sat back down without so much as casting a glance Javier's way.

"Sam, I believe you have some words you wanted to share with Abby?" the minister asked.

"Yes." Sam turned to Abby and took her hand. "Abigail Bingham, you are the girl I still want to wake up with every morning, the woman who surprises me each day with her good heart, and the bride who makes me laugh. There is no one else in this crazy world whom I'd rather hold at the end of the day than you. I love you. And with this ring, I hereby reaffirm my love for and commitment to you." He slid a sparkling band of tiny diamonds on her ring finger.

Then it was Abby's turn. "Samuel Bingham, you've had my heart ever since the day you took me out for Chinese food on our first date. I love you. I love the family we've built together." Her voice cracked. "May this ring be a further testament of my abiding love." She slid the ring on over his knuckle.

There was a beat of silence before the minister declared, "I now pronounce you man and wife! You may kiss the bride."

Sam planted a kiss on Abby's lips, and there was a shower of applause. Caroline, trying to hide her own emotions, jumped up to congratulate them, while Lee and Lacey gathered around to admire the ring. "It's gorgeous," Lee exclaimed, holding Abby's hand up to better let the ring sparkle in the sunlight.

"Okay, y'all!" Abby called out after a few minutes. "Let's head to the Reefs to celebrate!"

Caroline was secretly relieved; it was much too hot to stay on the beach any longer. Her dress was plastered to her body with sweat, and she couldn't wait to step into air-conditioned cool and get as far away from Javier as possible, maybe even in an entirely different room. Or hemisphere. Yes, another hemisphere would be good. She turned to join Lee and Lacey. Their plan was to get Lacey into a cab for the short ride to the hotel, but Sam stopped them.

"Sorry, Abby, but just one second before we do that," he said, holding up a finger. "I think we forgot something." *Oh, good Lord,* Caroline almost said aloud. She might faint if they didn't get into air-conditioning soon.

Abby turned, confused. "What is it?"

"Javier?" Sam asked. "Did you want to say something?"

Caroline's stomach dipped. *Oh, no.* Javier was actually going to apologize right here in front of all her friends? She didn't think she could bear it. It would just deepen her humiliation to make it public. *Poor Caroline,* they'd say. Javier was about to ruin Sam and Abby's perfect day. Caroline glanced around, panicked, looking for an imaginary escape hatch that she could disappear into.

"Yeah, thanks, buddy." Javier's voice warbled as he turned toward her.

Caroline shook her head, as if to signal to Javier, *No, not now. Please don't spoil this lovely day. You can apologize back in our room.* But as she attempted to silently convey all these thoughts to Javier, he approached her—and got down on bended knee. He reached for her hand, and Caroline felt the color drain from her face.

"Caroline Canton," Javier began. "I have loved you

since the first day I met you among those truly awful paintings." A small laugh escaped from her lips, despite herself. "No other woman I know carries herself with such grace and strength." Caroline bit her lip. "And, while I know you've been angry with me the past twenty-four hours, furious, actually—" He paused and shook his head. "I hope you'll forgive me. I really wanted to surprise you."

She heard Abby say, "Oh my goodness."

"Your friends' strong marriage is a testament to how wonderful such a union can be, and I hope that one day, we, too, will share our twentieth wedding anniversary together." Javier paused to clear his throat, then pulled a velvet box from his pocket. When he cracked it open, there was the ring she'd pointed out in the window at Tiffany's. "I guess what I'm asking is this: Caroline Canton, will you marry me?"

Caroline felt an entire ocean of emotions wash over her, and her knees buckled ever so slightly. She took a breath while she steadied herself.

"Javier Mendez," she said. "How dare you trick me into being angry with you!" She paused. "I'm so mad at you!" She stopped, breathed, and corrected herself. "*Was* so mad at you. Don't *ever* do that again." She noticed he was still looking at her, waiting. Her lips slowly parted into a smile. "And yes. Of course, I'll marry you!"

There was a collective exhale, and Abby squealed, "Hooray!" She pulled Caroline into a hug before Javier could even slide the ring onto her finger.

"Excuse me, but can a guy get a little room to put the ring on?" he asked.

Abby laughed and stepped out of the way. "I'm sorry, Javier. Of course you can. Have at it." They all watched while he guided it on, a perfect fit. He stood up and threw his arms around Caroline.

"I love you," he whispered. "I hope you'll forgive me for tricking you."

"No, I'm sorry," Caroline said now. "I was just so sure it was over."

"Never," Javier said. "I would never do that to you. I want you by my side always." He cupped her face in his hands and kissed her.

"Gosh, Caroline, you really made us sweat that one out," Sam said. "For a minute there, I thought you were going to say no."

"After what he put me through?" Caroline said. "Don't think I didn't consider it," she joked. "So who else was in on Javier's little plan?"

Abby shook her head. "Not a clue."

"Me either," said Lee. Everyone turned to Sam.

Sam shrugged. "Well, I only knew as of last night. Javier and I shared a couple of beers—after Caroline kicked him out of his room—and he spilled the beans. He wanted to make sure I wouldn't mind if he proposed right after our ceremony." Sam slapped Javier on the back. "I appreciated that, man."

Abby was glowing. "Good on you, Javier."

He grinned. "You know, I've had that ring locked away in the ship's safe ever since we set sail from Boston."

"You're kidding," said Caroline. She couldn't believe that he'd pulled off the entire proposal without even dropping a hint. Usually Caroline was good at reading other people. Well, she'd missed every single clue when it came to her own heart.

"You know," the minister piped up. "I hate to point out the obvious, but you do have a chaplain on hand." Everyone turned to him, considering his words.

"Oh," Caroline said, seemingly taken aback. "You mean—"

Abby clapped her hands together. "Caroline! You could get married right here. Right now."

Caroline and Javier exchanged glances, but Caroline shook her head. "Oh, no, we couldn't. Not right now. That's way too much excitement for one day. Plus, you know me." She shrugged. "I need to *plan* this thing. And, today is your day."

There was a pause while everyone waited. "Fine," said Abby finally. "But I almost forgot: we're not leaving this beach till we have some pictures. I want to freeze this day in my mind for as long as possible."

"Me, too," said Caroline and took her friend's hand as they walked toward the aquamarine water, the heat no longer bothering her at all.

18

They made it back to the ship with barely any time to spare. The wedding luncheon had been over-the-top with lobsters as big as dinner plates, fresh asparagus, and potatoes whipped into miniature volcanoes. For dessert, there was a strawberry lemon cake edged with papayas. Everyone watched while Sam stuffed a piece of cake into Abby's mouth, smearing frosting across her cheeks, and Abby grinned like a young bride all over again. The entire afternoon had been a page right out of a fairy tale. An island wedding, a beachfront proposal, the man and the friends she loved most in the world by her side. A sparkling ring not just on Abby's finger but on Caroline's own.

Never in a million years, especially after their fight, did Caroline imagine that she would be sitting here, on the tiny slip of a balcony, with her fiancé. *Her fiancé!* Just the thought of it made her want to shout it to the passengers who raced down below, trying to catch the ship in time for the five o'clock sail away. She watched while one couple trotted along the sidewalk, their arms weighted down with packages. In the eighty-degree heat and humidity, it felt like a mile. Caroline knew. She and Javier had just sprinted it themselves, fueled by pure adrenaline. That and the shouts of passengers already on board, who cheered on any latecomers from the top deck.

"It's so beautiful here. I'm not sure I can go back," Caroline said. Regal palm trees dotted the shoreline. On the point of the island, two ancient military forts stood sentinel as the distant sky began to turn a dusty rose. It was a gorgeous evening. After cooling off in the shower, Caroline had changed into a light sundress. Javier wore only a pair of shorts. A bottle of champagne that they'd ordered up for the sail off sat on a table with two glasses between them.

Javier nodded. "I know what you mean. Maybe we could both work remotely? Would that be possible? I'm sure there are plenty of fine island wines. And you could start up your own magazine here." He poured the champagne, already uncorked, and they watched it fizz up over the edges of their glasses before taking a sip.

"Mmm . . ." Caroline closed her eyes and imagined the possibilities. "Wouldn't that be nice. A girl can dream, right? I'm sure we're not the first people to plot their return to the island."

"No reason not to consider it at least. Maybe in a few years from now," Javier said. Her eyes flickered open as she smiled. She liked that Javier thought in big arcs of time, that, in his view, things were seldom impossible, just perhaps not immediate. Unlike her, he was patient, accustomed to waiting. Maybe it had to do with his job—a person had to wait years for a good wine to age, after all. But she suspected it had more to do with the manner in which he'd grown up. His childhood, she knew, had been difficult, his mother cleaning hotel rooms to support him and his sister. But then he'd been accepted at Columbia, and, from there, his life had blossomed.

At *Glossy*, Caroline was accustomed to people doing her bidding. The quick fix, the instant gratification, that's what fueled the magazine industry. What was hot last month was already old news by the next, and she'd trained her brain to think accordingly. Expect immediate results or else toss the product, the story out. In that way, she and Javier were a good match. Opposites. *What was it Abby had said about her marriage to Sam? That they balanced each other out.* Caroline wanted that, a counterbalance. At last, it seemed she had it. If only her parents were around to see it, life would be close to perfect.

"So, tell me the truth," Javier said. He was rubbing the inside arch of her right foot, her arches being where all the tension of the last few days seemed to have settled. "Were you really surprised?"

Caroline threw her head back and closed her eyes, the world spinning for a moment. "I don't think I've ever been so surprised in my entire life," she said. "Isn't it strange how I hated you one minute and loved you the next?"

Javier's eyes widened. "Really? You *hated* me?"

Caroline shook her head. "*Hate*'s probably too strong a word. But I was really, really mad at you. I couldn't believe that you were giving me such a hard time about wanting to get married. You made me feel desperate. I don't like feeling desperate."

"You? Desperate? Ha. Never." He set her right foot down and started in on the left. Caroline moaned in pleasure as his thumbs worked their way along the inner arch. "Exactly the opposite. You're a challenge. I had to do some of my best acting, pretending that marriage was such a chore. Such drudgery," he said.

"Well, I'd say you're Hollywood bound, because I bought your performance one hundred percent." He leaned over and kissed her, his lips grazing hers. They felt chapped from the sun.

"But that's exactly how it was supposed to go," he chided. "Still, it was hard to sleep last night, knowing that you were fuming at me."

"But you deserved it! Where *did* you sleep, by the way?"

He shrugged and set down her foot gently. "The library has some very comfortable couches. But I hope one night of agony was worth it for a day of bliss."

Caroline cocked her head. "Just one day? I thought I'd signed up for a lifetime."

"My mistake. Yes, a lifetime of bliss." Javier grinned at her. "Though I can't say you get the same accolades for acting."

"Why? Was it that obvious I wanted a proposal?"

He broke out laughing. "I'm not sure *obvious* is a strong enough word. Especially considering your behavior at the Swizzle Stick." Caroline groaned, both not wanting to hear it and hungry for details through his eyes. "You kept glancing at my pockets every few minutes," Javier continued, amused. "And you kept steering the conversation back to Abby and Sam, as if it would somehow jog my memory that marriage was a topic you were open to."

"Yeah, I couldn't figure out why you were being so dense," she said. He reached out to stroke her cheek with his thumb.

"You are so lovely," he said quietly. "I can't believe I'll get to call you my wife."

Caroline felt tears prick her eyes. How was it that the man knew exactly what to say at precisely the right moment?

He leaned in toward her, took the flute of champagne from her hands, and set it on the table. "Care to consummate the proposal?"

Caroline laughed. "Oh, really? I thought one only consummates the marriage."

Javier shook his head. "Different laws in Bermuda." He checked his watch. "And by my count, we have about fifteen minutes before we're out of Bermuda territory completely."

She smiled at him, a girl with nothing better to do.

"In that case, we'd better hurry," she said.

Lee hung by the railing on the top deck and watched the last cruisers race to catch the boat. She was trying to make sense of the past twenty-four hours that had left her feeling as if she'd been whipped around in a hurricane. Abby and Sam had renewed their vows. Caroline and Javier were engaged. Everyone was in a wonderful mood except for Lee. Because what did she have to celebrate, really? She was still alone, her daughter was limping around on a sprained ankle, and Lacey might have gotten herself pregnant—in college! Lee loved babies as much as the next person, but she wasn't ready to be a grandmother so soon, not when Lacey still had her entire future ahead of her.

Lee tried to determine the precise moment when she'd led her daughter astray. She'd warned Lacey how easy it was to get pregnant if she wasn't careful. In this day and age, she didn't really expect her daughter to abstain from sex in college, but she'd certainly counted on her to be smart about it. For Lacey's entire life, Lee had tried to prepare her daughter to be self-sufficient, to make good decisions. It struck Lee as one of the key jobs of parenting: ensuring that your children could survive on their own by the time they left the nest.

When Lacey had stunned her with the news last night, Lee had wanted to shout, "How could you!" Lacey knew how important it was to get her degree and find a job before falling for some random boy. *I told you so,* Lee had thought. *I told you that Tyler boy was bad news. I told you to focus on your schoolwork. How could you be so irresponsible?* She was furious that Lacey had put herself in this mess, that her daughter was setting herself up to repeat Lee's very own past. Every one of those uncharitable thoughts (and more) had passed through Lee's mind. And then—she'd surprised herself by pulling her daughter into a hug.

Because as angry as she was at Lacey, she couldn't bring herself to yell at her sweet girl when she'd looked into her eyes, so frightened, so alone.

Lee tried to talk herself through the different scenarios now. Maybe Lacey really was just late, and they could all go back to their ordinary lives, uneventful but safe. It was easy enough to find out. Lee had stuffed the pregnancy test from the doctor into her bag last night, out of sight, out of mind till after the vows ceremony. But now there was no more postponing it. When Lacey got back to the cabin (she'd gone to grab an ice cream cone with the boys), she was going to take the test. Mother and daughter had agreed that it made the most sense to find out. Either they could stop worrying, or they would have to start planning.

Lee watched the water ripple down below as the ship prepared for the sail off. Well, she thought, she'd screwed things up royally. She should have insisted that Lacey attend a college closer to home, maybe one where she could live at home and Lee could keep an eye on her. There were plenty of good schools around Charleston. Why on earth had she encouraged her daughter to look wherever she wanted? At the very least, she might have visited Lacey more often up in Maine. What if Lacey had been so homesick that she'd flung herself into a boy's arms out of desperation?

Or, was it possible that this was just straight-up rebellion? Was this Lacey's way of giving Lee the middle finger for raising her as a single mom? That seemed harsh, though, even for Lacey. Lee remembered reading in a parenting book that the closer you were to your children, the harder it was to separate when they went off to college. But Lee wouldn't have traded the bond she'd shared with her daughter all these years for anything. Lacey was her one true love. No one else.

Maybe that was too much love for a little girl to carry around, an albatross. But Lee didn't know any other way. She was loyal to a fault. If you were under attack, Lee was the person you wanted in your corner. And up until about twenty-four hours ago, Lee had always assumed that if you were a daughter, Lee was the person you'd want for a mom.

She would do almost anything for her girl. Even toss aside the possibility of love for herself. Because, yes, there'd been someone else in her life when Lacey was younger. A man named Charles, who'd made Lee feel as if she was the only person in the world. But that had been the problem—Charles hadn't wanted children, and Lee was a package deal. She came with Lacey, take it or leave it. She could never understand how Charles couldn't fall in love with her sweet child. Maybe he'd never really loved Lee in the first place. But how Lee had loved him! Probably a little too much. A bit too desperately.

Oh, she thought now with a ping of recognition. That was what Lacey had been trying to tell her about Tyler. Lee had almost forgotten the feeling.

As the ship pulled away and the silhouette of the island grew fainter, a sense of melancholy splashed over her, a feeling that she might have left something important behind. She ran her hands over her stomach and realized she was still wearing her lavender dress. It was time to get changed, time to meet Lacey back in the cabin. One thing Lee was sure of, though: she wasn't giving up on parenthood now. Not even close. She would steer Lacey through this, one way or another. They would get through it together, just as they had everything else in life.

19

⌒

When Lee stepped into the cabin, Lacey was already there, waiting.

"Hi, Mom," she said from her perch on the bed.

"Hi, honey. How's the ankle?"

"A little better, I think." Lacey began to peel back the Velcro strips on her walking boot. "It will feel good to get this thing off, though."

"I'll bet." Lee went to help her with the straps, then gently slid off the boot. "Oh, you poor kiddo," she said, when she saw Lacey's ankle. While the swelling had subsided, the foot had turned a deep, ugly purple. "That still looks pretty painful."

Lacey shrugged. "Maybe the painkillers are helping. Speaking of which, isn't it time for another?"

Lee checked her watch. "Righto. Six o'clock. You're due." She fetched a glass of water and a pill from the bathroom. On the bathroom counter sat the pregnancy test box.

"Here." She handed Lacey the glass and pill. "Bottoms up." She watched while her daughter swallowed, then drained the rest of the water.

"Thanks." Lacey handed the glass back. "I cannot wait to get out of this dress. Can you help me?"

"Of course." It was a struggle to get up without the ankle brace, but Lacey managed an awkward half stand while Lee unzipped the dress and pulled it over her head. She tossed the dress in the dry cleaner bag and grabbed Lacey a white robe from the bathroom. When she sat down on the bed, an awkward silence hung between them as they waited to see who would talk first. Lee reminded herself that she was the parent here, the responsible adult. It was up to her to get Lacey through this moment—and whatever might follow.

"So," she began and stopped.

"So." Lacey turned. Her eyes were wide with fear. "I guess this is the moment of truth, huh?"

"Oh, Lace." Lee pulled her daughter into a hug and squeezed. "It's all going to be okay, no matter what that little test says. If it's negative, then we'll keep living our lives just like we have been. If there's a plus sign, well, we'll deal with that, too. Together." She let go and combed a strand of loose hair around her daughter's ear. Lee felt as if she were looking into the face of four-year-old Lacey all over again, the little girl who would ask her mom to check under the bed for monsters each night. That child had been so afraid of being alone that

Lee had finally capitulated and moved Lacey's bed back into her bedroom. They'd shared a bedroom until Lacey turned thirteen.

Lacey nodded, pulled her lips into a line, then sniffed. "I know. Thanks. It's just, this is really hard." She nodded again, as if trying to reassure herself, though her eyes were wet with tears. "I just wish I hadn't been so stupid!"

Lee was stunned by the sudden torque toward anger. She knew Lacey was afraid, but she also suspected her daughter might secretly *want* a baby. Lee had been talking herself through this distinct possibility for the last twenty-four hours. Lacey was in love with Tyler. Lee tried to remind herself what that felt like. What she'd felt for Charles all those years ago. What worried her most, perhaps, was how Tyler would react if Lacey really were pregnant. Would he step up and support her—or would he flee? Lee fretted that her daughter might not like the answer.

But Lee had had an entire day to do some soul-searching, and, in the end, she'd concluded that she was in no place to judge. Lee, herself, had gotten pregnant with Lacey around the same age, and with a total stranger. True, Lee had graduated college by then, but were things really so different? Her own mother couldn't have been thrilled to learn that she'd be a grandmother at such a young age, and yet she'd never let on to Lee. Lee's mom had adored Lacey as if she were her own daughter. If need be, Lee knew in her heart that she would feel the same way about any child Lacey might have.

She'd promised herself that she wouldn't let her own hopes for Lacey's future cloud her response, whatever the test result. She would follow Lacey's lead. If Lacey were pregnant and wanted to keep the baby, Lee would support her. One hundred percent. If she felt differently, Lee would listen to that, too. She was here to hold her daughter up, not to judge or scold. Because, really, wasn't that the ultimate test of parenthood? To be able to show your children love even during the times when your instincts told you to scream, when it was the hardest of all to love them? That seemed to Lee the very essence of being a parent.

"Hey," Lee counseled her daughter now. "Don't be so hard on yourself. Remember, there's another person involved in all this."

"Pfft, yeah," Lacey said. "Like he even has to deal with any of it. He's got it easy. Tyler has no clue what's going on right now."

Lee nodded. "True, but eventually he will, don't you think? One way or the other?"

Lacey met her gaze. "Yeah, I'm definitely telling him regardless. It's not fair that he isn't here with me, worrying."

"Oh, honey," Lee said. "Haven't I taught you anything? Life's hardly ever fair." She paused. "Hey, there is something I want to share with you before you go in there and take that test."

"Yeah?" Lacey looked at her with big, soulful eyes.

"I know you think I've never been in love, Lace." She paused. "But I have. Not with your dad. But with another man who came into our lives later. You were still little, so you wouldn't remember him. His name was Charles." Here Lee felt her throat tightening. "He was a good man, Lacey. A really good man. We only dated for a year, but I wanted to marry him." She nodded as she revealed her one secret.

"What happened?"

Lee shrugged. "He didn't want to marry me. It was as simple as that. He had big plans. He was going to save the world, run for Congress, maybe be president one day."

Lacey's eyes grew huge. "Did he? I mean run for president?"

"No." Lee laughed. "Not even close. But he is a mayor, I think. Last I checked. That much I can tell you."

Lacey gripped her arm. "Who is it?"

Lee shook her head. "No way. I'm not telling you this so you can track him down." She sighed and her eyes locked with Lacey's. "I'm telling you so that you understand I *know* what it feels like to be in love. I also know what it feels like to get your heart broken. I get it, Lacey. I was young once, too."

"Wow." Lacey was quiet for a moment. "Can I ask you something?"

"Sure, shoot," said Lee.

"Why didn't it work out? I mean, if you loved each other?"

Lee had been bracing herself for this question. She couldn't tell Lacey that Charles thought being married to a woman who'd had a child out of wedlock might hurt his chances in public office. That's how shallow he'd been! But she hadn't realized it till it was too late. Why? *Because she'd been in love.* She patted Lacey's hand now.

"I think, Lace, he wanted to save the world. He had his sights set on big things. Turned out, he just didn't want to save me."

"I'm sorry," Lacey said quietly. "That really stinks."

Lee clucked her tongue. "Well, that's life, isn't it? Sometimes things work out, and sometimes they don't." She rested a hand on Lacey's knee. "So, do you think you're ready?"

Lacey took a deep breath. "Yeah, I'm as ready as I'll ever be."

Lee nodded. "Good. Do you need any help?"

Lacey shook her head. "No, I think I've got this part. If you wouldn't mind hanging out, though?"

"You know I'm here," Lee said. "I have the timer." She waved her phone in the air. "You just say the word."

Lacey hobbled into the bathroom and shut the door. After a few minutes, she called out, "Okay, Mom, ready."

Lee hit the timer button on her phone and held her

242

breath. *Oh please*, she prayed, *oh please, oh please*, although she wasn't sure what she was praying for exactly. The next three minutes might have been the longest of her life, until finally, at last, Lee could shout, "Time! Three minutes." She waited. "Lacey?"

When the bathroom door opened, she tried to read her daughter's face, but it was blank. Lacey held up the stick in her hand. And then a faint smile crossed her lips. "It's negative, Mom," she said. "I'm not pregnant."

"Oh, honey," Lee said, her voice threaded through with emotion, and went to hold her daughter tight.

20

~~

Abby was having trouble sleeping again. The doctor had given her a bottle of sleeping pills, but when they didn't help, he'd prescribed an antianxiety medication, a tiny blue pill to calm her nerves and pave the path to sleep. Because that was the real trouble: as soon as she lay down, her mind started spinning webs of worry. She was running on pure adrenaline after today's ceremony and Caroline's news. Earlier, when Caroline had come knocking on her door pleading with her to come out for the night—*C'mon, Abby, we have to celebrate more! Girls' night!*—Abby had bowed out, saying she was going to put her feet up, read a good book.

But the truth was, now that the anniversary celebration was over, Abby had bigger things to worry about. She and Sam had agreed not to say anything about her diagnosis until after the ceremony, but when was the right time? Tomorrow? Over brunch? Or maybe she was better off not telling her roommates until they were back in Boston. Everyone was having such a good time, she didn't want to spoil the fun. Perhaps she could arrange a dinner in the North End? But, no, that was a cop-out, and her roommates had to catch flights home. At some point, she'd have to tell the boys, too. They were beginning to shoot her curious looks whenever she grew absentminded. Another delightful side effect of the pills.

"Is it just my imagination, or is the boat rocking even more now?" she asked in the dark. Sam, sound asleep, snored peacefully through each dip and shudder. A few hours after setting sail from Bermuda, they'd hit some rough sea. *Nothing to worry about,* the captain had reassured the passengers over the intercom that boomed into their cabins. *There's some choppy water ahead, so we're going to close the pool and the cafeteria for a few hours until we reach smoother sailing.* Aside from a few off-balance moments, the ship's motion hadn't much bothered her on the sail down, but now with each new swell, a wave of nausea climbed in her throat. The little magnetic bracelets that were supposed to pinpoint delicate pressure points on her wrists were of absolutely no help. Abby tugged them off and threw them across the room. It occurred to her that she might need to knock on Caroline's door and hijack her Dramamine pills.

She shifted onto her side, listening to the bathroom door shimmy in its frame with each rock of the boat. Somewhere in the distance a foghorn blew. *Back and forth, back and forth.* It felt as if little men were tugging at her sheets. The clock on the bedside table glowed 2:16 A.M. *What was the use?* She pushed back the sheets, climbed out of bed, and crossed to the balcony window, where huge swells—at least three feet tall—slammed the side of the ship. The moonlight sliced through the dark waves, making the entire ocean resemble an eerie lunar landscape. Maybe the cafeteria had reopened and she could get some soda or seltzer water. At the very least, it might help settle her stomach.

Abby pulled on a pair of shorts and combed her hair with her fingers. When she headed for the door, the ship dipped sideways, sending her scrambling like a beetle. Sam groaned and rolled over. She flung open the door and quickly reached for the hallway railing. Though she hadn't given the railings a second thought earlier, she was grateful for them now. Gingerly, she made her way along the corridor, sidestepping an abandoned tray of steak and fries.

When she reached the cafeteria, a Closed Until Further Notice sign dangled from the buffet line, but the sitting area at the front, where guests could help themselves to drinks, remained open. A few passengers appeared to be in even worse shape than she was. One young couple tried to calm their screaming baby, while an older woman sat at a table with her head in her hands, moaning with each new tilt of the ship.

Abby made her way to the soda dispenser and filled a cup with ginger ale. In a far corner at the back, she found a table and sat down, willing her stomach to settle. If this was what cruising was really like, then this would be her last sail. Everyone had promised her the high seas couldn't roll a ship like the *Bermuda Breeze*, unless they came with hurricane-force winds, but what they were experiencing now was worse than anything she could have imagined. When she glanced up toward the front, she was surprised to see a familiar face. Javier. Abby waved in half greeting.

"This is something else, isn't it?" he asked as he came over, wobbling slightly as he walked. "How're you feeling?"

"Ugh. Awful. I didn't think I got seasick." She sipped her tepid soda. "Apparently, I do. Where's Caroline?"

"Back in the room, feeling miserable. I offered to get her some juice." Javier sat down and stared out the window behind her. "Do you think we're headed into a hurricane?"

"Hah. Don't even joke about it. They'd have to share something like that with us, right? At least I'd hope so."

Javier shrugged. "Maybe. Maybe not. Probably best not to stir up panic among the guests."

"Well, if it's any consolation," Abby said, "I'm not leaving this world because of a chance encounter with a hurricane."

Javier shot her an amused look. "Do you know something I don't?" he asked.

At that moment, the ship lurched violently to the

right, and her glass slid helter-skelter across the table. Javier caught it before it tumbled off.

"Good catch!" Her own hands white-knuckled the tabletop.

"Please," the moaning passenger begged. "Please get me back to Boston."

"Poor woman," Abby whispered. "I wish there were something we could do for her."

"Unfortunately," Javier said, "I think she has to soldier through it like the rest of us. But tell me again. How do you know you won't die in a hurricane?" A smile played across his lips, as if Abby had proposed they play a game.

She shrugged. "I guess I don't really, but I'm pretty sure when I die it will be of natural causes."

"And you know this because?" He cocked an eyebrow. "Because you've seen a fortune-teller?"

Abby shook her head. "More like a doctor. An oncologist."

Something—was it surprise? confusion? affection?—flickered across Javier's face. He frowned. "I'm sorry. An oncologist?"

Abby nodded. "Turns out I have leukemia." She waited a beat. "Which, by the way, no one on this ship knows about. Not Caroline. Not Lee. Not my boys. No one except for Sam." She paused. "And now, of course, you."

Without warning, Javier reached out and took her

hand. "Abby, I had no idea. I'm so sorry." His eyes swam with concern. "Leukemia? That's supposed to be curable, right? Are there medications you can take?"

"Yes and no," she said softly. It was the first time she'd heard true sympathy from anyone other than her husband. And even Sam didn't really sympathize with her. He was all about the Fight, about stopping the disease in its tracks, as if cancer were an intruder who'd entered their home and all Sam had to do was politely show it the door. Abby knew better, but she didn't have the heart to tell him.

"In some cases, it's curable. If you can find a match for a bone marrow donor, that is. In my case, probably not. So, I'm taking a lovely assortment of pills. My doctor assures me something else will kill me before the cancer." She shook her head. "I'm not quite sure how that's better, but he seems to think so."

Javier came over to wrap an arm around her. "I'm so sorry. You've hid it from us very well. How are you feeling?"

She laughed. "At the moment, not so hot."

"Right, of course."

"Anyway, we've known for a few weeks now. Sam and I." She swallowed more soda. "The pills I take are actually my chemotherapy. They're supposed to kill all the bad cells. The naughty ones," she joked.

Javier returned to his chair and stared intently across the table at her. "From what Caroline tells me, if anyone could beat this, it's you."

Abby nodded doubtfully. "Well, let's hope she's right."

Suddenly, a wave of regret splashed over her. Why on earth had she told Javier? How could she let the news slip so easily to him, when she could barely talk about it with Sam? *Because he's a stranger*, a voice inside her head whispered. *He doesn't know you well enough to let it break him. Because*, Abby realized with a start, *I'm protecting my best friends.* This wasn't about her being selfish or vain or a private person. It was about her wanting to guard her friends from the news that she was sick and could, quite possibly, get much sicker.

"This must be so hard for you," he said finally. "And to think of you guys today!" He shook his head. "Anyway, Sam didn't allude to any of this last night."

"No, he wouldn't." She massaged the cords in her neck, her fingers working out the tiny knots along it. "He's been sworn to secrecy."

Javier nodded. "And you will tell Caroline and Lee? Eventually?"

"Yes, I just didn't want to ruin everyone's vacation right off the bat."

He turned thoughtful for a moment. "That's incredibly kind and generous of you." Then he added, "But I think they'd want to know. Don't you? At least Caroline. I know she'd want to help you any way that she could. Find the best doctors in New York. Whatever it takes."

"Thank you, Javier." Abby wrapped her hands around

her cup. "I mean it. Your saying that means a lot to me. More than you know."

"Of course. You'll let me know how I can help?"

There was something refreshing about his old-fashioned chivalry. Javier's take-charge machismo, which initially Abby had found off-putting, was now welcome, as if he were offering her an enormous bagel after a monthlong carb-free diet. Sam was doing everything to help *except* talking about it. Which, she realized with a start, was probably the one thing she needed most right now. For Sam, Abby's illness was cut-and-dry: you attacked it with medicine, you killed the misbehaving cells, you carried on. There were no other options. For him, losing the fight, losing Abby was not an option.

But what if it was? She wanted to scream at him some days. What if the doctor was wrong and she had much less time than they thought? Any time she raised the specter of fallibility, though, Sam would dismiss it. Much like he did with his students, he'd play devil's advocate: Who was to say a branch wouldn't fall on his head and kill him on his walk to work the next day? *You can't live your days worrying about when the last one will be,* Sam counseled her. But what if Abby *needed* to let herself worry? Even a little? What if it was her way of getting her ducks in a row, just in case? For the boys' sake?

"It helps just to be able to tell you," she admitted now. "I haven't had much practice at it." She craned her neck back and forth. "Anyway, I guess you can't have your cake and eat it, too."

Javier stared at her blankly. "What does that saying mean? All my life, I've heard it, and not once have I understood it. How can you possibly have your cake and eat it, too? It makes no sense. In Cuba, we have no saying like this."

Abby smiled despite herself. "I guess I'm not really sure myself. I think it has something to do with wanting to enjoy the *anticipation* of eating the cake as well as the act of *eating* the cake. If you eat it, you can't look forward to eating it, right? Anyway, I think I should enjoy my cake right now."

"Oh, enjoy the moment, in other words."

"Yes, something like that." She drained the last of her drink and saw that Javier was smiling.

"Did you notice?" He waited a moment. "I think the rocking has stopped."

Abby looked around and realized her stomach wasn't hurting quite so much. It was true. The ship seemed to have leveled out. The woman who had been moaning was now sitting up straight and pleasantly chatting with another passenger. The baby had calmed with a bottle.

"You're right." She took a deep breath, exhaled. "Thank goodness. I guess you'd better go check on Caroline."

"Right. She'll be wanting her juice." He stood up and pushed in his chair.

"Hey, Javier," Abby said now. "I'm so glad you and Caroline are getting married. She's one of my favorite people in the entire world. You'll take good care of her, yes?"

"I promise," he said. "You have my word."

21

⌒

On Thursday morning, a thick fog blanketed the ship, as if to soothe the passengers after last night's rocking storm. A cup of coffee sat cooling next to Caroline. She was writing up her notes for her story before everyone else woke. Last night had been awful—she hadn't felt that sick since she'd gotten food poisoning from a Caesar salad in SoHo years ago. Given the smooth sailing now, however, it was almost easy to forget that she'd been hunched over the toilet last night, Javier rubbing her back and desperately trying to make her feel better. For a while, the cruise had felt like her own special version of *Deliverance.*

The only remaining pieces of evidence of the storm were the large puddles around the pool, where water had sloshed over, and the abandoned cocktail cups, wrappers, and flip-flops scattered across the deck. Caroline watched while a steward·swept at the mess with a wide-brush broom. It occurred to her that maybe he'd be willing to talk with her about the working conditions on the ship, but then she thought better of it. He was probably recovering himself from last night.

In her sleuthing, Caroline had learned that the *Bermuda Breeze* hired more than one thousand crew members from over sixty countries. She'd spoken with one woman, Jenna, who worked in the kids' clubs on the ship. Her own children, she said, were back in Burma, where her sister cared for them for the eight months she was at sea. It seemed an inordinately long time to be away from one's family, but almost everyone Caroline talked to acted as if they'd been granted a rare opportunity, their paychecks pennies from heaven that they could send home—and money that would stretch much further in those places than it would on American soil. Especially the young male stewards she'd interviewed seemed to consider working on a cruise ship a privilege. They enjoyed the perks—the travel, meeting new people, the food and entertainment—that came with it.

In her more cynical moments, Caroline wondered if maybe they'd drunk the Kool-Aid, convincing themselves that they were living lives of leisure when, in fact, they toiled for ten-hour shifts or longer. But who was she to judge? Her job was to report on the leisurely aspects of the cruise and the highlights of Bermuda, not prick people's conscience. It wasn't as if she was a journalist for *Mother Jones*, after all. Maybe another day.

She went back into the cafeteria to refresh her coffee. Whether it was due to last night's rough seas or the

fact that she'd been picking at the same food for several days now, Caroline found it difficult to glance at
the buffet. What had seemed like an ambrosial spread
the first night had transformed into a ransacked display
of muffins and bagels, bruised apples and bananas. The
kitchen, she thought, must be nearing the end of its
wares. Caroline had gorged herself on so many buttery
treats that even the blueberry muffins didn't tempt her
this morning. (She'd long since given up on working
out on board. What was the point? The caloric invasion
was swift and unbeatable.)

Like impatient toddlers, the passengers lined up for
the buffet this morning were getting pushy and belliger-
ent. There were those who cut the line, pretending not
to know better; the parents who juggled their own plates
and their children's and inevitably ended up dropping
food; and then the handful of finicky passengers who
demanded a gluten-free, dairy-free waffle that wasn't
available. It was this last group that got on Caroline's
last nerve. She wanted to ask them if their waffles should
be calorie-free as well. Yes, even in her newly engaged
state, she could still feel uncharitable toward her fellow
passengers.

Which probably meant it was time to go home.

Besides, she had a wedding to plan! It seemed sur-
real. She'd been so focused on the proposal that the
actual marriage part hadn't quite registered yet. There
was so much to do, so much to decide on before, well,

when? A fall wedding, she thought, would be nice. Yes, autumn in New York would be a lovely time to get married. Something small and intimate. Maybe in Central Park?

Across the room she spied Lee, nursing a cup of tea, and went over to say hello.

"Good morning. Glad to see you survived the *Poseidon*," she said. Lee peered up at her, big bags looming under her eyes, her blond hair flattened against her scalp.

"Very funny. Wasn't it awful? I think I got maybe two hours of sleep total. Between the rocking and the stuff with Lacey—" Lee stopped and sipped her tea. She hadn't revealed Lacey's secret to anyone.

Caroline cocked her head. "Uh-oh. Is Lacey's ankle worse?" She pulled out a chair and sat down.

Lee shook her head. "No, the ankle seems better actually." She debated whether to say anything. Would it be breaking Lacey's confidence to tell Caroline? Her daughter adored her aunt. Would she be upset if Caroline found out that she'd been "almost" pregnant?

"We had a little pregnancy scare," Lee whispered. "But it's nothing," she added quickly. "No need to worry."

Caroline fell back in her seat. "Whoa." She was quiet for a minute. "That's big. I had no idea. Is she doing okay? Are *you* okay?"

Lee nodded. "Yeah, it was quite a shock at first, I'll give you that. But now we're fine. At least, I think we are."

"Oh, lovey, I'm so sorry you were dealing with that. And here I was, only thinking about myself. I'm afraid I haven't been a very good friend lately; I've been so focused on things with Javier."

Lee shrugged. "It's all right. I didn't know myself until two days ago." She paused. "Besides, I'm really happy for you guys." And, as she said the words, it struck Lee that they were genuine. She was glad that Javier and Caroline would be together and that there would be another celebration to look forward to after the cruise.

"Aw, thanks," Caroline said. "I still can't believe it myself." Her eyes turned dreamy for a second, as if she were imagining a five-tiered wedding cake with fondant, then quickly refocused on Lee. "But what about Lacey? Do you want me to talk to her? Was it that boyfriend of hers—or some other loser—who almost screwed up her life?" Caroline grunted. "Sorry, poor choice of words."

But Lee laughed. It helped to have a girlfriend who wasn't shy about getting to the heart of the matter. She hadn't realized how much she'd been missing Caroline's no-nonsense attitude.

"Do we need Javier to fly up to Maine, maybe, and break the kid's legs?"

"I don't think that will be necessary," answered Lee. "I will tell you, though, I'm going to make a more concerted effort to visit Lacey this year. Get to know the boyfriend a little better. Give him the hairy eyeball and all that."

"Ooh, that sounds like fun." Caroline grinned evilly. "Let me know when you're going. I might invite myself along for a girls' trip. I think I'd like to meet this Taylor guy, lay down the law."

"Tyler," Lee corrected. "I always mix it up myself."

"What about Tyler?" Abby asked. She'd found them and was wedging herself into the last open chair at the table. Despite the gloomy weather outside, she carried a bag filled with all her pool gear, including her sun hat.

Caroline tossed Lee a look. "Oh, nothing," she said. "We just want to make sure that Lacey's boyfriend understands there are certain rules that come with dating our goddaughter."

"Why? What's going on? Do we not like the boyfriend?" Abby asked, easily falling into their routine of talking in the collective *we* when it came to forming opinions beyond their own rooming group. "Do we not like the dining hall food?" someone might ask or "What do we think of Professor Peterson?" It had always comforted Abby, as if their rooming group was a collective force, one person with three minds.

"We're not quite sure about the boyfriend," Caroline explained now.

"We think he's nice, but we don't really know him that well," Lee concurred cryptically.

"And we're thinking we should get to know him better since Lacey thinks so highly of him," continued Caroline. Abby felt as if they were speaking to her in code. She didn't know exactly what was going on, but she was pretty certain she'd be agreeable to whatever her girlfriends suggested.

"Okay?" said Abby.

"And we were thinking, more specifically, of taking a little road trip up to Maine this fall. You know, to visit Lacey, maybe introduce ourselves to Taylor. I mean Tyler." Caroline winked at her. "Are you in, Abs?"

"Oh." Abby thought she understood now. From the sound of it, Tyler had gotten Lacey into a bit of trouble and needed a talking-to. Well, the roommates had been down this path before, typically with their own boyfriends, when one or the other needed to be set straight. But the rule of looking out for each other naturally extended to Lacey and, Abby hoped, to Chris and Ryan.

She gazed around the table at her roommates' expectant faces, the friends she loved most, the girls who would traipse across the Sahara to give her water, if need be.

"You bet I am," she said.

22

Friday dawned sunny and bright, perfect weather for their last full day aboard. Abby and Sam sat in the cafeteria with plates of eggs and toast and multiple glasses of juice and coffee strewn around them. Sam's reading glasses were tipped on the end of his nose as he perused the two-day-old newspaper. It seemed like forever since they'd had a chance to read the paper together. Most mornings, Sam was out the door by 5:30, off to the gym and then the classroom or the office, while Abby and the boys slept in.

He lifted his eyes and caught her staring. "What?"

Abby shook her head. "Nothing. I was just thinking about how we used to go to that diner down the street from my apartment for Sunday brunch. This reminds me of it. Those mornings when we had nothing but time to kill."

"Oh, right. What was it called? Rita's? Renée's?"

"Renée's."

"Right. And they had the best blueberry pancakes."

He smiled. "Remember your place in the North End?"

Sam liked to remind her about her attic apartment with slanted ceilings, where Abby had lived for three years after college. Her place had always smelled of pasta from the Italian restaurant three flights below. She, on the other hand, liked to think of it as her pied-à-terre, which made it sound mysterious and romantic. Sam joked that he'd rescued her from a life of endless flights of stairs and potentially bum knees.

"Those were the days," she said now wistfully.

"Ah, pre-twins. Good Italian food. And lots of sex."

Abby laughed. Of course, Sam would remember the sex.

"But would you change any of it?" he asked. "I mean, can you imagine our lives without the boys?"

Abby shook her head. She didn't even need to consider Sam's question. Without the boys, their family would have been incomplete. It wasn't true for everyone, of course, but in her case, it was. She fed on the chaos and drama of family life and remembered the twins' swaddled bodies, one in each arm, the craziness of trying to synchronize naps and feeding times (impossible). Then suddenly they were toddlers, kindergartners, third graders, and middle schoolers racing to the rink for hockey practices. Where had the time gone?

Now they were full-blown teenagers, their faces speckled with acne, further evidence of their galloping hormones. Before she knew it, they'd be packing their bags for college. Even as angry as she'd been with Chris this vacation, there was no stopping her crazy, wild love for her boys. They were hers—the attitudes, the smelly socks, the occasional good night hug—all of it, the good and the bad. She and Sam would weather the storms of adolescence just as they had the sleepless nights of the boys' youth.

Sam pulled off his glasses. "Me either. I can't imagine it." He folded the paper and set it down on the table. "In many ways, we've been very lucky." For a moment, Abby wondered if they might talk about "it" now, about what might come next and how best to handle it. How would they tell the boys? And when? What else did they need to put in order besides their wills and their bank accounts?

Instead, he asked, "Feel like a walk?"

Abby hesitated, but a faint smile crossed her lips. No, Sam wasn't ready. She wouldn't push. Not yet. They still had some time. Abby worried about how little time, whereas Sam looked ahead to how much, but somewhere in between those two extremes lay a happy medium, she thought. Her condition, her diagnosis, whatever she called it, seemed dire only on her worst days, when she asked herself questions like *Why me? Why me, when I have two boys to look after?* It seemed outrageously unfair. But a piece of her, maybe the old Abby, also allowed herself to think sometimes, *Why not me?* Why couldn't she be the one to survive the longest, to beat the odds? *Why not her* when it came to imagining another decade or two with her family? It was possible, remote, but *possible*.

"Sure," she said now. "Couldn't hurt to burn off the three million calories I just consumed." She reached for her tray before remembering there were people here to tidy up after her, to take care of her when she needed it. It was a strange feeling, and she didn't know if she'd ever get used to it.

⌒

Out on deck, they walked briskly, Sam pumping his arms and Abby trying to keep up. Her husband was in better shape than she, but she was determined to match his stride for at least a few laps. They circled once, then twice, passing several other walkers as they went. Sam fell into the "serious" walker category, meaning he didn't like to talk while he paced. Occasionally, he would grunt in acknowledgment when Abby pointed out a loose shuffleboard puck headed his way or when she noted an interesting feature on the boat, like the hot tub on the bow, a few flights below.

By the third lap, though, she was feeling weary. Somewhere around the second lap, their leisurely stroll had evolved into a competitive speed walk. Abby was more of a lounge-by-the-pool vacationer than a walker.

"How many laps for a mile?" she huffed.

"Not sure," Sam replied, his elbows still pumping gamely. "Maybe four or five?"

Abby slowed her pace intentionally. "Phew! Well, I think I'll sit and rest at the next bench."

"Oh?" Sam slowed down, too. "Sorry, I didn't realize. I was enjoying our walk. I thought you were, too."

"I was!" Abby protested. "But I don't have quite the same energy I used to."

"Right. Sorry." He followed her as she headed for a bench. "You should have said something. Guess I got a little carried away. It feels good to stretch my legs."

"Yes, it does," Abby agreed. They settled next to each other and gazed out on the water while catching their breath.

"Everything okay?" Sam asked after a few minutes. "Are you feeling all right?"

Abby began to reply, automatically upbeat, but then stopped herself. "No, actually," she conceded. "Damn it, Sam. Don't you ever get angry? About how unfair this is?" She gestured out to sea. "All this beauty to share, and I may not be around much longer to see it?"

Sam stared at her, surprised. "Angry? Sure I do, but that's not going to change anything. I'd rather spend my time with you being happy than mad."

Abby huffed.

"What?" Sam pried. "What's wrong with that?"

"It's just so typical!" She stood up, her hands waving in the air, her voice rising. "Sam, the Saint. You always have the perfect answer for everything. Seriously, don't you ever get mad? I mean really, really angry that this thing has chosen me, our *family*?"

"Of course I do!" he exclaimed. "You think I like

any of this? That there's something inside of you, eating away at you? How could I possibly be okay with that? I hate it." He turned away from her for a moment. "Every morning," he began again, "I wake up and I have to remind myself that this horrible disease is our new reality. That it's not a bad dream but something you have to fight every day. That the person I love most in the world is sick," he said softly, his voice cracking. "And it breaks my heart, every single day. But I have to be strong for you."

"Oh, Sam." Abby came back and sat down next to him. She took his hand. "I love that you're my rock, but you also have to let yourself feel all those things. It's good to be angry, I think." She sighed. "I'm glad you told me. I was beginning to think you weren't human."

Sam reached out to smooth her hair. "Yeah? You mean, you don't think I'm a weak-kneed flimflam for admitting it?"

Abby laughed, finding herself again, hearing the old Sam in those words. "I'm not even sure what that is, but no. You've always been my rock. You know that."

He kissed the top of her head. "Oh, Abs, my dear, dear Abs. What would I do without you? Please don't leave us. You can't leave us."

Abby sighed again and faked her best smile. "I'll do my best, honey," she said. "I'll try my very best."

Because, really, she thought, as she looked out at the majestic sea, what was the alternative?

⌐

"What was I like when I was a kid?" Lacey asked. They were sitting by the pool, trying to squeeze in a few last rays of sunshine before docking in Boston tomorrow morning. Lee was reading a home-improvement magazine, and Lacey was working on a crossword, which involved more erasing of wrong answers than anything else.

"You were adorable," Lee said. "You had this long blond hair that you loved to wear in pigtails. And you were very good at entertaining yourself—a creative child. You would spend hours making up stories and acting them out. When it rained, you liked to sit on the porch with an umbrella and pretend it was your own little house."

"Really? I did that?" Lacey laughed. "I don't remember that at all. Was I a good kid or did I drive you crazy?"

"You were generally pretty good, although, around seven or eight, you'd have this maddening way of asking me what your punishment would be if I told you to stop doing something, like you were weighing the odds of whether it was worth it. You'd press me on the details—*How many more minutes in time-out?* you'd ask, or *How many more minutes of TV time will I lose?*" Lee smiled. "That's why giving you a warning hardly ever worked. You'd press me on the details when I was trying to invent something midair. You were usually better at thinking up punishments than I was."

Lacey rolled her eyes. "I sound so annoying."

"You weren't that awful. Really. Even if there were days when I wanted to lock myself in the closet for a few hours, you were still pretty amazing. I was Thelma and you were—"

"Your Louise. I know, I know," Lacey interrupted. That's how it had always been for the two of them, until recently. When Lacey was growing up, all her friends had thought her mom was the coolest, the prettiest. Like a big sister. And Lacey had agreed. Sometime during the summer of her senior year, though, things had shifted. Lacey was suddenly quick to point out her mother's flaws. She criticized her hair, her job, her clothes, even the way Lee answered the phone—*Hello, Minor residence*—in her pleasant, singsongy voice. Nothing her mom did was right. And though in the back of her mind, Lacey knew she was being unfair, cruel even, she hadn't cared. Because she was leaving for college, far, far away, and her mom couldn't stop her.

Now she wondered, had she been waiting for her mom to tell her not to go? Lee had given her carte blanche to apply to any college she might want. "Aim high, Lacey girl," she'd said. And Lacey had done just that, getting accepted at several top schools.

But she'd been confused when Lee hadn't pushed back even slightly once Lacey decided on a college in Maine. "That's a great school, Lace," her mom said, all congratulatory and proud. Later, after Lacey accepted, she'd panicked that she'd made a huge mistake. Why was she going so far away, when she and Lee did everything together?

The first few weeks at school, sure enough, she cried herself to sleep, missing everything about home. She missed their lazy Saturdays shopping at the Market and their walks through Waterfront Park. She definitely missed the warm Charleston nights. And the silly, insignificant things—like eating frozen cookie dough while they watched TV together—Lacey missed that, too. She'd craved Magnolia's pecan pie so much that she'd ordered one online, a little slice of the South delivered to her mailbox at college. And then Tyler had shown up, helping to dampen her loneliness ever so slightly.

It was as if Lacey's relationship with her mom had been cleaved in half over the past year. And Lacey missed it. Terribly.

But now she allowed herself to think that maybe with her pregnancy scare had come a blessing of sorts. It reminded Lacey why she'd missed her mom in the first place. She'd almost forgotten: Lee supported her, no matter what. She might disagree with Lacey (and would make those feelings known), but her mom would be there regardless. *Because the world is hard enough, Lacey,* she used to tell her. *I've got your back, always.* Lacey hoped Tyler would be supportive when she finally told him what had happened, but somehow his response mattered less now. Her mom knew, and her mom still loved her.

"Hey, Mom." Lacey turned to Lee.

"Yeah?" Lee lifted her eyes from her magazine.

"Thanks for being so cool about the whole—you know," Lacey said. She didn't say anything more, such as that this morning her period had arrived, as if her body had been playing a mean trick on her.

"You got it," Lee said. "My support, one hundred percent."

Lacey nodded, thinking for a moment. "Mom?"

"Yeah?" Lee looked up again.

"I was just wondering. Can I ask what you would have done? I mean if the test had been positive?"

Lee set down her magazine and studied Lacey for a moment. "The better question, honey, is, What would you have done?"

Lacey shook her head. She'd been trying to figure that one out. "I don't know," she said now. "I honestly don't know." It was the truth. She was relieved that she didn't have to answer that question quite so soon in her life. "I suppose I would have wanted to talk to Tyler first before making any decisions."

Lee nodded. "That makes sense."

"But I'm still curious. If you were me, what you would have done?"

"If I was you?" Lee's face broke into a radiant smile. "Oh, Lacey, honey, you already know the answer to that question," she said. "I'm looking at her."

23

~

That evening, Abby asked all the adults to meet her in a remote restaurant-bar at the back of the ship, Finnegan's. She had no idea how her friends would react. Or how she might react. But a secluded spot with dim lighting seemed the best place to reveal her secret. Earlier in the cruise, she and Sam had stumbled onto the cozy bar with supple leather seats and glass jars filled with peanuts. Every time they'd gone, a crotchety older man stood behind the bar, taking people's orders as if he'd rather not. It made them laugh to have found such a malcontent on a ship where everyone else practically hummed with enthusiasm. The walls were paneled in dark oak, the tables a polished cherry, a fitting spot for the news she was about to deliver.

Earlier, she'd felt nauseous, though she couldn't say whether it was nerves or the events of the last few days. Or her medicine. There were too many factors rolling around in her head. She knew she had to tell her roommates, and yet a part of her still wanted to guard her secret. To put it out in the open, to actually speak the words to her best friends, would make it all real. For the past eight days, Abby had been able to pretend she was perfectly fine, albeit a bit tired.

Sam sat next to her, a whiskey at his elbow. Abby sipped her iced tea. They'd talked it over, and they'd both agreed: short and sweet was best. No sense in prolonging the conversation. Abby would deliver the news and tell her friends not to worry. Just that it was the luck of the draw and Abby would ride it out, however her body saw fit. She might still outlive them all, who knew? They'd decided not to include the boys or Lacey tonight. Lee could tell Lacey on her own time, and she and Sam agreed that the twins could wait until they were back home, in a familiar setting with their friends.

Caroline and Javier were the first to arrive. Caroline, her skin bronzed the color of copper, glowed as she clasped Javier's hand. With her hair swept up in a loose ponytail, she looked twenty again, a beaming bride-to-be. Abby realized that marriage already suited her friend—Caroline was a natural.

"So, is this where you tell us that we've won an extended cruise, a whole extra loop to Bermuda and back?" Caroline teased.

"Ha, I wish." Abby played along. Just then, Lee arrived and pulled up a seat.

"Hi, sorry I'm late."

"No worries," said Abby. "You're not late at all." She

rested her elbows on the table and knitted her fingers together.

"So, what's the big news now?" Lee inquired. "I'm not sure my heart can handle much more on this cruise." Abby understood that Lee had been fighting her own battles with Lacey, but that the pregnancy scare had been just that, a scare.

"Well," Abby began. "As it turns out, Sam and I do have some news for you." She glanced at Sam, who nodded. "So, it turns out." She hesitated. "It turns out," she tried again, "that I have leukemia."

Lee fell back in her chair, and a small sucking sound escaped from Caroline. "Oh, no," she said.

"I know." Abby gave it a moment to sink in. "It stinks. I found out a couple of weeks before the cruise, and I didn't want to spoil everyone's fun. But I thought you both should know."

Sam stepped in. "We haven't even told the boys yet. We will, of course, when we get back to Boston. But Abby wanted you two to know."

Lee grabbed a cocktail napkin and dabbed at her eyes. "Jesus, Abby, I knew something was up. But this? I had no idea."

"Yeah, I figured you guys would pick up on the fact that I wasn't drinking much. Doctor's orders," she explained. "But I wanted to enjoy our trip. Celebrate twenty years of marriage. Of friendship."

Caroline's face was drawn and pale. "I'm sorry." She

shook her head. "I just can't believe it." She eyed Sam's tumbler of whiskey. "May I?" She took a long sip and set down the glass. "I'm so sorry, Abs." She reached across the table to take her friend's hand. "Well, one thing's for sure: you know we're here to help you fight this however you need to."

Abby swallowed hard.

"Leukemia is one of the curable ones, right?" Lee leaned forward, her eyes flashing. "We'll kill that bastard. Wring its little neck," she said, prompting a laugh from Abby.

"Right now I'm on all sorts of pills that are my chemotherapy."

Caroline's eyes widened. "You mean to tell us that you've been undergoing chemotherapy this whole time?"

"Yep. Tiny little pills. The miracle of modern medicine." Abby held her forefinger and thumb a centimeter apart to approximate the size of the pills she'd been swallowing over the last few weeks.

"And they're not making you sick?" Caroline pressed. "I mean, you've been acting perfectly healthy. Maybe a little tired, but healthy."

"Not really. At least I don't think so. Just a little queasy sometimes, but it's hard to know if that's the boat or the medication."

"So, Abby." It was Javier, the first time he'd spoken. She was grateful now that she'd told him earlier, a calm presence to help her steer her friends through the shock of her news. "What can we do to help?"

"Yes," Caroline chimed in. "Tell us. Anything we can do. I can fly to Boston on a moment's notice. I can go to your doctor's appointments with you. Or maybe we can help with the boys. Do you like your doctor? I know Boston has great clinics, but I can ask around about top oncologists in New York."

"Thank you. I appreciate it. I really do," Abby said now. "But I think we're all set for the moment. I have Sam, and my doctor is supposedly one of the best. My prognosis is pretty good, as long as I keep taking my pills. The doctor says I could live another twenty years. Of course, it might be closer to ten or five, but who knows?"

Caroline pulled her lips into a tight line. For once, Abby's roommates had nothing to say.

"Anyway," Abby pushed ahead, "it turns out only four in one million Americans get this particular kind of leukemia each year. So, there's that." She flushed. It was a stupid thing to say, but she was still struck by the infinitesimal odds.

Lee slammed her hand down on the table. "Damn it, Abby. It's just like you to go and get something that only three other people have." She shook her head. "I don't care how rare it is, we're going to beat this." And there it was, the collective *we*. Just like that, her friends had taken her disease on as their own. It was no longer only

Abby and Sam fighting this battle. She'd almost forgotten: she had her forever sisters. Through thick and thin.

"When will you know if the chemo works?" Caroline asked quietly.

"That's the thing. With this type of leukemia, there's no cure, per se. You just keep taking a low dosage of chemo for the rest of your life. My doctor called it a chronic condition, not a terminal one."

"Huh," said Caroline. Abby watched while her friends processed the information.

"I know, it sounds screwy to me, too, but apparently lots of people live with this for quite a while. Up to twenty years," she repeated.

"Well." Sam leaned forward. "Abby's not mentioning the one other possibility." Abby shook her head. "What?" he asked. "I think your friends would want to know." He paused, then forged ahead. "A bone marrow transplant. If Abby can find a match, then she'll be considered cured."

"Seriously?" cried Caroline. "Well, then that's what we'll do. We'll find you a match. How hard can it be?"

"Whoa, whoa." Abby held up her hand. "Not so fast. What Sam didn't mention is that my odds of finding a match are extremely slim, especially since I don't have any siblings."

"But isn't there a national database of some kind that can match you to a potential donor?" Lee persisted.

"I think so." Abby hadn't actually checked, assuming

it would be a shot in the dark. "But again, the odds are pretty slim. And, well, you know, it's not the easiest procedure. There are no guarantees. I figure why bother with that if I still have a good stretch of years ahead of me."

Caroline shook her head as if she couldn't comprehend what Abby was saying. "Um, because you'd be cured?"

"Look, I appreciate your can-do attitude," said Abby. "But I don't want to get your hopes up. This is something I can live with. As my doctor says, it's not the end of the world."

She caught Caroline and Lee exchanging glances and could see the wheels already beginning to turn in their heads.

"Okay," Caroline said cautiously now. "It's your thing, Abby, and you can deal with it however you want, but please tell us that at the very least you're going to put your name in that database to *see* if there's a match."

Abby hesitated and looked to Sam for guidance. The truth was, she hadn't considered searching for a match because she'd assumed the search would be futile. What's more, she'd convinced herself that she wasn't up for the procedure, that a transplant would be more than her body could handle. It wasn't as if she was signing up to get her tonsils removed.

"I can think about it," she said now deliberately, carefully. "I can do that much."

"Good." Caroline clasped her hands together. "Then it's settled."

Lee nodded across the table with an almost conspiratorial gleam in her eye, while Abby wondered what exactly she had just agreed to. One thing she knew for certain: it felt good to finally let her friends in on her secret.

24

Lee woke and pulled the curtains back to reveal the sky-line of Boston. The ship must have pulled into port at dawn while they were sleeping. Or sort of sleeping. Last night, she'd tossed and turned, thinking about Abby. Lee had suspected something was off with her friend, but she would never have guessed leukemia.

She clicked on her phone to see if they had Wi-Fi reception yet—and waited. Miraculously, the tiny green bars popped up at the top of her screen. She ignored the three-hundred-plus e-mails in her in-box and clicked over to Google. All they had to do was find a match for Abby. How hard could it be? The first thing she'd do when she got back to Charleston was get herself tested. What if she or Caroline were a match?

The ultimate confirmation that we are sisters, she thought. Lee knew she'd give Abby or Caroline her bone marrow, a kidney, whatever she could, just as she was certain they would do the same for her.

She scrolled down a list of studies, trying to be quiet, as Lacey rolled over in bed.

When she was back home, Lee would research the possibilities more. What if Abby's leukemia had been misdiagnosed? What if there was another treatment plan that could cure her without something as dramatic as a bone marrow transplant? Did radiation work with leukemia? Lee was grossly uneducated about the illness; she hardly knew where to begin. Well, she had the whole summer to figure it out.

At that moment, a text popped up on her phone from Caroline. Of course, Caroline had already been online doing research. *Hi! Wi-Fi working again. Did some checking this morning. 70% of Caucasian patients who need bone marrow transplants find a match! That's a lot higher than Abby led us to believe. Must discuss later. Xo, Car*

Well, there, thought Lee. Put Caroline Canton on the case and suddenly the skies brightened. It had been that way since Lee could remember. Caroline got things done, and what's more, she had connections. If there were specialists in New York whom Abby should consult for a second opinion, then Caroline would find them. It was a comforting thought.

Lee dressed and slipped out of the cabin before Lacey woke. There was one more thing she wanted to do before they stepped off the ship.

Abby, Sam, and the boys were sitting at a table in the Blue Wave, enjoying their final breakfast of omelets and French toast. In forty-five minutes, they were due to disembark. From above her coffee cup, Abby watched while more guests poured into the restaurant. It amazed her that, even after nine days, there still managed to be people whom she hadn't seen once on the ship. Some passengers wheeled their suitcases behind them as they went to sit down. Abby's family had tagged their bags last night so that their luggage would be waiting for them in the cruise port.

She bit into her French toast, drowning in blueberries and syrup. "I'm going to miss this food," she said.

"Me, too," agreed Chris.

Abby had enjoyed not having to shop or cook, so much so that she wondered if she might prolong her hiatus from the kitchen. Maybe she'd look into a home delivery service, where all the ingredients came freshly prepared. Sam thought she should be doing less anyway while her body adjusted to the medication, and she was beginning to see that he was right. It would do her good to slow down. For once in her life, she didn't feel compelled to tend to her family's every need. The boys were old enough. They could help out more, even make trips to the grocery store. It was time to loosen the reins. *More than time*, she thought.

Last night, when they'd had to pack up their luggage for the porters, she'd realized she'd written almost nothing in her leather journal. And she'd meant to include so much advice! To spell everything out for her boys, all that they would need to know in the event she had to leave them too soon. But it dawned on her this morning what a ridiculous plan it had been. The twins knew what she would say in most instances anyway. In fact, they'd already complained that her nagging voice followed them around everywhere in their heads. Well, one day, she supposed, when she was no longer around, they might appreciate that voice.

Yes, her boys would be fine, whether she left this world in twenty days or twenty years. Even Ryan, who seemed to be friends with Lacey again, would find his way. *Especially Ryan*, she thought.

She glanced around the table and was surprised to see everyone's head bent over his phone. *How quickly they all reverted to their old ways!* Here they'd spent seven full days out at sea, but now that technology was within reach, all the men at her table had retreated into their own individual bubbles. As if the need for civil conversation no longer applied.

Abby cleared her throat. "Isn't it amazing," she tried, "to think that after we step off the ship, the stewards are already getting ready for the next round of passengers? That at five o'clock tonight there will be another sail off?" She sipped her coffee, waiting for someone to respond. "I guess it's a shorter cruise by a day, though," she continued. "Leaves on Saturday and gets back on Friday next week." She glanced around the table. "Excuse me?" she said loudly. "Hello? Would anyone like to talk to me during our last few minutes of vacation?"

Ryan lifted his head and peered at her from under too-long bangs. He'd need a haircut when they got back home. "Sorry, Mom. It's just been so long, you know, since we've had any Internet."

"Sorry, honey," Sam said, without even bothering to look up. "I have a couple of work things I need to check." Chris slumped further down in his seat, pretending not to hear.

"Well, in that case," she said more to herself than anyone else, "it was nice seeing all your handsome faces for a week. Now I'm back to looking at the tops of your baseball caps."

⌒

Lee was the next person in line to pay her bill. She'd texted Lacey to meet her at the front, near the main exit for disembarking. She'd been waiting in line for thirty minutes now, but Lee didn't mind because she was busy combing through the brochures for other cruises. Despite the one rocky night they'd had, she'd discovered that she liked sailing and all its accoutrements. She could picture herself cruising to ports across the world. Maybe Italy or Greece next summer. A lot had happened in seven short days—Sam and Abby's anniversary, Lacey's pregnancy scare, Caroline's engagement, and now Abby's health news—and it made Lee realize that she needed to start living her own life again.

For so long, Lee's focus had been solely on Lacey. Shuttling her to ballet and gymnastics classes. Checking her homework, then her college essays. Making sure there was always enough money. It hadn't mattered that Lee had put on weight or that her cholesterol had skyrocketed. Even when the doctor had cautioned her that she was borderline diabetic, Lee had remained unfazed. So long as Lacey was happy and doing well, Lee was happy.

But it had taken the cruise to wake a part of her that she'd forgotten about herself. There was no reason for her to be the lonely mom left behind in an empty nest. Far from it! Lee had plenty of friends she could visit, and, even if she wouldn't admit it now, Abby would need their help eventually. Already, the roommates were planning their October trip to Maine to visit Lacey. Lee's life wasn't washed up quite yet. Thomas had been a fling, but he'd given her something important—a reminder of what it felt like to be attracted to someone and to feel desired. That elusive taste of fun that had been missing from her life ever since Lacey left for school.

Lee realized that she needed a plan, beyond what she was going to teach her preschoolers on any given day. She needed a life plan, one that would allow her to explore new places and one that, quite possibly, maybe even selfishly, would be about *her* happiness, not just Lacey's. Lee had gotten her sweet, slightly wiser, daughter back on the cruise, and she was tremendously grateful for that. But now, she told herself, it was time to get *herself* back.

The thought was so foreign she might as well have resolved to go skydiving. But there it was. Lee Minor resolved to do better by her life. Paying off the remainder of the cruise would be a step in the right direction, she thought, as she finally got her turn at the front desk. She'd already paid for their tickets (despite Abby's generous offer), but who knew what ungodly expenses she and Lacey had racked up during the week. She cringed to think it could be in the thousands.

When she gave the hostess her room number, however, she was informed that all expenses for cabin 1023 had already been paid in full. By one Mrs. Abigail Bingham.

⌐

It had felt good to pack up all her sundresses and cruise attire last night. Caroline couldn't help it—she was a New Yorker, and she was looking forward to getting back to the city. Plus, she was leaving the ship an engaged woman! There was so much planning to do, so much to look forward to. Already, a friend who worked at Vera Wang had left her a voice mail suggesting she drop by the store for a preliminary peek at wedding gowns. Because, of course, Caroline had posted the news on her Facebook account this morning, the very second Wi-Fi was restored.

She felt a twinge of guilt, though, when she glimpsed Abby and the boys falling into line for disembarking. Because Caroline was also leaving the ship knowing that her friend was sick, possibly very sick. She didn't yet have a handle on what Abby's diagnosis meant exactly—she suspected Abby had been glib in her description of it—but she intended to find out. Already, she'd e-mailed a friend of a friend who was married to one of the top oncologists in Manhattan. Surely, he'd be able to explain it to her, offer some advice, perhaps a referral.

"Are you sure that's what Abby wants?" Javier had asked her this morning in their cabin.

"What do you mean? How could it not be?" Caroline had demanded. "Abby's the kind of person who goes through life, come what may, without complaining. Sometimes she needs someone to take the bull by the horns for her."

"But what if she'd rather deal with things in her own way, on her own time?"

Caroline had shaken her head in disbelief. Was Javier really telling her to back off, to stop trying to do whatever she could to help her friend? *No way.* She'd felt the color creeping into her cheeks.

"I think I know my friend, Javier," she'd said curtly and turned on her heel.

But now she wondered if maybe Javier had a point. She'd have to be careful not to push too hard, to listen to what Abby wanted. It wasn't as if Caroline were charged with planning a wedding or a magazine spread for her friend—this was Abby's life. She took a moment to gather herself before approaching them. Should she tell Abby about the information she'd already found on donor matches and how encouraging it was? Or should she do what she really wanted to do at the moment, which was to pull her friend into a hug?

She glanced down the hallway and noticed one of the boys waving at her. *Chris.* Then it hit her: the boys didn't know yet. Abby and Sam were waiting to tell them back at home. Oh, the poor boys! Caroline would call later tonight to check in and see how things had gone. There would be no mention of Abby's predicament—or how they might go about solving it—this morning. That could wait. *We have plenty of time*, Caroline told herself.

"So, you better get ready," she said, as she clicked over to Abby's gang in her traveling heels, Kate Spade leopard-print mules. Abby stared at her confused. "Because I'm going to be bombarding you with wedding questions," Caroline finished.

Abby's face softened. "Happy to help however I can," she replied. "Though something tells me you already have the whole thing planned. Keep an eye on her, Javier. Don't let her go too far off the deep end, okay?"

Javier winked. "You bet. And, hey, we'll see you soon." He turned to Sam and the boys. "You guys are coming down for a Yankees game, right?"

"Yeah, but only to watch the Sox beat you guys. You

let me know the date," said Sam, shaking hands. "Congratulations, again. You're a lucky man. Guys have been chasing Caroline for years."

"Thanks. Same to you. What an amazing anniversary. Thanks for including us."

"Yes, thanks, lovey." Caroline squeezed Abby. "I'll call you tonight," she whispered.

Lee and Lacey pulled up behind them in line. "There you two are. All ready?" Abby asked.

"Well," Lee said, "if we have to get off the boat, I guess we will. Although Lacey and I were thinking of signing on as deckhands."

"I wouldn't put it past either one of you," said Caroline with a laugh. "Can I commission an article from you in that case?"

"Ha! Did you finish yours?" Lee asked.

"Hit *Send* this morning." Caroline made the whooshing sound of an e-mail traveling through cyberspace. "By the way, don't be surprised if you see yourselves quoted as 'experts,'" she added.

Their line inched closer to the porter who was checking passengers off the ship. Lee pulled Abby into a big, bone-crushing hug. "Thank you for everything," she said. "You weren't supposed to pay our bill," she whispered.

"Of course we were," said Abby. "I told you the cruise was our treat." They watched as other passengers handed over their room keys before checking off the ship. All too soon, it was time to say good-bye.

"Okay, so, no tears," coached Caroline. "You know how much I hate good-byes. Besides." She turned to Lacey. "We're going to see you in October."

"That's right," said Lacey. "And then for your wedding! Love you, Aunty."

"Me, too, sweetie. And, roomies, I'll be talking to you soon." Caroline waved as she headed down the gangway with Javier, the first to disembark. *Yes,* thought Lee. *We have a lot more to discuss.*

Lee handed her key card to the porter and hugged Abby one last time. "You take care of yourself. We'll see each other before you know it."

"You bet," said Abby.

Then Lee turned and followed her daughter down the walkway, onto firmer ground.

⌒

Abby stood at the railing and watched her friends depart. She told Sam she needed a minute. Soon, she'd step foot back on land, where her treatment and more tests and who knew what else awaited her. She'd been in denial long enough—the cruise had been a convenient way to keep her diagnosis at bay. But now she would have to confront it. She wanted nothing more than more time. But what was the point of bargaining for more time when she didn't even know if there was someone to bargain with?

Abby wanted to believe in a greater force, a higher

good. As a child, she'd attended communion and confirmation at her nondenominational church. She'd carried with her the nebulous underpinnings of faith, as if she might unpack them whenever a big trip demanded them. But her faith couldn't hold a candle to Sam's conviction, Sam who had been raised on the tenets of Catholicism since he was a baby. Like his lungs or a beating heart, Sam's faith was a natural part of him. How Abby longed for that certainty! She tried to imagine God granting her mom and dad a swank hotel room up in heaven, wanted to believe that one day she might come back as a robin, or a butterfly, to flutter around her boys. But it was, and would continue to be, she suspected, a struggle up until the very end.

She breathed in the morning air that had more bite to it than Bermuda's. But even here, in Boston's harbor with the brackish Atlantic, the water sparkled, the early-morning light skipping across it in silver arcs. It was crazy beautiful, impossible not to notice. And it was here, on the deck, that Abby promised herself: *I will not crawl into a hole and feel sorry for myself. I will put my name on the list for donors. I will remember to be amazed.* Amazed by the sun dappling the water. Amazed by the city's grand architecture. Amazed by the truly beautiful circle of family and friends that she'd built.

Abby was proud of each one of them—Lee, who'd raised a lovely, self-sufficient daughter all on her own. Caroline, who'd taken the world by storm and had at last found her life's partner. Sam, dependable, unbreakable Sam, who'd been by her side since she could remember. And her sweet boys, who would make their way in the world, with or without her. She'd done all the hard work already.

She thought of a sermon she'd heard during one of her infrequent visits to church, long before the diagnosis. The minister had talked about the Greek word for *perfect* or *telios*. But the full translation was "having reached your purpose." Abby had been struck by those words. Had she reached her purpose? If someone had asked her that day, she would have said that being a good mom, a loyal friend, a person who made the world a little better, was her life's purpose. But what if she was meant to do more? She'd always wanted to go back to the gallery once the kids were in college. What if she wasn't finished yet?

She looked down at the people below, hurrying to their homes or their jobs, at the gulls swooping in wide arcs above, at the warming sun hopscotching across the water, and was suddenly flooded with a sense of joy. Because what did it matter, really, if she was meant to do more? If she wasn't perfect? All around her was a world that bedazzled.

Abby had been satisfied that day in church, months ago, that she'd fulfilled her purpose already. There was only so much one person could do. So now, she would allow herself to be amazed. By all that she'd been given in life—and all that she'd been able to give back.

"Honey?" It was Sam. He was waiting for her at the gateway. She looked at her sweet, loving husband, his hand outstretched. "Ready?"

She paused for a moment, glanced out to sea, then turned back to him. "Yes," she said, reaching for his hand. "Yes," she repeated and offered him her most encouraging smile while silently reciting her new mantra as they stepped forward together.

If nothing else, remember to be amazed.

Acknowledgments

My thanks, as ever, to my editor, Trish Todd, who graciously helps every book tell the story it is meant to tell. To my agent, Meg Ruley, fairy godmother of all agents, who offers support, encouragement, and pixie dust, as needed. To my forever sisters of Kirkland House at Harvard (you know who you are!), thanks for always stepping up whenever one of us is in need of love or laughter. Thank you to the many other forever sisters I've been fortunate to have in my life—I'm continually amazed by the powerful bonds of friendship and the ways in which they sustain us.

We live in troubling times, but for anyone looking to be inspired by our world, look no further than Mary Oliver's poetry, especially her poem "Good Morning" (from *Blue Horses*). Her poetry reminds me to be grateful every day.

And to my family, Mike, Katherine, Michael, and Nicholas—thanks for telling me to keep writing, even when the meat loaf is burning in the oven.

About the Author

Wendy Francis is the author of the novels *The Summer Sail*, *The Summer of Good Intentions*, and *Three Good Things*. A former book editor, she has written for *Good Housekeeping*, *The Washington Post*, *The Improper Bostonian*, and Cognoscenti. She lives outside Boston with her husband and son.

Touchstone Reading Group Guide

The Summer Sail

Three former college roommates reunite for a twentieth wedding anniversary celebration on a cruise ship. As the liner sets sail and tensions rise, Abby, Caroline, and Lee realize that their secrets won't just disappear in a sunset cocktail or an ocean breeze.

For Discussion

1. Describe Abby, Caroline, and Lee. How do their differences complement one another? What do they teach you about female friendship?

2. Lee admittedly sacrifices her own happiness for the sake of Lacey's. But rather than feel appreciative, her daughter considers this cruel. To what extent has being a mother affected Lee's relationship and career choices? Are Lee's sacrifices unusual or all part of being a good mother?

3. Caroline decides that if Javier does not propose by the end of the cruise, their relationship is over. But she does not actually tell him this. Do you understand Caroline's rationale, or do you find her decision unreasonable? Should she be more up front with Javier? When, if ever, is it fair to deliver an ultimatum in a relationship?

4. While writing her article for *Glossy,* Caroline observes the passengers. What does she learn? Do you think the excessive eating, drinking, and partying offers a "larger commentary on American society in general"? Have you ever been on a cruise? What was your experience like?

5. Lee thinks her daughter is more preoccupied with her boyfriend than she is with her future career, and this often causes friction in their relationship. But Lacey is frustrated by her mom's expectations and resents the notion that she must "single-handedly carry the torch for all women." She thinks, "Women were already equal. If Hillary Clinton could run for president, then what was left?" And despite how grateful she is for her privileges, Lacey thinks: "sometimes it seemed like her mom's generation had gotten it all wrong. In their race to shatter glass ceilings, many of them had put their own families on hold." Do you think Lacey's convictions about women are outdated? Is Lee's concern for her daughter's priorities warranted, or is Lacey's behavior a prime example of a young woman blinded by love?

6. When first arriving on the Bermuda beach, Abby instantly feels her mood lighten and her stress subside. She thinks, "It was hard not to be grateful for every little thing." Do you believe in the healing power of nature? Is there a place that makes you feel at peace?

7. Despite having written an article for *Glossy* suggesting that women should feel free to propose if their partner is taking too long to do so, Caroline doesn't want to propose to Javier. Now that she's in this predicament, she realizes that it's "different in practice," and that she's still old-fashioned. What do you think of women proposing? Is there a stigma in society that shames women for taking the initiative? Do you think it's time this changes?

8. Abby hasn't yet told her boys about her health to "protect them for as long as she could." Do you think Abby is right to wait? What would you do? Are there some situations when it's necessary to withhold information from loved ones?

9. Thomas tells Lee that now that his daughters are grown up, he's going to try to worry less and let them make their own decisions. Lee considers this: "Maybe it was different for fathers. They couldn't wait for their kids to turn into miniature adults, even friends, while most moms Lee knew wished that the snuggling pockets of childhood would last a few years longer." Do you think men and women differ when it comes to parenting and wanting to protect their children for as long as possible?

10. As Abby prepares to renew her marriage vows, she admits that she loves Sam more now than she did on their wedding day—but that it's a different kind of love, describing it as "one that had mellowed over time, one that swam a smoother line." Do you think love evolves and changes over time?

11. Discuss how secrets are a major theme in the novel. Why do each of the women conceal parts of themselves to those closest to them? How do they ultimately grow as characters once their truths are revealed?

12. Lee believes that the essence of being a mother is "to be able to show your children love even during the times when your instincts told you to scream, when it was the hardest of all to love them." Do you agree? Discuss how Lee exemplifies motherhood by book's end. Do you think Lacey relates to her mother better?

13. How did each of the women evolve over the course of the trip? What did they learn about themselves? Are there any challenges that they still must overcome in their relationships?

14. When the ship docks, Abby promises herself: "If nothing else, remember to be amazed." What do you think of her new mantra? How can you incorporate it into your daily life?

Enhance Your Book Club

1. Friendship is at the heart of the novel; but unfortunately, many of us don't take enough time to express our appreciation to our friends. Show your friends how you care about them. Consider writing cards, inviting them over for dinner, or, better yet, organize a trip.

2. *Something's Gotta Give* is one of Lee's favorite movies. Consider watching it at your next group meeting. Why did Lee admire Diane Keaton's character? Discuss with your group.

3. Have you ever celebrated a milestone event with a girls' trip? If so, share your experience with your book club and bring in some of your favorite pictures or videos.

4. Consider these other summer reads for your book club: *Beach House for Rent* by Mary Alice Monroe, *Mystic Summer* by Hannah McKinnon, or Wendy Francis's own *The Summer of Good Intentions*.

A Conversation with Wendy Francis

Why did you set this novel on a cruise? What was particularly appealing about having the women interact on shipboard? And, most important, did you need to take any research trips?

To my mind, a cruise immediately says *vacation* and *summer*—two of my favorite words in the English language. A cruise ship also seemed the ideal setting for exploring the bonds of friendship among three women in need of a relaxing holiday. And where better to make tensions come to a head than on a boat hundreds of miles out to sea? So much can happen!

As for research, I've been on three cruises now. The first cruise I took was several years ago with my extended family, all eighteen of us, including cousins, aunts, uncles, and grandparents. Initially, I was a tad skeptical, worried that despite the beautiful setting, I might get seasick. But thankfully, you can barely tell you're moving on such large ships, and our cruise to a tropical island ended up being a wonderful time. It's easy to see why roughly twelve million Americans set sail on these luxury liners each year. With tons to do for the kids, adults can truly relax poolside; and once you dock, the beaches are pristine—a slice of heaven.

Sisterhood and strong female friendships are key elements to your novels. Is there a character or relationship in this novel that you can most identify with? Why?

Indeed. There are elements in all these women that speak to me. I share Abby's maternal, nesting instincts along with her aptitude for worrying about everyone and everything. I can appreciate Caroline's wanting Javier to propose already! Not that my husband dragged his feet, but up until my mid-thirties, I was fairly career driven. When I finally found the guy I wanted to marry, I was more than ready to tie the knot. And while I can't imagine the complexities of being a single parent, there is something about Lee that I find irresistible. I admire her no-nonsense attitude and her uncontainable love for her daughter. I imagine I'd share her frustration with Lacey's infatuation with her boyfriend, but I'd be equally relentless in making sure that Lacey finished college and pursued her passions, whatever those might turn out to be.

Each chapter is told from the point of view of one of the three friends, with a few sections told from Lacey's perspective. Why did you feel that it was important for Lacey to tell her own story?

If only we could all know what goes on in the teenage mind! I didn't set out to include Lacey's point of view, but she seemed to demand it the further I wrote into the story. It was that persistent, nagging feeling I sometimes get when my youngest accuses me of not listening (and he's usually right). So I tried to let Lacey whisper in my ear from time to time, to remind me what it's like to be a teenager so wrapped up in her own world. She's really a good kid at heart but has a lot to learn. By the end of the cruise, I hope she's a little wiser.

Your book comes out on the heels of an interesting political year. When Lee pitches the importance of women getting ahead in the world to Lacey, however, she doesn't mention the #MeToo movement or the various women's marches across the country. Why?

The easy answer to that is deadlines. Most of the novel had already been written before we knew just how crazy things would get in this country. Politics is a tricky thing to delve into in fiction—everything changes so quickly, and it's hard to know how relevant today's news will be a year from now, let alone next week. Though I didn't explore the current political scene, I trusted it was already pretty clear where Lee and her roommates stood on such matters.

Abby joked that traveling with separate suitcases was one of the secrets to a happy marriage. Is this one of your own secrets? Care to divulge any other tips to your readers?

Ha! My husband and I do travel with separate suitcases, but we usually end up sharing a suitcase with one of the kids anyway. A better way to ensure a happy marriage is to let Mom sit by herself on the airplane (preferably with a glass of wine) while her spouse entertains the kids en route. To that, I'd add one piece of advice a friend offered: If you find yourself in an argument with your spouse, sometimes it's best to say, "You're probably right," rather than roll up your sleeves for a full-out battle. That way, your partner thinks he or she has won, but you haven't completely ceded your point. My husband and I use this line every so often—at the very least, it lightens the mood. Just sometimes I put more emphasis on the word *probably*.

What was your inspiration for this story?

I'd been wanting to write a novel about college roommates—
and the strong friendships that form during those years—but
couldn't figure out the setting. Then one day it dawned on me
that an anniversary cruise might be the perfect way to bring the
roommates together again.

**Abby struggles to conceal her illness from her friends, often-
times experiencing anxiety, fear, and shame. How important
was it to you to show your readers the emotional distress an ill
person battles when trying to be open with their loved ones?**

This question is unfortunately personal for me: my mother was
sick with the same rare kind of leukemia that Abby has in the
book. For more than a year and a half, my brother and I watched
our mom struggle with the constant anxiety of wondering if—
and when—her condition would worsen. My mom was such a
graceful and accomplished person that I can only imagine how
difficult it was for her to weather this particular storm. She was
reluctant to ask for help beyond her immediate family—I sus-
pect she didn't want to be a burden to anyone, nor did she want
to worry her friends, much less invoke their pity. Beautiful, smart
as a whip, and funny as hell, my mom possessed a certain mid-
western toughness up until the very end. Having Abby reveal her
illness to her roommates was almost cathartic for me—I wanted
Abby to have the support system that my mother often refrained
from seeking out. Writing Abby's story also helped me revisit my
mom's illness with a more hopeful ending.

**Your novels are perfect for summer reading. What books do you
like to take with you to the beach? Are there any authors or stories that encourage your own writing?**

Thank you! I pretty much love anything by Elin Hilderbrand,
Mary Alice Munroe, Karen White, Patti Callahan Henry, Jane

Green, and Nancy Thayer. Summer is my favorite season, and those are all great authors of books to take to the beach. I'm also a fan of books that explore female friendships or family relationships, so other favorite authors include Liane Moriarty, Jennifer Weiner, Emily Giffin, Emma Straub, Ann Patchett, Ann Hood, and Lynda Cohen Loigman. I could go on and on, but I'd better stop.

Have you ever vacationed with girlfriends? Is there a particular destination you would recommend for a fun girls' trip?

Yes, it's essential to maintaining our sanity! Every year or so my college girlfriends and I reunite to share stories and recharge. Our getaways are typically short and sweet (a long weekend), but we pack a lot into those seventy-two hours. Our trips have included D.C., Cleveland, Boston, Chicago, New York, San Francisco, Charleston, and Austin. I highly recommend all these cities for their wonderful restaurants, museums, and walking trails. Such travels may sound indulgent, but off-season airfares can be reasonable—and sharing a hotel room with friends helps defray costs. After our getaways, I always feel as if I've returned from the spa, restored and slightly more at peace with the world. After all, no one knows you better than your college roommates/girlhood friends—well, except for maybe your spouse or partner.

What would you like readers of *The Summer Sail* to take away from the book?

There's so much that I hope will resonate with readers—the powerful, evergreen friendships women have; the challenges—and rewards—of being a parent; the solace and peace that the natural world can offer even in our darkest moments. In the end, though, I hope each reader will take away a little something different, whether it's nodding her head in recognition of Lacey's perplexing adolescent behavior or identifying with the humor and love that sustain longtime friendships like those shared by Abby, Lee, and Caroline.

Would you consider writing a sequel to *The Summer Sail*? What would each of the women be up to?

It's funny—I often get asked the same question about *The Summer of Good Intentions*, but I find that once I've written a book, I'm usually ready to let those characters go. If Abby, Caroline, and Lee continued on, I'd hope Abby would be living life to its fullest many years later; that Caroline and Javier would be happily married, maybe with a couple of kids, and residing somewhere other than New York. Perhaps Paris? Or Hawaii? As for Lee, I'd love for her to finally find true love and to see Lacey graduate and then go on to become a CEO of a Fortune 500 company while raising her own family—a modern-day feminist despite her teenage rebellions.

And, of course, the roommates would still be getting together every year. Maybe in their golden years, they could all live in one of those tiny-house communities.

Are there any relationship dynamics or familial stories that you haven't yet explored, but are interested in developing for future novels?

Yes, but I don't dare breathe a word of them so early—so please stay tuned!